Hostage of Islam

Phillip Strang

Dedication

For Elli and Tais who both had the perseverance to make me sit down and write

Chapter 1

Zebediah Johnson looked younger than his sixty-seven years. He was a man of moderate habits, with thinning hair, completely grey; his skin, tanned and leathered after years under the harsh African sun. His life as a missionary destined from childhood. His death, needlessly violent; God's will, he would have said.

'Africa is where you should go once you're ordained,' his father, Archibald would always reminisce about his time there with Zebediah's mother.

'It made me the man I am today,' he said. 'Broadens the mind, uplifts the spirit. Makes us realise how lucky we are here in the USA.' Zebediah's sustaining memory of his father would be of his love for Africa and the life of a missionary. 'We came back home to the States for you. If we could have been assured of a safe birth, we would never have left.'

The medical facilities in the Congo were dire and Zebediah's mother, Matilda had miscarried there a year earlier. Even then, she had to spend three months prior to the birth at the Baptist Hospital in Desoto, Mississippi.

'It's a boy,' the doctor proclaimed.

'We'll name him Zebediah, after my father,' Archibald said. His wife would have preferred a more modern name, but she was content with his choice.

Never a healthy baby, he was sickly and weak and subject to bouts of all the illnesses that children are prone. Two weeks off school for his classmates, he would require three.

The doctors all said it was due to his mother's weakened immune system. After so many years in Africa, they were probably correct. Both she and Archibald had suffered from malaria, and she had had a bout of typhoid. Dysentery had been unavoidable, the effects, debilitating. The privations of Africa had weakened both of Zebediah's parents, although his mother was to suffer the most. She remained frail for the remainder of her shortened life, susceptible to illness as the slightest provocation.

'We would have gone back with you to Africa, but it was not possible,' his father would say, sometimes sadly. 'Your mother was severely weakened after she gave birth, and you were far from healthy.' However, his father was not bitter. He loved them both dearly. 'By the time you reached eleven, your health improved, but then it was too late. Your schooling took preference.'

'I hope to go with Mary and continue your work,' Zebediah said. It was the day of his wedding, and he and his father were having a father-to-son chat.

'You will both love it as much as we did. You are both young. The two of you could make a difference.' Archibald was correct; they were young. Mary had just turned sixteen and Zebediah barely eighteen. They had grown up together on the same street and had been inseparable since they were toddlers running around the yard.

The wedding ceremony conducted in the Calvary Baptist Chapel in Jackson, Mississippi, with Pastor Archibald Johnson officiating.

'Wherefore, I now pronounce you husband and wife. And what God has joined together let not man put asunder. You may kiss your bride.'

The Pastor could not resist improvising on the closing part of the pronouncement of wedlock.

'Ladies and Gentlemen, I proudly introduce to you, for the first time as man and wife, Mr – and, hopefully soon – Pastor and Mrs Zebediah Johnson.'

It was to be another five years before Archibald's wish was to come true. Zebediah committed himself to study and Mary to providing the income. He emerged with two Masters Degrees, one in Theological Studies and the other in Divinity from the Houston Baptist University and the South Western Seminary in Fort Worth, respectively.

At the age of twenty-three, he became Associate Pastor, to his father's great delight, at the Chapel that he was proud to call his own, and where he and Mary had been married.

Two years later, Zebediah felt the call to Africa.

Mary only made one condition. 'If I become pregnant, I'll return home for the birth. I do not want to suffer as your mother did.

Mary, slim and athletic as a teen had changed more so than Zebediah since their arrival in Africa. She was now a short, portly woman with her grey, waist length hair tightly tied in a bun. Two years younger than her husband, yet she looked the older. The joy of motherhood had passed her by. It had caused her anguish in the early years, even tested her faith on several occasions but with time and the hormonal instincts diminishing, she had accepted it as inevitable. Zebediah said it was God's will, but he always said that when times were tough.

Within six months of his decision to embrace a missionary life, they arrived in the Democratic Republic of the Congo. To him, it was only logical that their first sojourn should be the country that his parents had left prior to his birth. To him, it felt like a homecoming. Assigned a small mission on the outskirts of Kinshasa, the capital, they quickly adapted to their new life. It was basic, and it was to be their home for the next thirty years. Apart from the occasional trip to the States, sometimes to England, to give lectures on mission work in Africa, they did not travel far.

In their thirty-first year in Africa, they moved to a township to the north of Johannesburg, in South Africa. They were to stay there for a few years before they moved to Liberia, followed by Kenya and, for a short while, Conakry, the hot and humid capital of the Republic of Guinea.

It was while they were in Liberia that they made another visit to the States. It was on that trip that they rescued Duncan Nicholson from a life of despair.

***

The most devoted of the Pastor's followers, Duncan Nicholson was a broken, homeless, shell of a man when Zebediah discovered him on a cold and wet wintry day in Detroit.

A lecture concluded at the Detroit Baptist Theological Seminary in Allen Park, and Zebediah was walking to his motel when he first saw the destitute man. It was part of his current lecture tour, speaking about missionary work, hopefully generating charitable funds. Always sympathetic to a soul in trouble and despair, he could not help but be drawn.

'Can I help you?' he enquired of the dissolute character in old dirty clothes, covered in pieces of cardboard in a vain attempt to keep warm and dry from the freezing, driving rain.

An indistinguishable grunt was the only response; the smell of urine, stale alcohol and sweat, overpowering.

'I don't know how long I've been here,' the man said on the third night.

'What is your name?' Zebediah asked.

'Duncan.'

'I am Zebediah. Would you appreciate a warm meal and some clean clothes?'

'Yes, thank you.'

Mary was not pleased when he turned up at the motel with Zebediah, but as always, she trusted his decision. After a shower and some clean clothes, Duncan was no longer recognisable as the person he had found under the cardboard.

'Would you please stay with Duncan while I continue my lecture tour down to Florida?' Zebediah asked of Mary. Two weeks later, he was back in Detroit. The change in the previously homeless man was staggering.

'I must thank your wife for my care,' he said, this time sober, coherent, and surprisingly articulate. 'Mary has told me of your good work in Africa. I would appreciate the opportunity to join you there.'

Another three weeks and Duncan was in Liberia with the Pastor and his wife. He never came to share their religious zeal, but they regarded him as the son they never had.

In his early thirties, he had served with distinction in Iraq during the Second Gulf War. 'I was a tank commander, a Sergeant Major, first wave into the country. I believed the propaganda of our government. Their statements of how we were taking democracy to Iraq, the weapons of mass destruction. It was all nonsense. If there were weapons there, we never saw them, and as far as democracy is concerned, it will not work. What I did see was our politicians aligning their business colleagues to take the majority of the oil industry for themselves. They had deceived us. It was not idealistic; it was purely money.

'I came back despondent to a society that saw me and thousands of others, not as conquering heroes, but as villains. I could not readjust. Eventually, I found comfort in the bottle.'

Dependable and liked by the locals in Africa, he was a rough diamond with a heart of gold. He loved the people, and they knew it. They loved him equally.

***

'Fatty, fatty Campbell.' It was what they had called her at the school since she had turned thirteen.

Helen Campbell was not what you would have called a beautiful child; that was reserved for her sister. The compliments were always for Theresa when the relatives arrived.

'You'll be a model when you grow up,' they would say, or, 'You'll be fighting the young men away from the front door in a few years.'

It was true; Theresa *was* the more attractive. Helen, two years older was heavy boned with a pleasant appearance and a tendency for chubbiness.

It was soon after she entered her teens when adolescence dawned. Within a few months, the acne appeared, and her glands went into overdrive. It was the age of junk food, and her constant craving to eat the wrong type of food exacerbated the fatty glands and added kilos around her waist. She started to waddle.

Never one to have many friends, she now had none at the school she attended, St Julie's Catholic High School in Woolton, an affluent suburb of Liverpool.

'Don't worry, you'll grow out of it,' her mother would say. However, for a young woman in her teens, that was not the advice she needed. Her parents were good people, but an adolescent looks to their peers, the other teenagers, for support. Instead, all they gave her was condemnation, bullying and teasing.

'*Fat pig*, why don't you stop eating?' Sally O'Rourke, the worst of her critics would chant. Attractive and slim, with firm, pronounced breasts and a tight arse, she was by the age of sixteen, highly promiscuous. Popular at thirteen, all the other girls wanted to be her friend; at sixteen, all the boys wanted to be up close and personal. She was an easy lay. Many a young stud lost their virginity on the village green, round the back of the bike shed, or on their parents' bed when the house was empty, thanks to Sally.

All of the girls in Helen's class seemed to be putting it about, as the saying went, all except Helen. She was sixteen and as interested in boys as anyone, but no one asked or cared. There was Fred Dagsworth, but he was one year younger, with a gammy leg, and had the worst body odour of anyone in the school. Stinky Dagsworth was definitely out of the question, even if he kept making suggestive comments.

'What do you say to a screw around the back of the school? I'll bring a condom.' She wanted romance, but all he was offering was a five-minute fumble and the need of a bath afterwards. Apart from that, there was no one else.

One week after leaving school, she ran into Sally O'Rourke, her main antagonist at St Julies.

'Helen, it's great to see you,' she said. 'I didn't see you on our last day. We must catch up for a drink.' They were under the legal age to purchase alcohol, but Sally could always talk someone into buying it for them.

It was that night that Helen finally lost her virginity.

Sally needed an unattractive friend; she did not want competition down the pub when she was choosing her playmate for the night. A fat friend of a beautiful woman and Sally was certainly beautiful, even if she was vain and vacuous.

'Meet me outside the Elephant Pub at 8:00 p.m. tonight. We can have a few pints and a few laughs.'

'Okay, see you then.' Helen was excited.

At eight o'clock that night, they met outside the pub in Woolton Street, the beautiful girl with the chubby friend. Helen, lacking in confidence and self-worth, was enamoured of the friendship of the one person that she had wanted as a friend at school.

Soon there was a group of local lads in their twenties, all well-oiled after a few pints of Carlsberg. Sally had chosen James Halsworthy, a strapping lad who played for the local football team. The others had also picked her but, as the night wore on, and the pints flowed, and then the shots of rum, they turned their attention to Helen. She was excited and equally drunk, and the more they drank, the more beautiful she became.

'I'll give you a lift home,' Bob Danvers said.

A detour round the back of the cemetery and there, in the back seat of a particularly uncomfortable Vauxhall, he had his wicked way.

'Come on, it's only a little kiss,' he said as he pulled the vehicle into a dirt track off the main road.

'I'm not that kind of person,' she pleaded unconvincingly.

Five minutes later they were naked, writhing, and uncomfortable, the buckle of the seatbelt in the back seat digging into Helen's backside.

'Hang on, I'm coming.' He was so drunk he could barely maintain an erection, let alone climax. In the end, and with her in a state of extreme excitement and encouragement, being as it was her first time, he finally came.

The next day at the pub, Bob, by then sober, walked straight past her without acknowledgement.

There were to be two more years of Sally or another promiscuous female with their fat friend. Two more years of drinking and drunken entanglements in the back seat of various cars where she was the runner-up's prize.

By the time Helen reached the age of nineteen, the weight had started to come off and the looks, although not beautiful, were of some competition to all those that had befriended her.

It was during those last few months that she had met up with Tom Marshall. He had actually liked her for herself. She had a boyfriend, but he had a dark side: he was a drug addict.

'Come on, Helen. It's only cocaine. Everyone does it, it's harmless.' She resisted for a while but then succumbed. She liked it.

'I want something stronger,' she eventually asked him. It was only a matter of months before she finally injected herself with heroin. She was addicted.

He died of an overdose one Saturday night. Hooked on heroin and in need of a fix, she ended up on the streets down by the docks on the Sunday.

Her parents had despaired.

'I need heroin,' Helen, desperate for a fix pleaded with the drug dealer on the Monday. She hadn't eaten, but the drug was more important.

'You've no money, go away. I'm not a charity.' He was rough and pushed her, face down, into the gutter with force. He was a businessman, interested in money, not some whining woman looking for a handout. However, he had to admit she was better looking than most of those that he saw hanging around.

'I'll do anything. Anything that you want.'

'Okay, I may be able to help,' he said. 'Here, come round the back of the building and give me a blowjob.' She did not want to; he was a short, fat, balding man with a ponytail who smelt of garlic.

She did what he wanted. She got the drugs; felt euphoria and then revulsion and guilt at what she had become.

The progression to selling herself to feed her habit did not take long. 'How much do you charge?' She had been standing on the corner down by the docks, an area frequented by drunken sailors and prostitutes.

'Fifty pounds for a blowjob. One hundred for a root.'

There was no need for small talk. Helen had never been one for bad language, but it was not a conversation that her customers wanted. They wanted the price, the service and she, the drugs their money bought.

By her late twenties, she had been on the street for over ten years. Sometimes, there was some accommodation, some periods where the drugs had not gripped her so completely, but mostly she had been selling herself to keep her drug dependency fed.

At twenty-nine, she had fallen pregnant. The father was unknown. He would have been some drunk, staggering home at night, having spent the remaining money from his weekly pay packet for fifteen minutes of her time.

'I know how to get rid of it. I've done it before.' It had been two months since her last period, and she knew what it was. Maisie O'Donnell was giving her advice.

They had shared the same street corner for some years, the same dosshouse when they could find a room. It was owned by a dirty old man in his seventies. Sometimes, he would take money, sometimes a blowjob or a quick screw behind the counter at reception.

Maisie was older, in her forties. However, it was not drugs; it was cheap whisky, cooking sherry, even methylated spirits. The meths had addled her brain, and she was slightly crazy. She was the last on the corner to be taken by the drunks.

'I could go to a hospital. They would deal with it.'

'Yes, and they would put you into a drug rehabilitation programme and strap you down until you screamed,' replied Maisie. 'And then they would ignore you until you stopped the screaming.'

She was right. Helen was too dependent on drugs to even contemplate a hospital.

'Here, drink this whisky,' said Maisie. 'The whole bottle, until you nearly pass out.' They had found a room in a cheap boarding house for the night. It was rough, but it was cheap, and it was where the abortion was to occur.

Maisie, neither qualified nor competent, was suffering the effects of drinking two bottles of a particularly unpleasant cooking sherry the night before. However, she continued to swig from a bottle of whisky while performing the procedure. Helen had bought two, given one to her as payment.

Maisie, unsteady of hand, shaking and coughing, set to work with a knitting needle.

'Just relax, it will soon be over.'

'Stop,' cried Helen. 'The pain, I can't take it.'

The aim was to break the amniotic sac inside the womb. Maisie kept missing the mark, and the pain was excruciating. Eventually, she made contact; the sac was breached, the miscarriage eventuated and the bleeding intensified. The drunken woman had perforated the uterus and infection soon set in. In fear of the hospital, Helen had resorted to massive doses of antibiotics. In a matter of a few weeks, the pain subsided, but she would never have children.

The abortion had triggered a change in her. Back on the street, and alternating between injecting drugs and smelly drunks lying on top of her while trying to French kiss her, she saw that her life had no purpose.

Two nights later, on a cold wintry night in a momentary period of lucidity, she jumped into the Mersey River. The intense cold of the water as she went under brought back memories, thoughts of what her life could have been. She realised this was not the solution. She struggled to swim and, somehow, pulled herself up on the bank.

'Oh, my dear, let me help.' Edith Smith had found her sitting on the riverbank, cold, wet, and shivering. She realised it had been an attempted suicide.

'Please, come home with me. Let me get you dry and warm.'

'I jumped in, but I couldn't do it. I don't know why; I wanted to.'

A kindly, pious and devoutly Christian woman, Edith had been taking her dog, Benny, for his nightly walk when she had seen an unusual shape by the water's edge.

She did not know why she had offered to take the woman home instead of calling the Police. She was of a nervous disposition, but something in Helen's face made her feel safe.

In the years to come, Edith would say it was God's will that she was there that night.

'We'll soon get you out of those clothes and warm. I have a warm fire at home. You will have to share it with Benny, though, he likes to hog it.' The dog was a sprightly little Jack Russell terrier, and he already loved Helen. He kept licking her.

Edith was in her sixtieth year and lived in a small, terrace house several blocks away from the river. There was nothing distinctive about it; it looked like every other house within a square kilometre, but to Helen it was heaven.

The back bedroom she had been given was cheery and bright, and she slept for twenty hours straight. Edith had made sure she had a cup of tea and a good feed ready for when she woke up. Sitting in front of the fire, she realised that the craving for drugs was still there, but it was manageable.

Three weeks passed, and she rarely left the house, although she sometimes took Benny for a walk. She phoned her parents after two weeks. For a number of years estranged from her parents, they had tried to help, but it was too difficult for them. They could only handle the situation by keeping away.

'Mum, I am okay. A lovely lady is looking after me. There is nothing to worry about. Let's get together in a week or so. Tell Dad I love him.'

They were delighted and, that night, they celebrated with a bottle of wine they had been saving for such a phone call.

'I am going to my Church tonight. There is a presentation on missionary work in Africa. Would you like to come?' Helen's saviour said.

Edith was a keen Baptist. Helen, although she had been raised Catholic, was not religious. Edith had asked before, but this time, she said yes. She was not sure why.

There was a small gathering of about fifty people in the little hall alongside the Baptist Chapel. Tea and cakes served to all on arrival, and, promptly at seven, Pastor Thomas Stewart stood to speak. Scottish, judging by his accent, he spoke at length about life in Africa, the challenges, the lifestyle, the people. He interspersed his talk with pictures.

Helen saw it as the life for her. It was alien from all she had known in her mainly troubled life, but she felt an affinity, a longing to travel to Africa.

At the end of the meeting, Helen with Edith had taken the Pastor to one side to discuss missionary work in Africa. Everyone else had gone home by then.

'I am sure. I would like to go and assist.' Helen was adamant.

With Edith's assistance, she quickly phoned the various people and she was accepted as a candidate for mission work. However, they required her to undertake some training in the religious aspects of the Missions, but she was not religious. She wanted to help, not preach. She decided to go anyway and soon decided on the Mission where she would go to first.

'I'm going to Africa next week.' Delighted as Helen's parents were to see her, the revelation shocked them. They had met at a local café near Edith's house. She still showed the effects of life on the streets, but she was calm, certainly fresher looking than the last time they had seen her.

'Africa!' her father exclaimed.

'It's all arranged. I'm looking forward to it.'

'And the other issue?' Her mother could not help but enquire about the *other* issue.

'I am fine,' said Helen. 'I do not feel the need for drugs; I don't think I will ever again. I cannot explain why, but there it is. Can you take me to the airport in Manchester next Thursday?'

'Are you certain?' It was a typical comment from concerned parents. *At least the sun will do her good*, they thought. They had never travelled and imagined she would be in the sun by the sea.

Thursday duly arrived, and Helen bid them farewell. Edith came as well, and they waved as she boarded a British Airways flight to Abuja, the capital of Nigeria.

Chapter 2

Pastor Zebediah had hoped that the Conakry Baptist Mission would last for another few years before they returned home to Mississippi. Mary was ageing; it was clear that she would need the medical facilities back home at some stage. The request had come unexpectedly from the Baptist Head of Mission in Nigeria to reactivate the Mission in Maiduguri after it had been neglected for several years. The previous Pastor wife had passed away, and he had retired back home to Florida. Zebediah could see no reason not to agree; he had to admit that the local team in Conakry was doing a fine job, more than capable to carry on the good work.

Three months later, they arrived in Abuja, the capital city of the oil-rich country. It was soon clear as to where the wealth was concentrated as they left on the three-day trip north to the Mission. The cities, the villages and the people progressively poorer, the further north they ventured. The temperature in the blistering sun nudged forty degrees centigrade, the cabin of the truck at least ten degrees hotter. It was unpleasant, uncomfortable, but no one complained. Years of trials and tribulations had inured Zebediah, Mary and Duncan, to what was always euphemised as 'local conditions.'

'Welcome to Maiduguri,' the driver said. A small town in Borno state, it was neither attractive nor pleasant. It was, however, where the Mission was located. As they entered through the gates of their new home, they were not filled with joy.

There were several run-down and neglected mud brick buildings with corrugated iron roofs. Substantial sections of the roofing were missing: the elements had claimed some, the locals the rest.

'There is a lot of work for you here, Duncan,' Zebediah said, aiming to maintain a sense of humour.

Duncan relished hard physical work. 'I'll soon get it sorted out.'

The main building was a large, rectangular structure with three bedrooms, living room, and a rudimentary kitchen. It was basic, unloved, but it was all that the Pastor expected and required. Electricity was a hit and miss affair and, whereas some in the community would have a diesel generator, he knew they would not; at least not on the meagre budget the Baptist Missions Board had allocated. The compound contained a small chapel and, judging by the numbers of seats, the attendance had never been more than a few dozen. Mor birds roosted under the partially collapsed roof than would be devotees of Pastor Zebediah's teachings.

There were some outhouses, a few broken chairs, miscellaneous tools of varying quality for maintenance, and some cans of paint, so old that Duncan would very quickly dump them in the nearest tip. On one side of the compound was a solid iron gate, wide enough for a vehicle to move through; the road outside, a dusty track.

'We need a horse and cart.' Zebediah was trying to communicate with a local supplier whose premises were not far from the Mission. There was meant to be an old truck at the Mission, but it was gone.

'Sorry, I do not understand,' replied Yabani in the local language. He spoke English perfectly adequately, any businessman did, but he was not going to let on; it would only weaken his bargaining position. He was a purveyor of horses, and the animal that the Pastor was interested in was old, beyond its use by date. Its kindly disposition, the limit of Zebediah's expertise in the purchase of horses, secured the sale.

Zebediah felt he had got a bargain, Yabani knew he had not. Thirty minutes had transpired on the transaction. Twenty minutes later, Sammy and cart arrived back at the compound. It was a silly name for a horse, but Mary felt it looked like a Sammy.

In a matter of weeks, Duncan had managed some essential maintenance and the main building, as well as the chapel, was useable if basic. Zebediah offered a prayer thanking Duncan at the first service in the small chapel.

'We thank thee, O Lord, for the humble surroundings that we find ourselves in. We thank Duncan for his good and hard work in the last weeks to allow us to use the chapel in the reverence of God.'

'Will you say a few words for Sammy?' Mary asked.

We also thank Sammy for his friendship and willingness to help us in our work.

Zebediah was as equally fond of the horse as Mary.

The horse was a friend, who would happily spend all day taking them where they wanted to go and then bringing them back. When they alighted in the small town, he would wait for their return. All he wanted was food to eat, water to drink and a few kind words. He had not been treated well during his life. A dumb animal understands kindness when it is given.

Surviving the first few months had been a battle. They had barely enough money, and the local traders were constantly overcharging. In time, the locals came to realise that these were good people, not of their faith, but nonetheless decent people and the overcharging ceased.

Services at the Chapel were held regularly and usually a few local Christians would come. However, as the insurgency of Boko Haram increased in intensity, the numbers dwindled. By the third year, nobody from the local community attended.

'We've been promised a truck from our fellow missionaries down in Lagos,' the Pastor announced after their fourth month. 'I am told it is rough and in need of some repairs. It sounds like a challenge for Duncan.'

'I'll fix it up, regardless of its condition,' Duncan proudly announced.

Sadly, the vehicle never made the trip north. What happened was to remain a mystery. Had it been dumped by the road? Maybe the driver took it for himself? Whatever the reason, they were to remain without motorised transport for some time.

At the conclusion of their first year, the Pastor, his wife, and their devoted follower were more than content with their simple life in the north. The local people invariably acknowledged them in the street and offered words of encouragement and goodwill.

'I am disappointed with attendances for my Sunday services,' said Zebediah, expressing his disappointment to Mary. He had ten once, but three to four was the average.

'The Lord preached to fewer numbers in the Holy Land two thousand years ago,' she replied.

'Maybe I should not be so disappointed. The Lord achieved success in time.'

'Apart from Conakry, we were always in predominantly Christian countries,' Mary said. 'Here, it is more extreme. The people are scared of the terrorists.'

***

'I have travelled from England to join your Mission.' Duncan could barely understand a word that she was saying.

'Sorry, you will have to speak more slowly.'

'I have travelled from England to join your Mission.' She tried to enunciate, but her English was not understandable to Duncan. Helen Campbell spoke scouse, a peculiarly Liverpudlian accent while he spoke with a strong American accent – and a Michigan accent, at that. He talked fast, slurred words and invariably dropped the last letter of every other word. Both spoke fluent English, both unable to understand the other.

It had been only five days since being seen off at Manchester airport by her parents and Edith. Benny, he would have only howled and annoyed the neighbours came as well.

'Please come in while I fetch my wife.' Zebediah had seen the confusion at the door; he came to assist. He had visited England on a few occasions and realised the regional dialects could be quite pronounced.

The Pastor had received many offers of assistance over the years; but, on the doorstep of a Mission in Northern Nigeria, such a broad British accent was unexpected.

Fair-skinned as befits the cold and damp climate of Northern England, with dark, shoulder-length hair, she was severely exhausted by the time she arrived.

'I'll run a bath, it's nice and hot.' Mary, practical as ever, dealt with the essentials. 'We can talk after. I will prepare a meal for you as well.'

'She has led a hard life,' said Zebediah. He knew the look of the street. Mary and Zebediah never concerned themselves with her past. They accepted people for who they were.

'I went to a presentation in Liverpool on missionary work. I felt it was something that I wanted to do.' A plate of chicken and rice quickly consumed; she spoke between bites. 'My life has not always been easy. I hope that you will let me stay.'

'You are welcome. Stay as long as you like.' Zebediah and Mary spoke in unison.

Over time, she would talk a little of her previous life to Mary, but she would never pry for more. Helen was the person they knew, not the person of the past.

Enthralled with her life in Nigeria, she became passionate in her dedication to the Mission. She felt as though she would stay forever. The Pastor and his wife loved her as a daughter.

In time, she regained the vitality and the fresh, young and tender look of her youth in the dry and dusty north of Nigeria.

***

'It's a beauty. I can't wait to start work on it.' No one could remember Duncan being so excited. The motorised transport had arrived, or at least a loose definition of motorised.

An old Bedford truck, at least fifty years old, had arrived at the Mission, not the original as promised. The tyres were bald, the main bearings clanked, the steering was imprecise and the brakes as effective as a stick pressed into the ground.

Red-haired with a susceptibility to the effects of sunburn, he had in the course of a few weeks managed to obtain some tyres of limited tread, fixed the bearings and worked wonders with the steering. He had also managed to resolve the brakes – they were never to be startlingly effective, but at the limited speed the old truck moved, they were acceptable.

He never managed to get around to cleaning the truck and the cabin smelt of something dreadful. Helen, in the first week of its arrival, had taken to the vehicle with gusto and had somehow magically transformed the cabin into something resembling a patchwork quilt. The seats were covered in local fabric, the floors with some straw matting, and the dashboard rubbed down and painted with white enamel she had found in a local store. It was clean and unique; she was immensely proud of her handiwork.

'It looks great. It's better than new.' Duncan was enthusiastic with the renovated cabin.

'I know it looks great, but I can't drive it,' she said. 'Every time I try to change gear, it makes a frightful noise, puts my teeth right on edge. I'll keep to Sammy.'

Duncan loved the truck. He had commanded tanks in the past; this was just a baby in comparison. The others liked Sammy equally, and Helen quickly became the horse's favourite; she was always giving him a carrot to eat.

***

The violence in Northern Nigeria had continued to escalate during the years they had been at the Mission. The call to pull out until the situation stabilised came by way of a formal request from the Baptist head of Missions. 'It would be appropriate for you to consider relocating to the south until the situation is more stable.'

'The people in the local community will look after us. For the present, we will stay,' Zebediah said firmly.

'I will respect your wishes, but if there is a dramatic increase in violence, you and your group will need to leave immediately. Is that understood?'

'I believe we are best positioned to judge local conditions.' Zebediah was obliged to agree, although he would be reluctant to abide by a decision made remotely. In times of decay and strife, that was when the Lord's work was most needed.

He was confident that they were involved in the Lord's work and his wife, Mary, was content to share her life alongside her beloved husband. Duncan was fully occupied, and Helen was truly happy. She had now been at the Mission for two years and had not seen her parents since that rainy day in Manchester.

'I am going to see my parents in Abuja,' she announced. 'They are coming over for a week. It is their first time out of England.'

'Ask them to come here, at least for a week or two.' Zebediah was pleased that she was reuniting with her parents after such a long time.

'My father recently had a hip replacement. He would not be able to handle the trip up here.'

'Please go with our blessing then.'

It was a bumpy trip down to Abuja, the surprisingly pleasant capital of Nigeria with its broad boulevards, luxury hotels and shopping centres. She certainly enjoyed the air conditioning at the hotel; but after two days, she missed her home in the north with a passion. It was her life, even if the Pastor's attempts to absorb her closer into his religion had not been the great success that he had hoped.

'We would not have recognised you,' her mother exclaimed at the airport when they first met. 'You look fantastic.'

Helen had left England that grey and miserable day, a woman aged beyond her years. She had a stooped posture and a facial complexion that showed every facet of her abuse at the hands of drink, drugs, and a life on the street.

'You look so young,' her father commented.

In Abuja, they saw a woman reborn. Her face was fresh and tanned; she stood upright, confident and looked ten years younger.

'We are so pleased to see you looking so well,' they jointly said.

'It is great to see you,' said Helen. 'I love it here. I do not believe I will ever leave Africa. It is my home now.'

Chapter 3

Somehow, Kate McDonald had avoided the inevitable wild youth of adolescence as the hormonal imbalance, and the first flush of adulthood took hold. There had been the late night sleepovers with her friends from school where she had drunk more than was good for her, but the abiding respect for her parents had limited her foolishness. There was to be no experimenting with drugs, no indiscretions with the local stud, and certainly no writhing half-naked in the back of a car, although there had been plenty of offers. She was attractive, slim, with long flowing blonde hair. Her parents adored her as she did them.

'Come on, it's no worse than a drink of beer,' Molly Barker would always say as she enticed her to down a shot of neat whisky.

Molly was her best friend, but they were as chalk and cheese. Kate was sweet and gentle; Molly was wild, always pushing the limits at school and at play. It was Molly smoking in the girls' toilets. It was Molly giving a blowjob to her latest boyfriend in the school gym. Regardless of their differing natures, they shared a genuine friendship, always looked out for each other. Kate covered for her the last time Molly had failed to turn up at school.

'Molly has a severe headache,' she had said. 'She will be in tomorrow.' Miss Epstein was enquiring as to her friend's non-appearance.

'If you tell me this, Kate, then I know it is true.' The teacher trusted Kate, and she felt some guilt afterwards about lying in this manner. She knew that Molly was giving Garry Spalding the ride of his life in the back of a Chevrolet SUV up at the lake ten miles out of town.

'It's only a cigarette. It will give you a high, nothing more,' Molly said, although she hoped she would not take it. Kate was the kind of person that she wished she could be, but her adolescence was playing havoc with her hormones. The desire to rebel and to screw every male she could get her hands on was irrepressible.

Molly, likewise, was the kind of person that Kate aspired to, but adolescence had not affected her with the same degree of vengeance.

A few boys had cornered her, or she had cornered them, at parties that invariably occurred every weekend during her later years at school and then at college. However, it had never gone further than drunken kissing, with plenty of groping and heavy breathing.

One of the rampant males had almost managed to score, but she had sobered up and pushed him away.

'Come on, everyone's doing it. You don't want to be the only virgin in college.' Glenn Smothers, an acne-ridden star of the football team, had tried to coerce her into relaxing.

'I can't.' She wanted to, but she wanted romance to accompany the physical act, and it was not love that he was offering. Next day, severely embarrassed, she feigned illness to avoid going to college and having him joking with his friends about how frigid she was. He didn't remember anyway, he had been so drunk.

The boys were always looking for and expecting more, but she somehow resisted and held on to her virginity when all her girlfriends, especially Molly, had given it away. It was usually to someone, such as Glenn Smothers, whose only attribute was that he was as drunk as they were, and in the right place at the right time.

***

Kate could have said to her parents that she was going away for the weekend with her boyfriend, but she still maintained the subterfuge of telling them that she was staying over at a girlfriend's place. She did not want to upset them, and they would have only worried about this quantum leap in her life.

She had decided to give up her virginity for her first serious boyfriend, Bill Cleaver, a bright but lazy student at the college they both attended. The anticipation, the pheromones, and the unrequited lust were strong as they drove up to a motel two hundred miles from New Orleans in Louisiana. He did not see the truck coming from the other direction in the half-light of dusk.

'Stop it, I can't concentrate on the road,' he joked with Kate, his eyes looking in her direction.

'Don't you want to see what is on the menu for tonight? I'm only giving you a little appetiser.' Both seized by forces that made sensible people foolhardy and unwise.

She was playing with his groin and cheekily flashing her breasts at him. At the last moment, he saw the truck. He slammed on the brakes, narrowly missing it. He did not, however, miss the embankment he had instinctively turned the steering wheel towards. The vehicle slowly rolled over and slid down the sloping incline into a small creek that flowed down into the Mississippi. It was not very deep, two metres at most, but the car had slid down on its roof, and the doors were jammed by the creek bank on either side.

He quickly succumbed, wedged as he was by the steering wheel, completely disoriented, and confused. He drowned within a couple of minutes of the vehicle hitting the water. Kate managed to free herself and found a pocket of air at the back of the car. The driver of the truck jumped into the cold water, smashed the back window with a wheel jack and somehow managed to pull her out.

***

Bob McDonald arrived at the Mission compound in Northern Nigeria unannounced one morning by helicopter. A friend for many years after Zebediah had approached him in Port Harcourt in the south of the country for some funding.

Zebediah was startled. 'Bob, what brings you here?'

'I have a favour to ask of you. Can my daughter join the Mission for a few months?'

'You are aware of the terrorist activities in the area. Do you think it will be safe for her here?'

'I will ensure that you receive enhanced security, regular visits by my people and a couple of reliable trucks. I will make sure you have a generator as well. Any sign of trouble and I will pull you all out.'

Bob explained. 'Kate was in a car accident with her steady boyfriend. It was fatal for him although she received no injuries. She is full of guilt, feels that she should devote her life to good deeds as a form of penance. No doubt she will eventually deal with her grief and move on, but in the meantime, I could not think of a better place and a better person to entrust her care to.'

A week later, she arrived at the Mission. Even Zebediah had to admit that she was a beautiful woman.

The local men, intrigued by her looks, could not keep their eyes to themselves; the local women, meanwhile, could not get enough of her. They wanted to be close to her, to enjoy her company, to express disbelief in how someone could be so white.

Never to be a dedicated missionary, she was religious in a conventional American, every-Sunday-to-church manner. She was not as strong a personality as Helen, but she helped the best she could. She made the living arrangements homelier, ensured the chapel had flowers, the Bibles well stacked and placed in the pews on a Sunday.

Her father guaranteed regular visits from the security company that he used for his burgeoning business in the Niger Delta. They did not enjoy coming, and they did not have the benefit of a helicopter. They had a couple of good, air-conditioned four-wheel-drive Toyota Land Cruisers, but it was still bumpy and long, and the dust still managed to get inside the cabin.

The promised Toyota trucks duly arrived. Helen loved them. At last, she could drive, although she was sure to make certain Sammy received due attention and plenty of carrots.

Duncan continued to use the cantankerous old Bedford, as challenging as it was.

The situation in the north continued to deteriorate; the fundamentalists were even committing terrorist acts in Abuja. There had been bombings of schools and bus stations, and the security at the entries into the city was becoming more intense.

Continuing escalation in the kidnappings of children, especially schoolgirls of marriageable age, some as young as fourteen, were being reported. Their fate was indeterminate, but it was easy to imagine that it was not pleasant. Forced conversion to Islam, given to the foot soldiers for entertainment, sold off for marriage across the border in Chad or Cameroon, were all put forward as scenarios, but there seemed to be no proof. The Nigerian military tried to control the situation, but there remained large parts in the northeast of the country deemed too dangerous for even them to enter.

Chapter 4

Abacha, a member of the Kanuri people, had never experienced love or affection as a child. There had never been the love of a mother's embrace, the nurturing at a milk-laden breast as a baby; or that of a father, proud of the son that he had seeded in his wife.

'Get out of my way, or I'll beat you.' His father was an angry and violent man who blamed young Abacha for his troubles.

It was only at the Madrassa in his village, in the remote south of Niger, close to the border with Nigeria, that he found respect and attention.

'Have you studied your Koran today, Abacha?' Mullah Ibrahim always asked every time that he saw him.

'Yes, I have.' Abacha was diligent in his study of Islam and embraced the religion. He could recite from memory, large sections of the Holy book of Islam by the time he had reached ten years of age. There was a varied education at the Madrassa, but religious studies predominated.

His mother was only fifteen when she had died giving birth to him. Her death was not because of him, but because his father, Harouna, was a stupid man. Illiterate and narrow-minded, he saw a woman of no worth other than breeding him sons, as many as possible. She had been screaming in labour for fifteen hours, but he did not concern himself with her anguish. A doctor could have dealt with the excessive bleeding and his wife's agony, but his father did not have the money to pay, or the intelligence to care. Eventually, the baby literally cut out of her by a local woman in the village. His mother died soon after of severe blood loss and shock.

The child, a male was strong and healthy, but it was to be his only son. To have only one son was a sign of weakness and failure and Harouna knew he could not afford another wife. He had laboured in the capital, Niamey for two years, to pay her parents, and he was not so young now. The miserable food that was dished up at the end of the day would not maintain his body for the relentless fifteen-hour workdays required.

The child grew firm and strong and at sixteen, Abacha was a handsome youth: tall and slim, with jet black skin. Considering the neglect and abuse of his father, it was remarkable. Mullah Ibrahim was more like a father to him than Harouna.

'You're not too old to get a clout from me,' shouted his father.

His father still attempted to hold control over him. That, however, was to be his final act of abuse. Harouna took a swing at him with a piece of wood that was lying on the floor of the yard. Abacha grabbed the wood and promptly hit his father with severe force He fell to the ground, bleeding and unconscious. He would never threaten him again.

Mullah Ibrahim, for all his good points, was a fundamentalist who believed that all one required in life was contained within the words of the Koran. He abhorred the West, although he had no knowledge of it. Islam and the Koran were the guiding principles of his life.

At the age of eighteen, Abacha saw the need of a wife. 'I will work hard and not complain,' he explained to the foreman at the building site. A wife cost money, and labouring on a building site was the only way to secure sufficient. He was following his father's approach by working in the capital of the country. Stronger than his father had ever been, he was back in the village within one year.

Samira, a first cousin chosen, and whereas she was pleasant to the eye, he could not view her with anything more than disdain. She was for breeding him sons, nothing more.

'Please leave me alone. I am scared and ashamed.' She pleaded with him on that first night. He did not care, or take any notice. He just ripped her clothes off and took her from behind with no feeling of remorse for her pain and humiliation. In fact, he had enjoyed it.

In two years of marriage, that was to be his method of intimacy. She had stopped complaining and crying, but he still appreciated the violence and subjugation.

She bred daughters, two in number; healthy and attractive, but they were females nonetheless. They were no use to him. He was worse than the father he despised – at least he had had a son.

Despondent with his life, Abacha saw the need for change. 'I am going to join with Boko Haram. They are committed to Jihad.' Mullah Ibrahim was impressed when he announced his intentions.

It was two months later when he made contact with the insurgents. He was an ideal candidate, genuinely devoted to their cause, although not yet fully aware of their brutality. A cruel man, his treatment of his wife and children, attested to that, but he had never shown them the brutality that he came to appreciate with Boko Haram.

***

'We will attack a school in the next two days,' Ismael, his commander, had announced.

Abacha, now armed with an AK47, the weapon of choice for terrorists the world over was ready. He had trained extensively, not killed yet. This was to be his initiation into the world of barbarism committed in the name of religion.

He was ready, confident, and full of religious fervour. In the distorted views of Boko Haram: criminal and violent activity, justified. Wanton and meaningless cruelty, encouraged. And infidels maimed, murdered and raped deemed acceptable.

'It's a boarding school for about fifty girls,' continued Ismael. 'They are Christian. We will attack at night. We go in fast, ram the gate, and encircle the compound either with vehicles or with men, but do not harm the girls; they will serve another purpose.

'Those in charge are of no value to us. Either they die during the attack or we will kill them before we leave.'

It was late at night when the insurgents entered, with Abacha in the lead vehicle. Still only a foot soldier and yet to be bloodied in battle, he was nervous, but it did not show.

A female, of about forty years of age, dressed in a nightgown ran out from one of the buildings. 'Stop, leave us alone,' she screamed.

Nervous and unpredictable, he levelled his gun and shot her repeatedly. Others rushed out, including some of the teenage girls.

'Halt the shooting,' shouted Ismael, firing a rapid volley from his AK47 into the air. 'We want the females alive.'

Quickly, the school was subdued, the teachers taken to one side, and the girls bundled into the back of a truck, suitably restrained and crying.

The female teachers not too old and grizzled were hustled into one of the schoolrooms and raped by all the soldiers in turn. Their throats cut, the school burnt before the attackers left.

He had enjoyed the experience. He was now bloodied, and the raping of the others, he felt was not a crime. It was a blessed activity condoned by Allah.

The schoolgirls they had been taken were separated on arrival at the camp. Those of some beauty, sold off to an Arab trader while a few of those remaining sold across the border into Cameroon or Niger as brides.

The least attractive: raped, abused, and forcibly converted to Islam; kept for as long their captors wanted and then traded. A pack of cigarettes or some additional bullets was sufficient payment for a human.

In the next six months, there were to be another three attacks. They all followed the same style; Abacha enjoyed them equally. Now a formidable fighter, he consolidated his power as second-in-command to Ismael.

The final attack suffered a significant fatality; Ismael had taken a bullet to the chest. It was a foolish shot from one of his soldiers. Some of them, trigger happy and stupid, no more than children in age and mental capacity, and far too dangerous to be holding a lethal weapon.

'Mustapha, stop firing or you will harm the females. They are not to be injured.' Ismael had shouted his last command.

Mustapha, barely sixteen, was on his first mission. Amongst a group of stupid men, he was the most stupid.

He swung around to accede to Ismael's command. In his inexperience, he failed to release his finger from the trigger of the AK47 he was holding. Ismael received a direct hit; he was dead before he hit the ground.

Abacha, a natural leader, took command of the group. Total loyalty from all that served with him was required; any deviation or dissent was not countenanced. Shekau, a surly individual, good with a gun, had answered him back when he had given a command he did not like. He would forever walk with a severe limp after the savage beating he received from four of his colleagues on instruction from Abacha.

His group were frightened of him, although he was always generous in giving out the Christian schoolgirls at the conclusion of a successful raid.

The Arab trader would pay well for an attractive virgin. He never knew where they went, although he assumed their fate was not pleasant. Not that he cared particularly; he always managed to keep a pretty one for himself.

'The more you resist, the more you will suffer.' He hoped they would fight; it always gave him the greater pleasure.

'Please respect me. I am a virgin; it will shame my family.' They always made the same statement. He did not care; they were only a female, and if they resisted, he would hit them into submission.

A cruel man when he joined the fundamentalists, his transformation to brutal did not take long.

Chapter 5

'For what we are about to receive, may the Lord make us truly thankful. And may we always be mindful of the needs of others, for Jesus' sake, Amen.'

None knew that Pastor Zebediah had given his last blessing for the meal that had been placed in front of them. Kate had proven herself to be an adequate if menu-limited cook; it was chicken and rice again.

It had been almost four years to the month since Zebediah, Mary and Duncan had arrived at their final home. Four years of striving, frustration, and ultimately contentment. In one violent assault, a group of people so alien to their beliefs and behaviour would replace it with savagery and barbarism.

'Not chicken surprise tonight, Kate,' Duncan joked.

'What do you mean? It is chicken.'

'I know, just joking. Not having chicken would be the surprise.'

The mood was jovial 'I'll give you camel tomorrow and then you will have something to complain about,' Kate replied light-heartedly.

It was soon after that the friendly ambience was shattered. It was Duncan who first heard the revving engines and the shouting outside the compound.

He quickly jumped up as the metal gates to the compound were ripped off their hinges.

'We're under attack,' he shouted.

His military training knew what was happening. The others remained where they sat. Kate's face went as white as a sheet.

'Allahu Akbar!' the people on the vehicles shouted as they came roaring into the compound. The lead vehicle, a beat-up dual-cab Toyota pickup, drove straight to the front of the main building, closely followed by a couple of old and battered Toyota

Land Cruisers. All the vehicles were old and in need of maintenance.

'Run to the back of the compound,' Duncan shouted. 'We need to get a message to the police.' Had he looked up into the sky, he would have seen the red glow from the burning police station. The terrorists had passed by there on the way to the compound. They had already killed five that day, the police at their station, their throats slit.

'There are at least twelve, heavily armed,' he continued. 'Stay out of sight and remain calm. None of you will stand a chance if you attempt to reason with them.' Duncan took control of the situation.

His time in Iraq had prepared him for the situation; he knew the calibre and the resolve of the attackers.

He reasoned that, if he could isolate one or two of them, then he would be able to even the numbers. A gentle and passive man, he would resort to what he knew well: how to kill.

'Surround the main building,' Abacha, the leader of the attackers shouted in Kanuri, the predominant language of the region. 'I want them unharmed.' He was not worried about the killing of anyone, but he didn't want any suitable females injured or killed. He had been told there was a white woman of unique charms and beauty; she would be his prize.

He was tired of reiterating commands to a motley group that was only controlled by his strict discipline. After so many killings around the countryside, they had become a lethal if degenerate rabble.

In the main building, Mary had grabbed hold of Zebediah. She was barely functioning. Helen, stoic, had jumped up. After so many years on the street, she had toughened herself to numbness. She was used to drunken hooligans on their way home, banging dustbin lids to wake the homeless, beatings from perverted customers blaming their lot in life on her. She had even had a gun thrust in her face once when the client had the need of her but not the money.

Kate, poor sensitive Kate, had entered a childlike state. Her feet were crouched up under her on the seat in a fetal position, looking for words to console and someone to hang on to.

'Get behind me and aim to rush out the back door if it is clear,' ordered Duncan. 'They will come in through the front door.' He had found a hefty piece of wood near the fireplace. It was ideal for his purposes.

'Come on, you bastards,' he shouted. 'I'm ready.'

He made a rush for the assailants as they bashed the door down. The first intruder's head entered through the door arch. With one massive swing, Duncan brought the piece of wood down on to his head. The assailant collapsed to the ground. He did not move, dead with one blow.

'Kill him!' Abacha screamed. Duncan's reaction was unexpected. They had expected minimal resistance; the capturing of the Mission, a simple, straightforward affair.

'One down, now for the others,' Duncan inflamed, was transformed; the man of peace and charitable goodwill had become a man of death. A second assailant and a second swing and another was waylaid and on the ground. This time, it was not a fatal blow, and the Boko Haram fighter raised himself groggily from the ground and retreated in haste, his arm severely broken by the force.

'Two of them will not trouble us,' said Duncan. 'I need a weapon; a piece of wood is of no use.' Years of military training were coming back to him. The second assailant, with his gun arm broken, had dropped his weapon outside the door. It was near.

I could kill all of these ill-disciplined and illiterate murdering thugs if I could reach that gun, he thought to himself.

He moved forward rapidly to grab the weapon when he took a bullet to the chest.

'I've hit him. Grab him!' Abacha shouted.

In Iraq, Duncan would have worn body armour, but here he had none. The wound was not fatal, but it stopped him and he collapsed to the ground.

'You bastards will pay for this.' It was an empty statement. There was nothing he could do and there would be no assistance from the others in the Mission.

'Drag him into the open,' Abacha, enraged and violent screamed. The first fighter who had died at Duncan's hands was one of his best fighters.

Duncan muttered incoherently as they dragged and pulled him to the centre of the compound. Screaming was beyond him, the blood loss sapping his strength.

Abacha took the first shot, and then the others indiscriminately emptied their AK47s into Duncan. His death had been quick and gruesome.

'Check who else is in the building,' Abacha shouted.

The attackers, following his command, rushed through the open door where, moments before, Duncan had valiantly attempted to protect his colleagues. The attackers spotted Helen and Kate.

'Get your filthy hands off me, you dirty bastards.' Helen had experienced abuse and violence before in her past and screaming for help had been the best deterrent.

Quickly tied up, groping hands all over them as they were restrained, Helen and Kate were powerless to stop their disgusting behaviour. If the insurgents were enamoured of Helen, they were beside themselves with Kate: her whiteness, her blonde hair, her slim and lithe figure. They, with their bravado, were quickly discussing who was to be the first to enjoy her, and where, and when, and how many times she would need before she would be satisfied.

'Leave me alone,' Kate cried and screamed, tears running down her cheeks.

'They won't listen, don't resist,' said Helen. 'They've killed Duncan. They will do the same to us.' She had resigned herself to their fate. It was now about survival.

'Please leave me alone, I am not that kind of person,' Kate, a quivering wreck pleaded. 'My father will reward you.' Their captors were now in a fever pitch of groping and prodding.

35

If she had understood what they were saying, she would have been totally ashamed and confused.

Helen's initial outbursts of rage had subsided. Her background of abuse, whether by her own hand, or by some fat, smelly and booze-infested man who had bought her off the street had ingrained a behaviour of detachment.

She had very quickly fallen back into that state of mind and, whereas unable to assist the others, she was able to handle the current situation. There was nothing they could do to her that would invoke a response, or a cursing, or a reaction.

***

In their excitement of having discovered Helen and Kate, the Pastor and Mary had been overlooked.

'Please, do something,' said Mary. 'Go and talk to them. Let them know that we are peaceful people only trying to help.' She was irrational, somehow believing that Zebediah could bring calm to the situation.

'My talking to them will have no effect,' he replied. 'They have already killed Duncan.'

'Are we going to die?' she asked.

'I do not know. We must believe that whatever happens is the Lord's will.'

'I will not live without you,' she said.

Zebediah knew that without him, she had no purpose. How he was going to salvage anything from this disaster was beyond his comprehension. All the years in Africa and miraculously they had experienced very little trouble, apart from the inevitable bouts of dysentery, malaria, and the endemic corruption and pilfering that plagued the continent.

'Check the building for others. There must be more here,' Abacha commanded, although he had to fire a gun in the air for his fighters to take notice. The men still rejoiced in Duncan's death, and Helen and Kate interested them far more than looking for others.

Three of the attackers searched the other buildings in the compound while five entered where Duncan had been standing five minutes previously. Zebediah and Mary had attempted to exit through the back door, but they were quickly cornered and captured.

'May the Lord bless and forgive you,' Zebediah spoke. 'As-salamu alaykum.'

A traditional Islamic welcome served no purpose and their age did not garner any special treatment. They were roughly dragged outside in a similar manner to Helen and Kate.

The Pastor was whiplashed across the face with a pistol, held by an unpleasant, lame-footed individual with no teeth.

'Infidel! That is for your heathen religion.'

Mary was mortified and intervened when he went to take another swing. 'Leave him alone, you unpleasant little man.' She was too much of a lady to swear.

Her strength of character had confused 'no-teeth' and he ceased to hit the Pastor. The insurgents, for all their violence and hatred of anything Western, still maintained a degree of civility towards an elderly woman, regardless of the fact that she was a Christian.

Zebediah sensed they would not harm Mary, and that they would possibly leave her behind when they left the compound. He had to save her.

'Forgive them for they know not what they do.' He was desperate to save her. 'Mary, you must protect yourself. They will not harm you if you stay calm.'

Zebediah had determined that he needed to focus their anger towards him. He had to direct their violence at him, and hopefully abate any further killing. Duncan was gone; Helen and Kate's fate, unknown. It was only Mary that he could help.

'Jesus suffered for his faith. I can do no less,' he said to Mary.

'Stay with me. They will not harm a servant of the Lord,' she pleaded.

'These people do not believe in our Lord. To them, we are heathens, infidels. We are of little interest to them. I do not believe they will harm you, though.'

He quickly kissed her on the cheek and made a bolt for the chapel. They fired as he ran, but he avoided the bullets and entered through the front door.

From the sanctity of the chapel, he called to Mary. 'Please do not resist, do not aggravate the situation. Save yourself. I love you.'

'Let me go. My place is beside my husband.' She was distraught.

'Set their house of religion on fire. It is an affront to Islam,' commanded Abacha. 'If the old man stays inside, then he will burn with it.'

No-teeth found some petrol cans close to Duncan's Bedford truck and threw the petrol liberally around the chapel's porch. It was old, mostly wood and tinder dry. It would burn with ease.

'Set it on fire,' Abacha shouted.

'I will do it.' No-teeth enthusiastically applied himself to the task.

Some old petrol-soaked rags, a few matches and the flames started to rise. They quickly spread to the roof.

Psalm 23 could be heard emanating from the chapel. It was a favourite of Zebediah's.

The Lord is my shepherd; I shall not want.
He maketh me to lie down in green pastures.
He leadeth me beside the still waters.
He restoreth my soul.
He leadeth me in paths of righteousness for his name's sake.
Yea, though I walk through the valley of the shadow of death,
I will fear no evil: for thou art with me.
Thy rod and thy staff they comfort me.
Thou preparest a table before me in the presence of mine enemies.
Thou anointest my head with oil.

My cup runneth over.
Surely goodness and mercy shall follow me all the days of my life.
And I will dwell in the house of the Lord forever.

He repeated the psalm, his voice quivering with terror as the flames came ever closer.

'I must be with Zebediah,' the devoted Mary shouted. 'Let me go.' With almost superhuman strength, she shook herself free of her captors and made a dash to the chapel and her husband. 'My life is with you, Zebediah,' she cried out. 'I will not stay here without you.'

She reached the entrance to the fiery building and made the only decision possible.

Rushing through the door, she grabbed hold of him and hugged him tightly. The reciting of the psalm, interspersed with screams of agony echoed throughout the compound for at least another sixty seconds. Even the attackers were moved by the poignancy of the moment.

To Helen, they had been like parents and as much as she loved her birth parents back in England, the relationship with Zebediah and Mary had somehow been more. She cried silently, but otherwise remained impassive. She would mourn another time.

Kate, in severe shock and denial, unable to comprehend, cocooned into herself.

'The dark-haired one is for me,' Abacha said, pointing to Helen. He had decided that she would suffice as his reward. She was Christian, older than normal, yet she had a look that appealed to him. The fair-haired female, he knew was not for him. The slave trader would pay well for a beautiful virgin. If any harm came to her, he would be answerable to Mohammad Murtada, the Boko Haram supreme leader.

Murtada, the fundamentalist leader and Abacha had no feelings of compassion towards a woman, no matter how white and beautiful she was; it was purely commercial. To wage their religious war, they needed money and weapons; the slave trader could supply both.

'The one with the light hair is not to be touched. There is a buyer for her,' Abacha shouted.

He needed her in pristine condition. He had to ensure she remained unmarked, untouched and unharmed. His soldiers, after the burning of the chapel, had returned to their pawing of the two women.

'Get you filthy hands off her! She is not a stupid village woman,' Helen screamed. Molested as well, she had already retreated mentally to a place where, whatever they did to her physically, would not affect her.

Kate, not capable of anything more, wriggled to free herself from her shackles and her captors, but it was in vain. She was close to unconsciousness, reduced to no more than a rag doll.

'Leave the women alone. They are not for you,' Abacha screamed. 'If you do not stop, I will kill all of you.'

One of the soldiers, another unpleasant and unattractive character of no education and no willpower, was oblivious to the warning. He was overly excited, caressing Kate's breasts and trying to rip her dress off; he had not heard. As he attempted to open his trousers and press his erect member up against her, Abacha took his pistol out of its holster.

'I have warned you,' he shouted one more time. Realising that it was hopeless, he levelled his weapon at the head of the disobedient fighter and pulled the trigger.

'I told you I would not allow them to be harmed.'

Kate collapsed on the floor, splattered with blood from the dead fighter. She had fainted. The ardour of the other soldiers diminished in an instant.

'Kate, stand up,' shouted Helen. 'Don't let them see your fear. You must not give them the satisfaction of knowing they have subjugated us.' Hearing her words, Kate revived sufficiently after a few minutes.

'They have killed Duncan, and Zebediah and Mary,' Kate bleated. 'What are they going to do to us?' Tears rolled down her face and she was shaking like a leaf.

Helen did not want to tell her the obvious, and Kate must have realised what their fate would have been had the leader of the attackers not intervened. In her torn dress, she lifted herself up and sat on the steps leading up to the main building. Her hands were still tied at the front, but somehow she managed.

'You must stay strong and calm,' continued Helen. 'If you show weakness, it will only be worse.'

'Were they going to rape me?'

'Probably, but they were stopped. They are keeping us alive for a reason. Screaming and shouting will not help. These are violent people, and you are something they have not seen before. It is because we are young and female that we are not dead on the ground.'

'I am so frightened,' Kate nervously spoke, her voice quivering.

'So am I, but I have experienced violence before. I will not allow them to control my mind. What they do to my body is transient.'

'Do they intend to rape us?' Kate asked again.

'You need to separate yourself physically and mentally. I will try and help you if we are given a chance.'

'My father will come for us.' Kate maintained confidence in her devoted father's resolve to rescue her.

'I hope you are correct. In the meantime, we must survive.'

'We leave,' Abacha commanded. 'Put the women on the back seat in my vehicle. Make sure they are secured, do not touch them.' His soldiers were temporarily subdued after the shooting. 'Take any vehicles that you can start.'

They attempted to start the old Bedford truck but were unsuccessful. Duncan had a skill that no one in the compound had ever mastered successfully. The two vehicles that Kate's father had given, started and driven out through the main gate.

'Get in the vehicle.' Abacha gestured to the women, pawing Helen at the same time.

'Do not touch me.' She attempted to pull away from him.

I look forward to taking her. She will fight me with a passion, he thought. It would be his first white woman.

'Come on, Kate,' said Helen. 'Stand up straight and walk to the vehicle.'

'I will not go.'

'We have no choice. If we resist and cause too much trouble, they will rape and kill us before they leave. If we go, there is a chance.'

Kate realised there was no alternative and walked slowly to the vehicle, supported by Helen. They climbed into the back seat of the Land Cruiser, a fighter pinning them in on either side.

'Burn whatever you can,' shouted Abacha. 'We must leave an example to others who feel that they can come here and preach their infidel religion.'

The compound was well alight as the vehicles headed north out of the town. Abacha, the Boko Haram leader at the attack was pleased with their night's activities.

Chapter 6

The security team from Counter Insurgencies did not relish their fortnightly visit to the Mission. The insurgents had become more brazen in recent months and the risk of attack, a distinct possibility. Steve Case, the CEO of Counter Insurgencies, had agreed with Bob McDonald to keep an eye on his daughter, Kate, and to pull her out at the first sign of trouble. To Aluko, the head of the team, the time to pull her out had long passed. He did not know it, but Steve had already told Kate's father that it was no longer safe. Bob McDonald had given in to his daughter's request to stay.

It had been two days since the attack, and their visit was on schedule. They were prepared for an overnight stay, check everyone was okay and then commence the arduous trip back down south. What they found on arrival was unexpected.

'The compound has been attacked.' Aluko called on the satellite phone he carried.

'When did this happen?' Steve Case asked, distressed at the news.

'There's no one alive. It's all gone.'

'I need you to calm down. We need the facts.'

'We arrived about ten minutes ago. They have attacked the local police station. The locals shouted at us to get out of the city quickly, but we had to check the Pastor and his people first.'

What have you found? Steve asked. 'After many years in Afghanistan, and in recent years as the CEO of Counter Insurgencies, he knew an emotional reaction from him would serve no purpose.

In his mid-forties, he had set up the company some years previous. Based in Washington DC, he had grown up in Rock Hill, South Carolina. The company specialised in the recovery of Western expatriates hijacked by fundamentalist or gangster organisations around the world.

He realised instantly that he would have to break his promise to Megan, his Australian-born wife; they had met twelve years earlier in Afghanistan when she had been working for a non-governmental organisation in Kabul. His position of communications engineer proved to be an ideal cover for an active CIA operative.

He did not like breaking promises to her. She had been there for him in the years following Afghanistan and the treatment that he had received from Hassani, the educated Taliban torturer. She had been there when he suffered from guilt over the senseless deaths of Andy Scott and Phillip Tenant, his fellow housemates at the company house they shared in Kabul. The Taliban were after him, but they ended up with their throats cut in a ditch.

He had been in Iraq, drumming up business, when he received the first call from Aluko. Within four hours, he would be on an Emirates flight down to Lagos, the crowded, bustling and seemingly chaotic megalopolis of twenty million people situated on the Gulf of Guinea. An Arik Air Boeing 737-800 would complete his journey for the short flight to Port Harcourt.

'Duncan is dead,' Aluko was saying. 'He's lying face down in the middle of the compound. He's been shot multiple times.'

'Are you sure it is Duncan?' Steve needed confirmation.

'It's him.'

'What about the others?'

'We've seen no one else so far. We're still searching.'

'Keep looking. Contact me in ten minutes with an update.'

'The two Toyota trucks that we brought up here have gone,' added Aluko. 'Duncan's old truck is still here.'

'The trucks are unimportant, the people are,' said Steve. 'If they're alive then there is a chance. How we are going to get them back is another issue.'

'There are two more bodies, the attackers probably. One of them has been shot in the head, the other looks as if he has had his head caved in. Duncan may have killed them.'

'Conduct a full search. Ascertain what you can from the locals and then pull back for the night.'

'That's what we will do.' Aluko did not intend to stay at the compound if there were no people to be rescued. The risks were too high.

Steve trusted Aluko implicitly. He had joined Counter Insurgencies some years previously down in Port Harcourt. A small, well-built man, originally from Enugu, the former capital of Biafra, the centre of a violent and bloody conflict in the 1960s. He was stocky and brave.

Ten minutes later, he was on the phone again.

'We have found the Pastor and his wife.' He was almost in tears.

'Are you sure it is them?' Steve knew that Bob McDonald and the Pastor had a solid friendship, and that Bob would take the news badly.

'There are two bodies in the chapel, unrecognisable. They must have been in there when the chapel burnt down. We found them with arms wrapped around each other. The height of the bodies identifies them and besides, who else could it be?'

'What about Helen and Kate?'

'There not here. One of the locals told us that the attackers left with two white women. God help them.'

'If they're alive, there is always a chance,' Steve said.

Bob McDonald had entrusted the security of his daughter, Kate, while she was at the Mission to Counter Insurgencies. Regardless of the fact that he had failed to heed the advice, it remained Counter Insurgencies' fault. Steve took his negligence in not forcing her father to comply personally.

Regardless of errors made, advice ignored, it was his company's responsibility to rectify.

Aluko knew that if Helen and Kate were in the hands of the poorly educated and heavily armed fundamentalists, their position was very tenuous. He did not want to state it to Steve, but in his mind, it would have been better if they had died in the compound.

'We are pulling back eighty kilometres to a Nigerian military base,' said Aluko. 'We can do no more here.'

'Understood and agreed. Stay in position to your south. I will contact you within the next day or so. I'm on a flight to Nigeria in the next thirty minutes.'

'What about the bodies in the compound?' Aluko asked.

'Are you able to move them?'

'Yes, I imagine we could.'

'Take them with you. We'll get them flown out to the States in due course.'

'It's all very sad,' said Aluko, a sentimental soul.

'Focus on the living. The dead can be mourned later.' Steve realised that all focus would need to be concentrated on the two women. 'We need to find Helen and Kate.'

As he sat in the departure lounge at Baghdad International Airport waiting for his flight, he had one final task, the most difficult. He had to phone Bob McDonald, Kate's father.

Chapter 7

The convoy of vehicles from the compound headed to an unknown destination. The Land Cruiser of Abacha with Helen and Kate in the back seat, took the lead. Following at a close distance were the vehicles that had entered the Mission at the time of the attack as well as the two trucks that Bob McDonald had supplied. As they travelled, the vegetation became sparser, the signs of civilisation more infrequent. Helen preferred to stay mute and calm; Kate could not.

'Where are they taking us?' Kate wedged tightly in the vehicle asked.

'I've no idea,' Helen replied. 'It appears to be north.'

'Why don't you ask? Tell them we are only trying to help their people. Let them know that my father will pay them well for our return.'

'Kate, you're naïve. You saw what happened to Pastor Zebediah and Mary. You saw how they killed Duncan.' She saw survival as their primary interest, not the destination.

Both of the foot soldiers that they were wedged between kept rubbing up close to Kate and Helen, inadvertently grabbing their breasts, ensuring that their hands slipped down between their legs. The one on the left was particularly aggressive. His excitement was making him lose control. He slipped his hand up inside Helen's blouse and grabbed her bare breast.

'Take your filthy hands off me, you perverted degenerate.' She had lost her patience. She had experienced similar abuse on the streets down by the docks in Liverpool, and her reaction had been instinctive. 'If you do that one more time, you'll regret it.'

There had been countless unwarranted abuses and unwanted men pawing her body over the years. This one was no worse or no better than most of them.

Abacha, sitting in the front passenger seat, turned around on hearing the raised voice of Helen. His reaction was immediate.

'I told you to leave them alone. You saw what happened at the compound. I killed one of your friends because he could not leave the light-haired one alone. Now I will have to kill you. Stop the vehicle!'

As soon as the driver had pulled to a stop, Abacha quickly ran round to the rear left-hand door. He grabbed the excitable soldier by the scruff of his collar and dragged him out, pushing him roughly to the ground.

'Please, I was wrong,' he cried. 'I will not do it again. Please, let me live.'

'You do not deserve to live,' shouted Abacha. 'You have disobeyed my command. I am going to kill you.'

'I am your best fighter. You have told me many times; you have always given me one of the captive girls on our previous raids. The dark-haired one is so desirable. It will not happen again.'

'It will not because you will be dead.' Abacha knew that the forlorn and repentant individual was one of his most accomplished, most vicious fighters. He would not kill him, but he would make sure that he did not transgress again.

'Beat me, but don't kill me. I deserve to be beaten.' The now repentant, hand wanderer realised that there would be a punishment, severe probably, for failing to adhere to his leader's orders. Better a savage beating, than a bullet to the head.

'You know that the dark-haired one is for me. The fair-haired beauty is for the slave trader. Any more violation of these women and I will kill all of you.'

All the vehicles had stopped by the side of the dusty road, and the soldiers were crowded around Abacha to see what he would do. He had to be violent in his actions, but he no longer had the will or the anger to kill the man. He raised his rifle and, with its butt, commenced to hit him repeatedly. The beating lasted for five minutes and when he ran out of energy, others replaced him. At the conclusion of the beating, the soldier was covered in blood, his left leg, right arm and four, possibly five ribs, broken. He would live, but he would always remember Abacha.

'Throw him in the back of one of the trucks,' Abacha commanded. 'We still have a long way to go.'

The vehicles continued to trundle north – at least Helen thought it was north. It was more northeast and the border with Chad.

'Helen, what is to happen to us?' asked Kate quietly.

'Stay calm, stay quiet and do not annoy them. You've just seen what they did to the gunman that was pawing me.'

'Their leader is protecting us. Perhaps we will come to no harm?' Kate said.

'He is not protecting us to maintain our virtue. He is keeping us pure for another reason.'

'They intend to rape us?' Kate looked for assurances that Helen could not give.

'You need to calm down. If they intend to rape us, they will, and they will do it whether we resist or not. They are not averse to violence. Women are no more than chattel to them, traded and abused as per their dictates. They do not care about us or our feelings.'

'I am frightened.'

'So I am, but this is the reality. It will not help if you continue to believe in fairy tales. You have heard the stories in the north of the female schools attacked, what happened to the women. You may wish to think it's not true, but it is.'

'I will not let them touch me,' Kate said.

'You cannot stop them. If you resist, they will beat you savagely until you submit. I have experienced rape and sex with violent, drunk, fat, and smelly men before. I know what they're capable of.'

Kate sobbed and dozed as the kilometres passed by. The vehicles stopped only for sustenance, fuel and prayers. It was dusty and hot and the roads became progressively worse.

In the early hours of the morning, just before daylight, they reached a remote location from where they could see no signs of civilisation.

'I think we have stopped,' Helen said. 'There appears to be some sort of camp.'

'What will they do with us?' Kate asked again. Helen was becoming annoyed with the constant questioning.

Abacha came round to the back door of the car, dragged them out, and made them sit on the ground. Hands and feet bound, they suffered the glaring eyes of the insurgents in the camp, and the pawing from many. Abacha saw what was happening.

'Leave them alone! Their fate is a decision for our leader, Mohammad Murtada. Anyone who harms them will suffer his wrath.' It had only a momentary effect on those assembled.

'You have set a dangerous precedent,' said Mohammed Murtada, the leader of the insurgency. 'I am not pleased. A few local girls will raise some concerns, but it is only rhetoric from the West and the Nigerian military; they cannot do much. White women and we will have the weight of the Western military coming down on us.'

While Abacha was distracted, some of the men started ripping the clothes off the woman.

'Don't touch us!' Helen screamed. 'Your leader has killed some of you for touching us. He will kill you.'

It was to no avail. Deprived of women apart from the occasional captured black schoolgirl, and never having touched a white woman, they were out of control.

'Help, help us,' Kate screamed at the top of her voice.

Abacha heard and came running. He quickly grabbed the women and pulled them to safety. Still some of the men came following at speed, oblivious to Abacha and Murtada.

'Stop or I will shoot,' Abacha shouted.

'We want the women,' one of the men shouted. 'They are our right, our gift from Allah.' With that, Abacha levelled his

AK47 and emptied its barrel. Five died before he regained control of the situation.

Chapter 8

Mohammad Murtada was an intelligent man, the most determined of the Islamic fundamentalists: Intelligence that had allowed him to gain the leadership of an organisation that did not value education or at least a Western education.

At the age of thirty-five, Allah had spoken to him in a dream. He had commanded him to reject Western influence and to embrace Sharia.

His upbringing as the second eldest son of a wealthy trader in Kano, in the North of Nigeria, was in stark contrast to the austere life that he led now. Gifted with a good education and a command of languages, he spoke fluent English and Arabic. He had joined, embraced and, in a matter of years, achieved the leadership of an organisation rooted in the dark ages. An organisation whose primary tenet was the abhorrence and total rejection of the education that he had received.

He had left the confines of a comfortable life in the suburbs as a dignified and upright man in his mid-thirties. In time, and with the demanding lifestyle of a jihadist constantly on the move, his personality and appearance had transformed from distinguished and agreeable to dishevelled and unpleasant.

'Abacha, you have brought immeasurable trouble for us. You should never have brought these white women here. Better they were dead at their compound than alive here.' It confused Abacha; he saw them as valuable assets, not as difficulties.

'I thought you would be pleased. They will bring a good ransom, and the trader will pay highly for the fair-haired woman.'

'I am not pleased. You have not considered the situation. Do you think the Western governments will allow their women to be taken?'

'They are infidels. What can they do? Besides, they are only women.'

'Then you are more stupid than I imagined. Do you not realise the strength of their militaries? Heathen, non-believers

52

they may be, but they have weapons of which we can only dream. They will make our life extremely difficult.'

'Then I was wrong.' Abacha did not understand, but Murtada was wise, he was not.

'Yes, but now we must deal with the situation. It is too late to take them back. We must attempt to gain some advantage of the situation. The slave trader will be interested in the fair-haired woman. The other one we can try and ransom back. What is the condition of the women?'

'They are safe and isolated from the men. The fair-headed woman is very nervous; the dark-haired woman is calm. There was trouble when we captured them; the fighters were unable to control their hands. I shot one of them in the head.'

'You see the trouble that these women cause. A black female is of little concern, but white women will drive any of the men in the camp mad with lust.'

'The one I killed in the compound was one of my best fighters. I nearly beat another to death for the same reason.'

'It is up to you to ensure that your men fear you more than the passion they feel for these women. Any problems and I will hold you responsible.'

'I will ensure they are safe and secure.'

'I wish to see the women now,' Murtada said. 'I want to know that the risk you have placed us under will be compensated by a suitable financial gain.'

Abacha took Murtada to a small building on the far edge of the camp. Mud brick and surrounded by a wall, it offered some privacy from the prying eyes and the amorous advances of the men. There were close to two hundred men in the camp, and none would have maintained control for very long. Even Abacha's retribution for violating his orders would only serve as a minor deterrent. The two women had received food and water and were free to move around in their confined enclosure. The guards posted at the entrance constantly undressed them with their lecherous glances.

'What is happening?' Kate asked.

'Kate, you keep asking,' Helen replied. 'I assume they are figuring out what to do with us.'

'Do you think my father knows?'

'Probably, but what can he do?

'Are they going to rape us?' Kate obsessed over her possible violation.

'I don't know. You saw the young women on the way in. I think they came from the Christian School attacked a few weeks back. Some appear to be with the men.'

'Will they do that to us?'

'I have no idea,' replied Helen, exasperated by Kate's questioning. 'I just don't know. Worrying about it will achieve nothing.'

Murtada entered alone into the enclosure where Helen and Kate were confined. 'I apologise for your treatment,' he said in perfect English. 'I will endeavour to ensure that you are both kept comfortable.'

'Why are you holding us? Why did you kill our friends?' Helen said angrily.

'Please Helen, he speaks English.' Kate had misinterpreted fluent English for a compassionate man. She was severely wrong. He was not concerned about how they were. He knew the repercussions if they were poorly treated or physically harmed.

'My father will pay well for our return.'

'Kate, say no more.' Helen could sense the foolishness of what she was saying.

'My father is Bob McDonald. He has a lot of business in Nigeria.'

'Where is he?' asked Murtada.

'I don't know. I assume he will be in Port Harcourt now. He will pay well for our return.'

'Then he will be contacted.'

'If you do not send us back immediately, he will send people to free us.'

'That would be foolish. You have seen what my people are capable of. If there is any attempt, rest assured that the two of you will be killed before you could be freed.'

'Kate, don't you see?' said Helen sharply. 'He speaks English, but he is as savage as those who killed our friends.'

'You are wiser than your friend,' said Murtada with a slight smile. 'I would not kill you, or anyone else personally, but I would have no hesitation in ordering your execution. You are merely women and Christian women at that. You are an asset that I now need to rid myself of.'

It was clear to Murtada that the dark-haired female was more knowledgeable about the realities of the world. The fair-haired woman was innocent, naïve and simplistic; she may even be a virgin. He would tell the slave trader that she was.

'The food and water we have been given is making us ill,' Helen said. 'We need medicine and a doctor.' Both of them were suffering from severe stomach cramps and diarrhoea.

'We are both ill,' she added. 'We cannot keep any food down for more than a few minutes.'

'It is the same food and water that we have,' Murtada responded sharply. 'You need to adjust to local conditions. This is not the decadent West.'

'It was you who said that we were to be secure and comfortable,' replied Helen. 'It will be of no advantage if we are dead.'

'You are correct. I cannot allow you to die.'

The rebel leader issued an immediate order to the guards at the entrance. 'Get a doctor. I cannot have them in this condition. Also, clean clothing and warm water for washing. Get some of the captured women to come and look after them.'

Within the space of a few days, Helen and Kate's treatment, although measurably improved, was far from ideal. The accommodation, roughly constructed, was comprised of two rooms, with a basic kitchen and a toilet that consisted of a hole in the ground outside. Walled in and held securely, the two women were supplied with some food – rice and chicken mainly – and bottled water. The women assigned to look after them did the cooking and their health improved. With their renewed strength and vigour, however, came the inevitable grief. Kate was often in tears.

She should have not been at the Mission in the first place, Helen thought. Grieving as she was, she suppressed her feelings. She had decided she would grieve later; for now, she needed to stay resolute for the two of them.

It was some time later that Murtada met with Abacha. 'They will bring a good ransom, especially the fair-haired one. We will conduct an auction with her father – she gave me his name – and the slave trader. The dark-haired one is older, and not so beautiful or innocent; he will not want her.'

'What does he do with them, the slave trader?' Abacha asked.

'I have not asked.'

'Have you thought how much to ask for the fair-haired woman?'

'You ask too many questions. That is not of any concern to you. Your interest is to ensure that they are secure and unharmed. The fair-haired female will attain a substantial price; I am sure of that. Apart from that, it is for you to take your responsibility seriously. Too many men have already died because of these women. I do not want anymore.'

'Normally I would take one of the females as a reward,' replied Abacha. 'I would have taken the fair-haired one for myself.' He was angling for Helen.

'Do not even consider it,' Murtada replied.

'May I have the dark-haired female?'

'Yes, but she is to be treated well. She will still command a substantial ransom, and whether she is raped or not will not impact on her value.'

'Thank you.'

'She is yours until the ransom is received,' added Murtada. 'But remember, if she is harmed or marked, then I will have you killed. Is that clear?'

'Yes, I understand.' Abacha was delighted.

***

'Leave her alone, you filthy swine,' Kate shouted, trying to drag Helen away from the firm grip of Abacha.

'Kate, don't interfere,' Helen said, trying to keep her voice steady. 'He can do nothing to me that I have not experienced in the past. I can calm him down, control him. He will ensure we are well-treated as a result.'

'But, he's going to rape you.'

'It is only rape if I resist, and I have no intention of allowing him to use force.'

'How can you let him touch you? He is foul. He killed Zebediah, Mary and Duncan.'

'I know what he did. Just calm down, we are going to survive. It's only my body he wants.'

Kate relented. She knew of Helen's past and, besides, she was a more resilient character than she would ever be.

In the confines of his hut, the murderer of her friends attempted to take Helen the way he had with his wife and the schoolgirls they had captured in the past.

'Stop!' she screamed. Having got this attention, she sat him down firmly on a chair and gave him the full treatment of her skills. She was tender, loving, gentle, and he loved it. He had never experienced anything like it before. She had shown nakedness, whereas before he had to enforce it. She had kissed him in return, instead of his mouth hard against the woman's until forced open.

She pretended to enjoy the experience, but could not with the man who had been responsible for the deaths at the Mission and the kidnapping of both her and Kate. Besides, she had decided long ago that men and sex no longer had a part in her life; any pleasure in the physical act driven from her after years down by the docks in Liverpool.

She showed him how to savour lovemaking; that it did not need to be force and subjugation, and then penetration until his lust was sated. With Helen, the ecstasy prolonged for hours.

For Abacha, he felt euphoria, a feeling he had not experienced before. He felt tenderness and a fondness for this dark-haired white woman. He did not know what it was, but it was love. She only wished him dead, but she still had to protect Kate and herself. Once free of his clutches and safely ensconced back into civilisation, she would have been glad to hear of his death.

Chapter 9

Soboma Tom was a criminal. However, he did not see himself as such. He believed he was a visionary leader, a freedom fighter for his people in the south.

Life had been tough in the Agip waterside shantytown in Port Harcourt, Nigeria. His father he never knew; he could have been one of the many men his mother had entertained over the years.

'Get off to school,' his mother would always say, but she was not often there. She may have been interested, but she still had to put food on the table, keep a roof over their heads. Schooling from the age of five to nine was infrequent; after that, it was virtually non-existent. Naturally smart, he was literate and could do his sums. By the age of eleven, he joined his first street gang; he became an area boy, that peculiarly Nigerian term for a group of hooligans.

'You can start by begging down in the centre. Look as though you are starving and desperate. If you get a chance, when they open the window to give you some money, grab whatever you can.'

His introduction to a life of crime was to the point. Dele was the leader of the 'area boys' in the shanty town where he lived. A swaggering, tall and skinny elder of sixteen, he had the look that appealed to Soboma.

Dele carried a knife. 'I've carved up a few with this. I even killed one old man who wouldn't give me his car.' He proudly bragged as though it was a badge of honour.

Soboma was not shocked. He had seen violence – you could not avoid it living in an impoverished shanty. He had even experienced it; he had walked in on his mother with her latest client, an unpleasant swarthy man who went by the name of Blade.

No one seemed to know his real name, but he was vicious and the name fitted his claim to fame: swift with a knife and always ready for a fight. His mother, Fortune, had been on top of him, her pendulous breasts bouncing up and down; he was breathing heavily when Soboma innocently walked in.

'I'll kill you for interrupting me when I'm busy,' Blade screamed.

'Sorry, it was an accident. Please don't hurt me.'

'Leave him alone. He meant no harm.' Fortune tried to intervene.

Quick as a flash, Blade jumped off the bed, grabbed Soboma by the arm and thrust a knife aiming for his throat. Soboma was fast. He was only six and he got away with a small cut on the shoulder. Fortune leapt in to defend him; she received a swift kick in the face and a knife to the abdomen. Two weeks in the hospital and then there was another man on the same bed with her. She had to earn a living.

By the age of sixteen, Soboma, a natural leader, had his own group to hassle cars, pick the pockets of careless people, and extort money from foolish old people that were out at night. He now had a knife, like Dele's, only his was bigger. He had not killed anyone yet.

His mother died of AIDS by the time of his thirteenth birthday; he did not miss her greatly. She had never been a good role model, and anyway he had moved out three years earlier.

He had one redeeming trait: he liked to read. This, coupled with his naturally good intelligence, gave him a solid if unusual education. He was certainly smarter than his fellow hooligans, most of whom were barely literate.

'It is time for me to take the leadership.' He had issued a challenge to Dele for the control of their local group of area boys. Dele, past his prime at twenty-one, and besides, the group already looked to Soboma for instruction.

The leadership to be decided by a knife fight. First to concede would be the loser. Down by the docks, a hidden patch of ground where they would not be disturbed. The local gang, over thirty members, assembled to watch the proceedings.

Dele was nervous. He knew Soboma was going to be a tough nut to crack. He knew he would have to kill him. Soboma, equally nervous, was at least sober; His opponent had consumed some Dutch courage, courtesy of a bottle of whisky.

'First to concede is the loser' Bobby, a member of the gang, was to be the referee, not that there would be much need of interpretation of the rules of engagement. There was only one rule: concede or die.

Soboma had the advantage; he had read up on the subject of street fighting in preparation. Dele's solution had been to get drunk. The group of onlookers formed a rough circle, with the combatants in the middle. Dele had a bandana tied around his head; he thought it made him look cool and menacing, but it did not. Soboma was dressed as usual in a t-shirt, jeans, expensive sports shoes, and a cap, peak turned to the back: standard area boy uniform.

Dele made the first lunge with the knife he had used to kill an old man. At least, it would have been, had it been true. He had made up the story to look bigger and stronger than he really was.

Soboma quickly sidestepped, Dele missed his mark. Soboma responded; he had the bigger knife and cut Dele across the left cheek. He had been lucky; he had been falling over in an attempt to get away. Sensing the deteriorating situation, he had tried to get out of the circle. The excited watchers, baying for blood pushed him back roughly.

'Coward, get in there and fight.' All the onlookers were shouting for action and Dele was not going to get away.

'Kill him!' they shouted to Soboma. They wanted blood.

Forced to fight and now frightened, Dele started to bring the action forward. He slashed wildly, cutting Soboma severely on the left arm; it bled profusely.

'Come on, Dele!' Their allegiances changed with whoever appeared to be winning. 'Stab him in the guts.'

Soboma did not like violence, but now there was no option. He could not back out; he had to finish the fight, and he had to finish as the victor. There was no alternative, Dele had to die.

He hit Dele hard with his fist. He fell, dazed and, by now, sober.

'You've got him!' the baying crowd roared.

'Stick the knife in!' they shouted.

With one stride, Soboma leapt on top of Dele and pushed the knife that was in his right hand through Dele's heart.

'Soboma! Soboma!' the crowd cheered. 'You've killed him. You are our leader.'

He was victorious, although he felt no joy, sickened by what he had done. He would get others to fight for him in future.

One more casualty of the violence that gripped the city, Dele's lifeless body would be dumped in a gutter.

***

'Our people live in poverty and starve. At the same time, oil companies keep their people in five-star hotels and drive around town in expensive cars.' In the six years since Soboma had killed Dele, he had consolidated his power. No longer the leader of a group of thirty area boys, he had managed to bring several warring factions under his leadership. Others were rushing to join his group; there was more money with him.

He had formed a cooperative to pool their illicit earnings, a fund to look after them and their families in time of need. There were three hundred under his leadership now and it looked like swelling to over one thousand in the near future.

'Let us help our people. We know how to make money on the street, but the big money is with the oil companies. If you let me organise, then we can take them for all we can get. If we set aside a percentage, we can use that for all the people in the shanties.'

There was little debate from those assembled. Soboma was so far advanced in intellectual capacity and organisational skills that he stood unquestioned; a villain with a brain, a formidable combination.

'We can break into their premises and steal a few vehicles, a few computers, or we can go for something more substantial.' He was aware of the benefits of hostage taking for ransom around the world.

'We should rise above petty crime and hustling. We should kidnap their Westerners for ransom. They will pay millions in American dollars to get them back.'

He had become idealistic. His reference point, crime; it was what he knew, and he could see that crime in an honourable pursuit was not a crime at all. It was not a logical conclusion that he had made; but, as with many ventures in life, the end justifies the means.

'What we must do is organise, train, and plan.' Those that listened trusted in his wisdom.

***

In less than a year after Soboma had put forward his idealistic plan, the numbers of hooligans, street kids, and gangsters under his leadership had increased to well over the projected one thousand. He could number close to one thousand five hundred and yet more came to join.

'You are our leader,' they would shout.

'We are ready for your commands,' they would proclaim.

He was to them a messianic figure that could do no wrong. His intellect should have protected him from their false worship, their hanging on to his every word, but it did not.

'When are you planning to attack the first rig and take some Westerners?' Ngozi asked.

She was one of his latest playthings. As befits a messianic leader, it was important to maintain at least three women in his entourage. She was slim, young, and readily available. He would keep her for another month or two and then change her for someone slimmer, more nubile.

'Why do you ask me? You are here to serve my needs, not to question,' Soboma replied angrily.

'The men are frightened to ask,' she said. 'They are afraid of how you might react.'

'So they have coerced you to ask when I am exhausted, when you have worn me out.' He was certainly at his calmest. She had just finished bouncing up and down on him; he had to admit, as a lay she was exceptional.

'They did not ask me.'

'If you ask me again, I will remove you from my presence, and have you thrown back on to the street. Is that clear?'

'Yes.'

'If you had asked at any other time, you would have felt the back of my hand.' As irritated as he was with her for raising the question, he would not have hit her. He had killed Dele, but he did not enjoy the act of violence. There was, however, no issue of ordering others to perpetrate it on his behalf.

'It is time for our first attack,' Soboma stated at a meeting a week later. Ngozi, irritated as he was at the time, had reminded him that it was time for action.

'There is a drilling rig in the Niger Delta swamps,' he continued. 'It is ideal for our first operation, sufficiently remote for the rapid response security forces. There will be high security on the rig. They will be heavily armed, ex-Nigerian military, at least six of them. Do not underestimate their capabilities.

'We will need to be in and out within thirty minutes. There are always some Westerners on board and we need to capture and remove all of them to a location of our choosing. Do not harm them. Dead, they have no value; alive, they command substantial money. Anyone who kills a Westerner will be killed themselves. Is that clear?'

'Yes, understood.' They either nodded or affirmed verbally.

'The training we have conducted these last months has ensured that all those who are coming on this mission know how to shoot and to shoot accurately, so I will accept no excuses. If any Westerner shoots at us, aim for their legs to disable them. Do not aim at the body or the head.'

***

'Stand by that pump. Be ready to switch it off.' Larry Herbert, a hardened oilman from Texas, was dealing with the latest crisis. A pump channelling the extracted oil was leaking badly. He had to isolate and transfer the oil to the standby pump.

The rig, set in shallow water in the Niger Delta swamp would normally have upwards of fifty personnel. On this night, at the end of a six-week shift, the number had dropped dramatically. Soboma knew the details; he had a contact within the oil company's administration office in Port Harcourt.

'There are only twenty-five on the rig and we know at least four are Westerners,' he said, giving his last-minute briefing before the imminent assault. 'We want those four unharmed. Remember, a dead hostage has no value. There will be security on the rig, they will be heavily armed and they will shoot.'

The two launches mounted with machine guns at the front headed up the winding tributaries of the Delta.

'Keep quiet,' Soboma whispered. Stealth was paramount as they closed in on the oil rig. They could see its derrick rising into the night sky. The people on the oil rig could not see them. 'Keep the motors off until I give the word.'

The boats were silent, save the splashing as they manoeuvred closer, using their paddles.

At the ideal moment, Soboma gave the command. 'We go now.' There was a distance of a hundred metres of open water and the full moon and cloudless night would give them little cover. The motors fired into life and, within fifteen seconds, they were alongside the rig.

'We're under attack!' Idris shouted. He was the first to see the boats coming at speed. A tall, well-fed, Nigerian ex-military sergeant, he was as tough as nails. They paid him well to protect the rig. Tonight, he was going to earn his money; tonight, he was going to die.

The approach had been rapid, the machine guns mounted at the front of both of the boats firing at full force. Idris and his team had responded as best they could, but it was a moving target, and all they could do was empty their automatic weapons in the direction of Soboma and his people.

'Keep firing!' Soboma shouted. 'Remember, it is for our people.' He was inspirational, even though he sat close to the back of the second boat. This was not his scene. He had come this first time as the great leader at the head of his troops as he led them into battle, but he was no Alexander the Great. He vowed that, if he survived, he would never partake in another similar activity. This was dangerous.

Quickly, as soon as the boats touched the side of the rig, the freedom fighters were off and onto the rig. The fighting was intense; Soboma took a bullet in the foot and fell to the ground. He soon recovered, just in time to see the crew of the rig being subdued.

'How many did we lose? he asked. He was weak and unable to stand without assistance.

'We've lost at least ten,' Benjamin, one of his lieutenants replied.

'The Westerners, did we get them all?' Soboma was more anxious for this news.

'One of them was killed. It was an accident; he took a bullet to the head. He had picked up a weapon from one of the guards that we had taken down, and he was firing at us as we drew alongside. One of our men failed to heed your instruction.'

'Who was it?' Soboma responded angrily.

'It was Akin, one of our best fighters. He was carried away by the excitement of the attack.' Benjamin attempted to defend him.

'There is no excuse. You know what needs to be done.'

'He is a good person with a wife and two children,' Benjamin explained, attempting to obtain a compromise.

'Discipline must be maintained. I cannot show weakness. Do it now, and do it quick.'

Benjamin realised it was futile to debate more. Raising his pistol, he shot Akin in the head.

'How many Westerners do we have?' Soboma asked.

'Three, they are all unharmed.'

'Get them into the boats quickly. This place will be crawling with security personnel soon; we cannot hold out against them.'

'What about the locals on the rig?' asked Benjamin. 'Eight of them died, but some of the security guards are still alive.'

'Kill them all. There are to be no witnesses.' Soboma's command implemented immediately. 'Take the hostages to our camp in Ogoni. Make sure they are bound securely and blindfolded. Do not harm them.'

He took off in a different direction; he had a foot that needed medical treatment.

It was his first attempt at ransom, and it had been successful. The three captives fetched seven hundred thousand dollars in total.

With some of the ransom money, new teachers were brought into the school he had rarely attended as a child, attendance compulsory. A new medical clinic established; no one would die of malaria or the myriad of diseases that perpetuated those areas.

Soboma was a hero, a benefactor of his people.

***

With time and the money acquired through ransoms and oil theft, it took only a few short years before Soboma had transformed from visionary back to criminal.

The amount flowing to his people in the shanties reduced. There were expenses: foreign bank accounts, luxurious properties to renovate, expensive women to maintain. The priorities reprioritised with the school and the medical centre at the bottom of the list.

The poor and honest people who had believed in him soon came to realise that he was like all the others before him, whether politician or businessman. They were all in it for what they could get, and the common person was just to receive the verbiage and the dregs at the bottom of the substantial money pot.

He now travelled in a fleet of four-wheel drives, with guns bristling. His home was a luxurious compound and the women were as plentiful as was the money. He did not care about the misery that resulted; the deaths did not cause him any sleepless nights. The campaign for justice, corrupted. He was satisfied that a man such as he could achieve so much.

His pronounced limp from the first oil rig attack, a result of the bullet in his left foot. It was to him, a badge of honour, and he would proudly recount the tale of how it had come about for all to hear.

'There were twenty of us that night,' he would brag. 'It was late, and the oil rig was heavily defended. We came in fast, two boats moving fast, machine guns mounted on the front. They had the advantage of a stronger position and certainly better weapons than we did, but we were smarter. We lost some of our people, at least ten, but we made up for that. We killed all of theirs and took three hostages – two Norwegians, one Englishman. We took them off for ransom.'

'It is truly impressive; you must be very proud of what was achieved. What was your role in this?' He had told the story many times and always someone felt obliged to ask. If no one asked, Soboma Tom would have flown into a rage at their insolence in not indulging him his moment of glory.

'I was in the lead boat, I was the leader and I was the first off the boat and onto the rig,' he would say. 'I was ruthless in cutting down those who had fired at us and I made sure that their leaders were dealt with first.' A gasp of admiration heard from the assembled group of sycophants.

It was a great story but, as with Dele before him, it was not true. He had been on the second boat and last on the rig. Time and success had transformed him. He believed in his infallibility, his benevolence, his bravery.

He had used his superior intellect to control a group of poorly educated people. A benefactor initially, but now no one benefited from the money apart from himself and a select inner core of fighters, and his bravery, an illusion.

Some knew the truth of that first raid, but he had ensured that they had long passed on. Five had met their deaths in gang-related violence; the remainder had died leading attacks.

Chapter 10

Eight years had passed since Soboma Tom's first hostage taking. The success and the ensuing confidence had led him and his group to attempt increasingly ambitious raids and kidnappings. Some had failed, most had been successful; but, with enhanced security and the Nigerian military showing greater resolve, he had reasoned that their luck was bound to run out at some time.

He was not concerned about his fighters; they were expendable. His lifestyle concerned him. It was time for him to put his money and efforts into legitimate business endeavours. The transition from a street hooligan, to the visionary leader, to gangster, to honest businessman was almost complete.

'We have had a good run,' he said, addressing his core group of lieutenants, 'but it is not going to last. We need to consider the next assault as our last attack. I propose we attack an oil platform out at sea. The financial gain will far outweigh the risk.'

A master strategist, he had calculated the attack carefully. He only needed to convince his people of the benefits. His core group had become wealthy, lazy and risk-averse. He knew that he had, but with one final raid, he could retire from crime, become respectable. In his early thirties, he had risked his life too many times and besides, he was not brave, regardless of what the others believed. He feared being shot, as much as the next man. So far, he had made sure that it was the next man who had been on the receiving end of the bullet.

'I will be in the lead boat,' he said. 'We will go for the maximum number of hostages, and this time we negotiate hard and long until we get what we want. I can see close to ten million dollars.' The teams always functioned better when he was there. He had sent them on their own before, but invariably something went wrong. His presence always maintained their motivation and enthusiasm.

'Exxon has an oil platform,' he said. 'It's about twelve kilometres off-shore. We will follow our practice of getting close and, once the sun dips below the horizon, we move in fast – three boats, heavily armed and at least thirty fighters. The advice that I have been given indicates there should be at least six foreigners, and most will be Americans. They always pay the best. This time we ask two million dollars for each one. Any delay, any attempt at negotiation and we'll send those procrastinating over the money various body parts.'

'We will follow your advice,' the assembled members of his core group echoed in unison.

'Fine, then we will plan the raid for next week. This is to be the big one. Make sure all those you bring are aware of the special bonuses. Remind them, anyone that kills a foreigner will receive the same fate as the person they have just eliminated.'

***

Up till now they had concentrated their kidnappings on oil rigs and boats transporting workers out to the rigs within the confines of the Niger Delta tributaries. A raid across open water, a new challenge, but that was where the high price targets were, the most senior personnel brought in by helicopter. Soboma Tom knew the risks and they were proportional to the reward.

The three boats were ready, sheltering behind a sandbank close to shore waiting for the light to dim. The sky was cloudy, the moon largely concealed, and the security on the platform would be complacent. The oil companies always felt more secure when there was open sea separating them from the coast.

'How did production go today?' Fred Hewitt enquired. This was to be his last job as Operations Manager. He was in his fifties, still looking good for his age, and fast approaching retirement back home in Akron, Ohio. After some twenty-five years out on oil platforms and rigs around the world, he had seen enough. He had a hundred-acre farm that he intended to run some cattle on, grow his own vegetables and live a simple life, as self-sufficient as he could make it.

'The centrifuge on number four rig gave some trouble, but we soon fixed it up,' replied Gerry Wrightson. 'I can't wait to get back on terra firma.'

He, like Fred, had spent too many years sitting out in the sea in some depressing part of the world. Not that he had much to show for his years of working. It was invariably three weeks on, two weeks off.

Unlike Fred, who always took the opportunity to go home to his wife, Victoria, the three kids, and four dogs, Gerry headed for the fleshpots of the world. Two weeks of whoring, drinking and over-indulging, and there was his pay down the drain. Still, he enjoyed it, but now he regretted that he had not put some aside for the eventual rainy day. His lifestyle, coupled with the exotic tattoos and the earrings that some whore on a commission had talked him into when he was drunk, gave him the look of a loser. Still, Fred had to admit, he was the best Maintenance Manager on any of the Exxon rigs.

'How long is it before your next break, Gerry?' Fred asked.

'Two weeks.'

'Where is it this time?'

'Bangkok.'

'You must have run out of places and girls there. How many times is it now?' laughed Fred.

'It must be at least ten or eleven. I always seem to end up there. Believe me, you can never run out of girls there.'

'I don't know where you get the energy from.'

'I get the energy from them. They are very obliging.'

'It's your money they are after, not your charm.'

'I know that, but for a few weeks it's harmless and then I can handle another three weeks on this old heap of metal. For the first week I'm glad of the break; now I can't wait to get back to them.'

'These raids on the rigs in the Delta are disturbing. Either of you guys worried?' Harry Greenock asked. He was the drilling superintendent on the rig. The North of England was home, and he longed to return. The climate was just too hot and even if the weather in the UK was abysmal, he preferred the drizzling rain and the damp underfoot. Even the slushy snow in winter, the car sliding across the road, appealed to him. England, the home of the British pub, and there was nothing he cherished more than a pint or two down at the local watering hole.

'As long as the company takes us on and off by helicopter, then I'm okay,' Fred replied.

'I'm okay, although I don't like the ride from the heliport to the airport in Port Harcourt, even with the security,' Gerry answered.

'That's how I see it,' Harry said, 'the ride to the airport.'

All three, experienced as they were in matters pertaining to oil and its extraction, were naïve in the cunning and stealth of Soboma Tom. As they spoke at the end of a long day, Soboma and his cohorts were closing in on the platform. Security was tight and it was good, but it was not tight enough for the events that were to unfold within the next thirty minutes.

'We want the Westerners unharmed and alive.' Soboma gave his last instructions before they commenced their rapid advance. 'Don't shoot any of them, even if they shoot at you. They're worth at least one million dollars each, possibly two, and I am not going to have one of you excluding us from that money.'

He knew he had to drum it in constantly. Willing, enthusiastic, and invariably brave – at least, braver than him – they were not too bright. An AK47 in their hand, and they would be showing off to their colleagues.

'Ten minutes and we move in fast,' he continued. 'Remember, they'll have good security. We head for the central platform and the main office. You can see it standing proud.'

As darkness came, the boats moved in quickly, Soboma in the lead. However, as his driver knew, once they were close to the docking bay, he had to ease the throttle and let the other two boats reach the ladder leading up first.

Security on the platform was good, mainly ex-Nigerian military, although this time with Exxon's Security Chief, Barry Duffield on board, they were at their most diligent.

Duffield, in his forties, hailed from Sydney, Australia and, as with all oilmen, he was weary of the travel, the isolation that accompanied the job. There was no weariness with the salary that he received. He had spent it well: a couple of investment units in central Sydney provided a reasonable return, together with a house up on the Northern Beaches for his family. Every two to three weeks he was out of the office and out to an oil rig somewhere. The last one was in the South China Sea, this time, Nigeria; next time, he was not sure.

'Security is not bad,' he had confided to Fred Hewitt earlier in the day. 'They need some more discipline, stronger adherence to the guidelines, but overall, not too bad.'

It may have been good, but it was not perfect. Soboma had the advantage of a contact at Exxon's office in Port Harcourt, a friend from his childhood whose life had taken a different road.

Emmanuel was a good person but, with a burgeoning family, his wife expecting again, he needed the money. Exxon, for all its visible wealth – the office manager drove around in an armour-plated Range Rover – yet, he was barely able to put food on the table. He had tried to be honest and decent, but those that he attempted to look up to treated him with indifference.

Soboma Tom may well have been a criminal, but he was more honourable than the company Emmanuel worked for. Soboma would hold to his word, and ten thousand dollars in local currency was a fortune. How could he resist? He could not bear to go home and see his children complaining of being hungry, his wife in discomfort with a difficult pregnancy. She needed to be in a good hospital, and now he could give that to her.

'Anyone black, shoot, whether they are holding a gun or not. White, do not shoot,' Soboma shouted as the first boat made contact with the rig. At least ten of Soboma's men killed in the first couple of minutes; it was not going well.

'Get up there and take control!' he screamed at the other fighters, who were cowering behind a metal structure down one level from the main deck. 'Either you go up or I will shoot you from down here.'

With such incentive, they moved forward. The two in the lead, dead before they had moved ten metres. Barry Duffield had felt obliged to enter the fray. As the head of security, he could not stand up in front of his superiors at the inevitable grilling over the incident and state that he stayed safe in the office.

Soboma had seen the white guy and he did not want him dead.

'Leave the white guy with the gun to me,' he shouted.

Soboma had to admit it was not a bad shot; he managed to hit Duffield in the shoulder. Incapacitated and in severe pain, he would make a good ransom.

With the security subdued, they took the main office with little trouble. Three Westerners, as well as the Westerner with the gunshot, made four.

'We need more whites. Find two more,' Soboma commanded. 'Look in the living quarters down below.'

In two minutes, three of his fighters returned with a couple of frightened men.

'Where are you from?' Soboma shouted.

'Canada,' the taller individual replied.

'America,' the other said.

'They'll do. Secure the area; we leave now. Six is enough.'

Chapter 11

The morning after the kidnapping of the men off the oilrig, Steve Case received a phone call from Sam Anders, Deputy Head of Exxon Security.

'I need your team down in Nigeria.'

'They're busy with a rescue in Southern Iraq. What's the problem?' He realised the reference to the team could only mean one thing – a kidnapping. He had met Anders back in the States a few years earlier. They had been thrashing out a contract for Counter Insurgencies Ltd to take the lead role in ransom negotiations and the rescue of Exxon's personnel worldwide.

'There's been an attack. Six expats have been taken.'

'Send me the details. I'll get the team working on the situation. I can have them there in three days. Any ransom demands?'

'Two million dollars each, or else they'll send body parts as an incentive for us to pay. They appear well organised. If they say body parts, then I believe that is what they will do.' Anders was obviously agitated and anxious. He had been a calm, impassioned negotiator when Exxon had been discussing a business relationship with Steve previously.

Steve would have expected Barry Duffield, Exxon's head of security, a friend of the family to make the phone call, not Sam Anders.

'Who will we meet in Port Harcourt?' You or Barry?'

'Barry's one of those kidnapped.'

'How did that come about?'

'It was coincidental. He was making a random check on one of our platforms.'

'Coincidental sounds too easy. Your Head of Security will command a high ransom. I suggest you check all the people in your office that could have passed information. Look for unusual behaviour, obvious signs of newly-acquired wealth.'

'When can you be here? We need to act quickly.' Anders was impatient for support.

'The ransom and rescue team will be available within three days.'

'Is it the same team that we know from Iraq? Is Yanny with them?'

'The same team, and yes, Yanny is with them.'

Sam Anders remembered Yanny from a previous meeting. He, like most men, went week at the knees in her presence. In her mid-thirties, she had a unique and distinctive beauty, the result of a German father, and a Senegalese mother.

Her mother promised since childhood to the youngest brother of the last King of the royal house of Jogo. Her father, Hermann Schmidt, the senior engineer for a large engineering company upgrading the container loading facilities at the port. They met, fell in love and married after a short courtship. Fatou, Yanny's mother, immediately disowned by her family. At the age of seven, Yanny and her family relocated back to Hamburg in Germany.

She remained there until her early twenties. Academically gifted, she graduated from the Hamburg University of Applied Sciences with a bachelor's degree in Foreign Trade/International Management. She was part way through a degree in International Business when approached by German military intelligence.

'Warum willst du mich?' Yanny asked.

'Please, English,' Major Baumgartner had said. 'It gives us a little more security to discuss openly, and I am well-aware that your command of the English language is flawless. So, are your French and Arabic?' Seated in the library at the University, there were people who would feel the need to eavesdrop for no apparent other reason than sheer nosiness.

'What do you want with me?' she had asked. 'I have never shown any interest in the military. I'm studying international business.'

'It is not the military per se that requires you.'

'Why? What could I possibly bring that you must already have amongst your enlisted personnel?'

'You have certain attributes that are unique. One being your command of languages, and your distinctive looks. It will allow you to go undercover in a society where a blue-eyed German man or woman could not.'

'Are you saying this is dangerous?'

'Yes, extremely dangerous. You would, however, receive the best training, the best support possible – and, of course, all your academic studies, current and future, will be fully covered by the government.'

'Danger is not necessarily the major issue, but I will need full details and an open and candour disclosure of what is required.' She had an adventurous spirit, and study, no matter how much she enjoyed it was becoming tiresome. She needed a break and this appeared to be an ideal opportunity.

'Next week is a break at the university,' said the Major. 'If you can come to our office in Berlin, we will explain. All expenses paid, of course.'

'I will be there,' Yanny was intrigued by what she had heard and excited at the possibility of meeting the Major again.

Six months later, she was in Afghanistan, fluent in Pashto, and exceptionally well trained in the use of weapons and hand-to-hand combat. An admirable fighting machine, she would don a burka and go undercover. There had been two lovers at the University, neither long term. Major Baumgartner was to be her third at the end of the week in Berlin.

For her, it was love, for him as well. The Major was to die in Kabul three months later, the result of an explosive device placed under the armoured vehicle he was travelling in on the outskirts of the city. Vowing never to fall in love again, there was the occasional one nightstand, before a major operation that could result in death.

'You realise what we're asking of you?' Colonel Smyth of the British Army had said. 'You understand the risks? We may not be able to rescue you.'

A veteran of several campaigns in Afghanistan, he realised that a woman suitably clad and with a submissive manner would be able to get in closer to sensitive Taliban positions. They derided women and as much as they would hurl abuse and throw stones, even hit with a rifle butt, they would not come too close in case she was unclean, menstruating.

'Your ability to integrate into the local community is uncanny,' Smyth complimented. 'I have never seen anyone else as capable as you at such a deception.'

'I understand different cultures,' she replied. 'I came from a family background totally different to the Western ideal. I do not aim to understand how the local society operates; I just sense it and adjust. My fluency in Pashto is almost perfect, although my accent sometimes raises comment. Apart from that, I am virtually indistinguishable.'

'We need you to go down into Helmand Province. There is a small village in the Upper Gereshk Valley, about forty-eight kilometres from Lashkar Gah, the principal city in the region. We believe there is a substantial bomb-making facility located in the mosque. We want to knock it out, but there are too many civilians close by. The best way is to get in close on foot and identify precise locations; a drone will deal with removing it. Are you willing?'

'In the past, it's always been surveillance from a distance. On some of these, I have received severe beatings with rifle butts, been pelted with stones. Is it critical?'

'We are planning a major offensive, the biggest so far. We need to ensure the ability of the Taliban to respond is curtailed. We cannot risk a random bombing; there would be too many casualties. A drone will do the job if you give us very precise coordinates. The locals have no great love for the Taliban, but they would embrace them if we kill too many of their innocent relatives.'

'I will do it, but I need a male relative with me. Anyone you trust?'

'Najib can be trusted. The mission starts in two days.'

It was with the forewarning of danger, the fragility of her life that the usually calm and sensible Yanny felt the need to rebel, the need to party, the need of a man. She had met a handsome individual at the German restaurant in Kabul; his surname she never asked, and she barely remembered his Christian name the day after, seriously drunk as she had been that night. He was American, attractive and available; they hit it off instantly.

The next morning, she left him curled up in bed and headed off to her assignment. It was to be some years in the future that she would realise the person interviewing her for a position as an operative of Counter Insurgencies Ltd was, in fact, the same man from that one-night stand. She had been attracted to him then, initially as a lay before a mission; however, at the interview, she realised the attraction had been more than a fleeting moment. For her, she saw love, but Steve Case in the interim had met Megan, now at home looking after his two children. It was complicated and embarrassing. Steve calmed the way.

'Yanny, I want you on the team. The past is a wonderful memory, a wild night where we both gave it to the moment. No one will ever know.'

***

'We've just received part of someone's ear, complete with earring,' Phil Marshall said.

'It's Gerry Wrightson, the maintenance manager. He is the only that matches the description,' Yanny replied.

It had been ten days since Steve's team had arrived in Port Harcourt. Well-seasoned, they had been together for a few years.

Phil Marshall, the oldest of the team in his mid-fifties, was especially handy with a knife, not squeamish to use it. He had worked undercover in Afghanistan and Iraq with the Special Air Service Regiment, an elite branch of the Australian military. He was adept at adopting local dress and mannerism, and picking up the local languages. With a tendency to overcompensate in his physical and sexual prowess to deny the ageing process, he was susceptible to the charms of the local women of the night and fond of a few beers. A laconic, laid-back character of medium height with dark hair, he had a ruddy complexion indicative of the outdoor life that had been his childhood, and an accent straight out of a *Crocodile Dundee* movie.

'This is getting serious,' said Yanny. 'We have six hostages and it appears that three have been mutilated. This is unusual behaviour for Southern Nigeria. It's purely money with these guys, yet here they are damaging the merchandise.'

'They've either become Islamists or else they are copycatting their style. They'll be an execution next.' Phil immediately realised it was an unnecessary flippant comment.

'They won't do that. They want the money. We will pay for damaged goods. Destroyed, there is no value.' She knew the psychology of the gangsters. She had experienced jihadists in Afghanistan and these were not jihadists. They were purely gangsters. 'They're tough negotiators, not willing to prolong the discussions and then accept a meagre return for their effort.'

'Meagre?' said Phil. 'At this rate, Exxon will pay two million for each one.'

'They probably will. It's unusual to find a ransom situation where there is no compromise. The only issue for us is to bring them back alive after the money is paid.'

'That's how Harry and I see it,' Phil said. 'We are close to locating where they are being held. Once the money is paid and they start celebrating, we move in. To us, it's a rescue mission. Drunk and they start waving guns and threatening our people. We cannot guarantee they will return alive even if the money is paid.'

'Never trust anyone involved in this business. It's up to you and Harry to get them out,' she said.

'We have the informant at Exxon's office in Port Harcourt, name of Emmanuel. You can't help but feel some sympathy – he only wanted to pay his wife's medical bills,' Phil said.

'This is no time for sympathy,' replied Yanny firmly. 'Extract what we need.'

'It's just unfortunate that an innocent pawn, desperate for money, will no longer be able to help his family. No doubt he'll end up in one of the local prisons for an extended period.'

'We all feel for these people, but we're professionals tasked to do a job. Our inner beliefs and morality are suspended for the duration of the rescue operation.'

'Agreed, we know our responsibilities,' said Phil. 'Anyway, he is singing like a bird. No roughing up necessary.'

Harry – or, more correctly, Lord Harry Warburton – the third member of the team, was grilling the informant.

'Emmanuel, you realise the trouble you are in?'

'I did it for my family, my wife.'

'We know. The only way to help them now is to give us what we require. Where are they holding the hostages? If you help, it will go better for you.'

'I don't know,' the frightened man replied. 'I only gave some information about who was on the platform.'

'Did you tell them about the senior people there?'

'I may have mentioned it.'

'He's only playing you for a fool,' Victor interjected. Sturdy, burly, and ex-Nigerian Army, he had spent time in the north of the country fighting Boko Haram. He knew how to get the truth. 'I'll beat the answers out of him.' He stood in front of the man being grilled in an intimidating manner.

'You're going to tell us all you know. Aren't you, Emmanuel?' Harry said. He and Victor were playing the good guy/bad guy routine.

'Yes.' Emmanuel was close to vomiting with fear.

'That's better,' said Victor. 'Let's start at the beginning. Why did they contact you?'

'I grew up as a child with their leader.'

'That's better. What's his name?'

'He'll kill me if I tell you.'

'If you don't tell us what we want, and quickly, we'll release you back on the street, and put the word out that you were most helpful. Is that what you want?' Victor enjoyed playing the villain.

'Don't do that, I will be dead within the day. His name is Soboma Tom.'

'Then tell us all that you know,' said Harry. 'Some will be killed, maybe even your Soboma Tom. That's your best protection. You help us, we help you.'

'What about my wife? If I go to prison, they will kill me in there. She will have no one to support her.'

'We can only help you if you help us. It may be possible to keep you out of prison if you assist us to get the hostages back.'

'We're wasting time here,' said Victor. 'Let me soften him up.'

'He's going to tell us all he knows,' Harry replied confidently. 'Let's get back to Soboma Tom.'

'We were children in the slums, played together. Later, when we were around ten years of age, he joined a street gang. I joined a church group. He found crime, I found God. I saw him occasionally, always flaunting his power and the whore women he attracted. I knew he remembered me from our childhood. Sometimes, he would acknowledge me with a cursory glance. Apart from that, we had no contact until about three weeks ago.'

'Victor, what do you know about Soboma Tom?' Harry asked.

'He's bad news. Smart, streetwise, sees himself as a freedom fighter for his people. Some years ago he may have been. His talk of redistributing the riches of the oil companies to help the poor made sense to me at the time. Not much of the money goes their way now.'

'Where does the money come from?'

'Street crime, extortion, robbery, most of it comes from the oil companies.'

'Oil companies, I've never heard of this guy?'

'The word on the street is that he has been involved in a number of hostage situations. He is well educated. If anyone threatens, or attempts to expose him, they end up dead in the gutter. We should not underestimate him. The police and the politicians are almost certainly in his pocket.'

It was time to raise the heat on Emmanuel, a frightened and lowly paid employee of the oil company.

'Where are the hostages?' Harry intensified his questioning.

'I don't know. I only gave the information.'

'When he approached you, where was it? What did he ask?'

'I was on my way home. A four-wheel drive stopped, I was bundled into the back seat and taken to his compound. They tried to ply me with whisky and women. They thought I would appreciate their life, but I do not. I am a servant of the Lord. They do Satan's work.'

'Carry on,' said Harry. 'What happened?'

'Soboma asked me to keep him informed about the platform out at sea. I said that I would not. I stated that I was loyal to my company and my promotion opportunities were excellent.'

'How did he react?'

'He laughed, said I was a fool and they were only using me for cheap labour. He knew about my wife needing a hospital, my financial situation.'

'When did he offer you money?'

'It was soon after. He offered me ten thousand dollars. Five immediately and the rest once I had told him the best time to attack and when the most senior people were on board.'

'What did you do? What did you say?'

'I agreed. I had no option. He threatened my family. Besides, I could give my wife the medical care that she needed. It caused me great anguish, and I prayed to God for forgiveness in the days that followed.'

'What was God going to do for you?' said Victor in a derogatory manner. 'You sold out.'

'The Lord had been tempted by the devil and resisted, I did not. I had failed my religion. I was hoping for forgiveness. It did not come. I am a sinner.'

'Where are the hostages?' Harry asked again.

'I don't know. I told you before, I only provided the information.'

'Did you overhear anything, no matter how small? Remember, until Soboma Tom and his group are captured, you and your family are not safe.'

'I did hear something. If you make a move on them, they will know it was me. If they cannot get to me, they will go after my wife and children. I cannot tell you, I cannot risk my family.'

'I understand,' said Harry. 'Let me talk to my superiors and see what we can do.'

One hour later, Yanny, Phil and Harry were in communication.

'We need to do a deal with this guy,' said Harry. 'Exxon has to absolve him of all crimes and guarantee to look after his wife and children.' The others agreed. It was for Steve to speak with Sam Anders.

***

'Sam, we need your agreement on a sensitive issue.' Steve opened what was to be an awkward conversation.

'Tell me what you want.'

'The informant we found in your office in Port Harcourt. We want your company to grant him amnesty.'

'Hell! You know we can't do that,' Sam exclaimed, clearly annoyed. 'This guy's been indirectly responsible for a number of deaths, as well as the capture of six people who are being returned to us in pieces.'

'We have no option. He knows the location where the hostages are being held. We need him on our side.'

Phillip Strang

'Can't you beat it out of him? How does he know the location?'

'He overheard it mentioned. He is dead if he gives us the location. We need to give him and his family protection as well.'

'You're asking too much. How do you know the information is accurate?'

'We don't, but it's our only lead. We'll check before we give him a full pardon.'

'I have no option, do I?' said Sam. 'Give him what he wants, but don't expect me to offer him congratulations for seeing sense.'

'What about your senior management?'

'They'll have to accept. Besides, they have given me full authority to do whatever is necessary. Just get our people back.'

It was later in the day when Steve got back to the team; he was still in Iraq. 'Okay, Exxon have agreed. Give him what he wants. Just make sure his family are safe, and his wife has access to decent medical facilities. Phil and Harry, check out the location as soon as he gives it to you. Yanny, keep up the discussions with the kidnappers.'

'Okay, you have a deal,' said Harry, turning to Emmanuel. 'Where are the hostages?'

'I need it in writing.'

'You're asking too much. We'll put it in writing and ensure your family are safe.'

'You're too soft,' Victor added, staring at Emmanuel. He just wanted to beat it out of him. His cousin had been a guard on the platform and he was now dead.

'There is a small community by the name of Esynma in Bomadi,' said Emmanuel. 'Soboma Tom has a compound there, isolated, about fifteen kilometres out from the village.'

'How do you know so much?' Harry asked. 'You must be involved more than you are telling us.'

'I know Bomadi, and besides, people on the street know no more than you do. They hear it, but they do not inform. They know the penalty if they do.'

86

'We'll check,' said Victor. 'If it is correct, we keep to our agreement.'

'It is true. I swear it in the name of God.'

***

Yanny updated Steve as to the current situation. 'I've agreed to pay the money in the next three days at a location in Port Harcourt. They have chosen a busy shopping centre with an easy getaway for them. They will hand over the hostages down in the delta at a location to be given once they are in receipt of the money.'

'We can't trust them,' replied Steve. 'They may decide to kill them anyway. Harry and Phil are in location close to the compound in Bomadi.'

'Then we adopt our standard practice. We pay the money and give the kidnappers at Bomadi a couple of hours. As soon as they relax and start drinking, we move in quick and fast.'

'The money is unimportant. Exxon will just have to write it off as a business expense,' Steve said.

Negotiations had been progressing for some weeks, and there had been no concessions from the kidnappers. It was two million American dollars for each of the six hostages. Each time, Yanny had become adamant for a concession, they sent an earlobe or a finger. Exxon and Steve's team realised it would have to be the full amount, and agreed. It was up to Yanny to seal the deal and agree to the time for the transfer.

***

'They're going to give us the full money,' Soboma Tom announced to his lieutenants.

'When will we get the money?'

'Set it up for three days from now.'

'What about the hostages?'

'Get the money first. After that, I don't care what happens.'

He had a private plane ready to take him out of the country with the majority of the cash in his possession. What happened to the hostages after that was of no concern.

'The money is to be handed over Friday, three o'clock, in Port Harcourt.' Yanny said over the phone to Phil and Harry, who were closing in on the hostages in the delta.

'Give us notice of payment,' Harry said.

They were both keen to commence with the hostage rescue. Two white men in the area would raise an immediate alarm. They had spent the last few days keeping out of sight, holed up in a derelict barge ten kilometres downstream from the kidnappers' compound. Dirty, smelly, with no light or the possibility of warm food, they were both feeling miserable.

They were not alone in the area, as six of Counter Insurgencies' best locals were close by. They were able to blend in and their time, if not pleasurable, was at least endurable. Surveillance indicated at least eight men guarding the hostages, heavily armed and, judging by their behaviour, well trained.

'These guys are a cut above the normal riff-raff we have to deal with,' Phil observed.

'We need to be careful here,' replied Harry. 'If they sense us coming, they will shoot the hostages.'

'As soon as the money is handed over, we'll move in closer to the compound. Stand to, about fifty metres out. We wait the two hours and then go over the wall. Any random shooting by the hostage takers, then we will just have to risk it, go straight in.'

'The helicopter comes in as soon as the area is secured,' added Harry. 'The Nigerian military will come in at full strength soon after.'

'I hope the military keep to their agreement,' Phil said.

'They should be okay. They can take the glory afterwards. Failure and they will be blamed. Success and they will have no hesitation to announce their leadership in the rescue.'

The Friday payment of the ransom proved to be a test run. Soboma's people wanted to check that Steve and the team were playing by the rules, no additional heavies waiting to pounce. Counter Insurgencies had made it clear, Exxon had agreed, the money was expendable and there was to be no attempt to capture those picking up the ransom or tailing them. The release of the hostages was of primary importance; nothing was to interfere with that operation.

'Any issues with the test run?' Soboma asked.

'We saw nothing unusual,' Stanley, one of his lieutenants said.

'Good, then set it up for tomorrow, Saturday. Same time, change the location.'

With the new date confirmed, Yanny informed Phil and Harry. 'Saturday, same time, different location. They were testing us the first time. Prepare yourselves for a rescue.'

'Yanny, we'll be ready,' replied Phil. 'Harry smells a bit off after so many days here.'

Phil did not know, very few did, but he was making a joke at the expense of the heir apparent of an English Earldom. Harry had studied at Eton, the educational establishment of choice for male heirs to the British throne, a true blue-blood. However, he disdained the privileged upbringing, the rigid class structure of his country of birth. To all, he was Harry, the African poacher hunter. How a service rendered to Charles the Second, in reclaiming the throne after Oliver Cromwell in the early seventeenth century, entitled his family to an Earldom was beyond his comprehension. He had not done anything that set himself superior to his fellow man, nor had his father. His father revelled in the title. He did not.

His talents to the team had not come from any military training with an elite group of the British military. It had come from the African bush, in the pursuit of poachers aiming to slaughter elephants and rhinoceros to satisfy the insatiable demands of the Chinese medicine practitioners and the devotees of anything ivory.

His childhood, apart from frequent absences at foreboding and austere boarding schools, was a large, exquisite Georgian mansion in the North of England.

Steve Case knew the story from their initial meeting. Harry had brushed aside his impending elevation to an Earldom and the considerable fortune he would inherit on the death of the current Earl, his father due to a lifetime of overindulgence and numerous, increasingly younger women.

'I'm sending you to a game park close to Victoria Falls in Zambia,' his father, the Earl Hampden, said. 'I have a substantial financial interest in the park. They will look after you well. It will do you good.'

It was not the truth, but Harry was delighted. The truth was that, now in his late teens, and no longer at boarding school, the young and virile Harry posed a threat. The mistresses were getting younger and the Earl was getting older.

Harry formed an immediate love of Africa, the people, the wildlife. Some years later, when he was twenty-seven, he gained a Masters in Wildlife Management from the University of Pretoria in South Africa. In his fifth year on the continent, he had visited the Odzala-Kokoua Park in the Republic of Congo, where ivory poachers were active.

Money had never been an issue, as he stilled received a substantial allowance from the Earldom. He had gone out with a local tracker, Vianney Moupele, who had found where the poachers were heading. On the way, they had seen a slaughtered elephant. It had been butchered, shot and had two substantial spears sticking out of its side. The tusks sawn off, close to the skull.

'Why do they do this?' Harry asked of Vianney.

'They do it because they are hungry. They need money to look after their families.'

'Do they not feel for the suffering of the animals?' Harry had been long enough in Africa to know the answer; he just wanted to hear it from the tracker.

'They feel nothing. That is for people with money and food in their belly.' It was an indirect reference to him; he chose not to comment.

Harry could not defy the logic. There was only one solution: remove the poachers by any means possible. He vowed to have no compunction to dispatching them with a bullet.

Vianney, wiry and jet-black, his skin dried hard by the incessant sun led the way. The three poachers were camped in a clearing at the side of a tributary of the Mambili River. They were loading their ill-gotten gains into a canoe, a small outboard at the stern.

Harry, without hesitation, entered the clearing, raised his South African-made Denel R4 assault rifle and shot them dead with the thirty-five rounds in the magazine. He had never killed a man before, but it gave him no qualms or concerns, no sleepless nights.

'Why did you kill them? They were only trying to make a living,' Vianney shouted.

'I cannot let them kill defenceless animals. If they can't earn a living without resorting to savage cruelty, then they must die.'

Vianney appalled as he was at the manner in which Harry had dispatched the poachers, could not dispute his passion. He was a conservationist, but also an African of the bush; he had known what it was like to have an empty belly. He had empathy with the poachers; death was too severe a solution.

Harry was to become a leading authority in the control of poachers in Sub-Saharan Africa. Whenever there was a problem, they would call for him. Money was never mentioned, just accommodation, vehicles, weapons and trackers as required. Vianney would spend a further six months teaching him all the tracking skills he knew: how to move through the terrain, open savannah or tropical forest without being seen, without leaving tracks.

He knew he had been lucky; he did not have the necessary training to enter a compound with guns blazing. When his time concluded with Vianney, he enrolled at the Tactical and Defensive Action Centre in Johannesburg to learn advanced rifle, handgun and knife usage. Dismayed by the insensitive attitudes of some of those taking the courses in post-apartheid South Africa, he kept his views to himself. He had no issues with anybody, regardless of colour or creed; he only had a problem with those who killed and maimed wildlife in the name of profit.

It was on a very rare visit to England that his father had caught his latest mistress acting provocatively towards Harry. He had done nothing wrong; even tried to repel her, but she was over-amorous, high on some unknown substance. She would not take no for an answer. Regardless of Harry's protestations, his father cut his allowance. He, therefore, needed to work to maintain his lifestyle. Counter Insurgencies had been the solution.

'It's today. Are you guys ready?' Yanny asked.

'We're ready,' Phil replied. 'If you feel sure, then we'll move in closer.'

It was a risk for two white men to move openly in the region. Adept as they were at keeping out of sight, there was bound to be someone who would see through their disguise. Dark glasses, broad-brimmed hat, darkened faces may conceal most, but the way they moved, always harder to camouflage.

It was often a child that seemed to be the most perceptive. In their innocence, the child would happily and proudly announce to all that there was a white man dressed funny. They had recently concluded a rescue in Southern Iraq; their mannerisms adjusted to there, not Southern Nigeria. The businessman in Baghdad for the sake of a deal had disregarded security instructions and gone to a restaurant with people he thought were interested in the company's products. The lure of a juicy bonus had overridden his good sense, and he went for dinner with his kidnappers. The bonus he was anxiously pursuing could easily have been a slit throat.

His company issued the mandatory reply. 'We do not negotiate with terrorist organisations.'

A YouTube video of him severely beaten by a gang of thugs, and a sword to his throat at the conclusion, changed their approach. His company negotiated then, but it was going badly, and those responsible for the negotiating were inexperienced and looking for a quick resolution. After the second video and a more severe beating, the company relented and brought in the best, Counter Insurgencies Ltd.

In a matter of days, they ascertained the hostage's location, agreed on a deal, a drop-off point for the money, and for the exchange to occur. The team realised that he would probably not come back alive; he had seen their faces at the restaurant.

A rescue mission set in place with the assistance of trusted locals, and Phil and Harry had gone in with them while Yanny concluded the ransom drop. They rescued the severely weakened and badly beaten businessman. The hostage-takers that survived claimed the money. Four had died; Phil had been responsible for two. Harry took a bullet to the leg, minor, and, apart from some soreness, he was fine.

***

After sometime since the last phone conversation Phil phoned in, 'We've secured our position. We'll wait until nightfall before attempting their release.'

Relieved to be free of the rusty boat, they had managed to approach within the pre-determined fifty metres of the compound.

'Is the compound difficult to take?' Yanny asked.

'It should be okay, no more than a few run-down shacks used by local fishing boats.'

'They've taken the ransom,' she confirmed.

'You don't need to tell us. They've started drinking.'

'Can you see the hostages?'

'No, but we can see and feel the mosquitoes. It's pretty grim here.'

'How long before you go in?'

'Let's give them another ninety minutes. I will move in first with Harry and see if we can protect the hostage before our local guys come in. The hostages are probably freaked out by now, and not in good health.'

'Helicopter in twenty minutes once you give the word,' said Yanny.

They were not to get the ninety minutes. The kidnappers, excessively drunk on bottles of Johnnie Walker started firing guns in the air after the first hour.

Phil and Harry were quickly over the wall. They took out a couple of the kidnappers on the way, knives to the throat.

'Hostages, hut to the right.' Phil signalled to Harry.

'I'll check it out,' Harry signalled back.

He moved over to the hut. The kidnappers had not sensed that anything was amiss. The whisky had dulled their senses, not their trigger fingers. There was only a padlock on the hut door, very light security considering the value of its contents. Through a gap, he could see why security was minimal. A thumbs-down to Phil conveyed the poor condition of those inside.

It was clear to Phil that they would need to maintain security for the hostages. Their local colleagues needed to come in and deal with the kidnappers. It was not ideal.

'Come in fast. We'll protect the hut on the right,' Phil said into the two-way radio in his hand.

'What about the hostages? Are they alive? Are they okay?' Victor asked. He had been at Emmanuel's interrogation in Port Harcourt; he wanted to be at the conclusion of the operation.

'They're in a bad way. Most of them will have trouble walking.'

'Okay, let's set our watches for one minute. Give us covering fire if the kidnappers come running out.' Victor said.

As Victor and his team came in, they quickly dealt with five of the kidnappers. Another three, alive and armed, headed towards the back of the compound and the hostages.

'They're pointing a gun at the head of one of the hostages,' Phil shouted. While the action had been continuing at the front of the hostages' hut, Phil and Harry had failed to secure the back of the building.

'Rush the door,' Harry shouted to Phil. 'We have no option.'

'Some of the hostages may get shot.'

'It's a risk we have to take. They'll kill them all if we don't act fast.'

Two of the three kidnappers dispatched with comparative ease; the third continued to hold the gun close to the temple of one of the hostages.

'I'll shoot him if you don't give me safe passage out of here.' The kidnapper was nervous, sweating profusely.

'Anything you want, just don't shoot.' Harry agreed to his demands immediately. 'Drop you weapon and we promise you will be safe.'

'I don't trust you. If I let him go, you will shoot me. Put down your weapons first.'

'Okay, we are putting them on the ground now,' replied Harry.

With Phil and Harry lowering their weapons, the kidnapper eased his hold on the hostage. At that moment, Phil reached carefully behind his back and pulled out a knife and, with one swift movement, pierced him cleanly between the eyes.

'That was remarkable. I've never seen anything like that before,' Harry said.

'Area secured,' Phil radioed in to Yanny.

'Helicopter is on the way. What's the situation?'

'The kidnappers have all been taken out. No serious injuries on our side.'

'What about the hostages?' she enquired.

'Alive, just, but they look to be in a bad way. Stretchers for all; there is a distinct smell of gangrene.'

'They'll be in Port Harcourt within the hour.'

'We have another situation to deal with in the north of the country,' added Yanny. 'We need to meet with Steve tomorrow.'

'It seems we're in a growth industry.' Phil attempted a humorous comment, aiming to defuse the seriousness of the situation they had just survived.

Meanwhile, Soboma Tom, oblivious of the activities down in Bomadi, was flying at thirty-five thousand feet with ten million American dollars in cash, his take on the latest ransom. He was heading to parts unknown and respectability.

Chapter 12

The man that Steve Case met that morning at the Novotel Hotel
on Stadium Road, in Port Harcourt, was a shadow of his former
self. Bob McDonald, a tall, well-built man in his fifties, did not
exercise as much as he should and it was starting to show in the
slight paunch protruding from above his belt. The kidnapping of
his daughter, Kate, had left him a shattered man.

'I will do anything to get Kate and the other woman
back,' he said.

'Helen,' Steve said.

'Helen, of course. I met her at the Mission. What about
her parents?'

'I phoned. They are distraught. They said they would sell
their house to raise money for a rescue.'

'Tell them that I will cover all costs,' Bob said.

'That's what I told them. They wanted to fly out here
straight away. I've dissuaded them for now.'

'What do we know?' Bob asked.

'The details are vague. We believe the Pastor and his wife
are dead. They'll conduct DNA testing although it's not
necessary. Duncan Nicholson is clearly dead; he was recognisable
and lying in the compound. Of Helen and Kate, we have no
information and we must assume the attackers took them. That
would be their usual modus operandi although this would be the
first time they have taken white women.'

'What do they want with Kate and Helen? Is it ransom?'
Bob looked for appeasing words, but he knew that ransom was
only one component – rape was a strong possibility.

'Ransom is no doubt the primary reason,' Steve replied.

'Is there another reason?'

'You know the answer to that question.'

'Yes, I do.' Bob sighed heavily. He looked close to
collapse.

'We must stay focussed, deal with the facts,' said Steve. 'My team are wrapping up a hostage situation not far from here. They will be here tomorrow.'

Bob McDonald came from an influential Louisiana family that stretched back many generations. There had been a Mayor of New Orleans back in the 1920s; numerous family members over the years had sat on the boards of the various schools and institutions in the city. One had even contemplated running for the Presidency of the United States back in the 1940s.

Unfortunately, for Bob, his father, Samuel, the black sheep of the family, squandered the substantial fortune that the McDonalds had strived for and accumulated over the years. Samuel had been a speculator, whether it was financial futures, the stock market or the roll of the dice. He always felt that a dynamic thrust, the right attitude would win through. He was sadly wrong and the last venture failed spectacularly. A broken man by the age of sixty, he simply resigned himself to the disgrace he had brought his family. He slowly faded away and died within a few years while Bob was in his early twenties.

All that was left was a sprawling, run-down Louisiana mansion, a couple of hundred thousand dollars in the bank, and an insatiable desire on his part to reclaim the family fortune and prestige. He reasoned that the best way to make money was to go where the money was, and that was oil. To drill a hole in the ground and pray there was a gusher sounded like speculation and he had inherited none of his father's less admirable traits.

No, he figured the best way to make money from oil was to supply the machinery and materials to those who were involved in its extraction. He registered Oil Extraction Ltd with the Louisiana Dept. of Revenue with him as the Chief Executive Officer. At that point, he was the CEO of a company consisting of one person, namely Bob McDonald. He did have, however, the savvy of generations of successful McDonalds. It was not long before he started to attract significant business.

Initially, he focussed on the oilrigs in Louisiana, then out into the Gulf of Mexico, then, after a number of years, to all the major oil fields around the world. Oil Extraction Ltd was to become one of the largest suppliers of drilling equipment in the world with a staff of over two thousand.

'I know you told me to pull everyone out from the Mission earlier,' Bob said. 'I listened to my daughter and Pastor Zebediah. I was wrong. I blame myself for what has happened.'

'The past is history. For now, we must focus on the present,' Steve replied.

'With my daughter, I am putty in her hands. You told me on several occasions, you even put it in writing, that you could not guarantee the Mission's safety. I chose to ignore that advice.'

'We're all putty when it comes to our children,' Steve said; it was of little consolation.

Only the Louisiana McDonalds' tenacity held Bob McDonald's emotions in check.

'Do whatever necessary to get them back,' he said. 'Money is not an issue'

'Kate may have listened to you,' Steve replied. 'The others, no matter how strong the message would not have left.'

'That's possible, but I should have been more determined, provided them better security. I did nothing.'

Steve attempted to change the subject. 'Our local team are staying in the North until this is resolved. They'll follow through on any leads, try and ascertain where they've gone.'

'Do they have any ideas?' Bob asked.

'North is the assumed direction.'

Bob rested his head in his hands and sighed. Steve paused for a moment before continuing.

'It would be preferable if this is kept out of the media for as long as possible,' he said. 'It always complicates the situation. Kidnappers tend to panic if there is undue pressure.'

'How quick before we get them back?'

'The time is immaterial. What is important is that we get them back in one piece, healthy and unharmed.'

'You did not mention untouched.' Bob sounded alarmed.

'Healthy and unharmed is our primary focus. If we act too fast, go in too soon with guns blazing, they will be compromised. You have to realise that we are dealing with irrational, emotive people who place little value on the sanctity of human life. The majority are fostering an opinion that what they do is condoned and in the service of their God.'

'I must respect your expertise,' said Bob. 'I just want to go straight in and grab Kate.'

'Your emotion is understandable, but you must place your trust in us.'

'I will. It's not easy to stand by inactive.'

'You have done all that is necessary,' said Steve. 'You must leave it to us.'

***

Yanny, Harry and Phil were exhausted, but jubilant. Bob McDonald had not slept in days. It did not bode well for the meeting at the Novotel Hotel in Port Harcourt the next day.

'Sorry, guys,' said Steve. 'I realise you need a good rest, some time off. But in this instance, we must focus on Kate and Helen's rescue.'

'We understand,' Yanny replied on behalf of all three.

'What do we know?' Phil asked.

'Not a lot,' Steve replied. 'We know that the Pastor, his wife and Duncan Nicholson are dead. There is nothing more we can do for them.'

'We have to focus on those still alive,' Harry said.

'I need you to find my daughter and her friend,' Bob McDonald said.

'Kate and Helen,' said Harry. 'What do we know? Where have they gone?'

'Our information is limited,' Steve replied. 'Aluko is in the area. He believes they have most probably headed north or northeast towards the border with Chad.'

'Any ransom yet?' Harry asked.

'Not yet. We'll receive one in due course.'

'*Due course!*' shouted Bob in exasperation. 'What do you mean in due course? My daughter is out there with a bunch of savages. God knows what will happen to her.'

'Bob, we spoke about this yesterday. Emotional responses will not help here. We have to be rational, methodical. We have to get them back unharmed and alive. Rushing in, out of a fear of what may happen, will not assist.'

'You're right. I will try to follow your advice.'

'Thank you. You have given us a clear mandate to conduct this operation, and sufficient funds. If it is too difficult, then I will be required to ask you to leave the meeting.'

'I will comply with your instruction.' Bob attempted to hold his emotions in check.

'So, where do we go from here?' Harry asked.

Yanny, in such a situation, would have expressed an honest evaluation of the likely scenario. However, with the grieving father being present, she decided on a more diplomatic approach.

'Women have a value other than monetary. Their lives will at least be more secure than a man.' She attempted to remain subtle, not to use the 'R' word. Bob McDonald knew exactly to what she was referring.

There was a knock on the door and a bright, very dark woman in her late thirties entered. 'I've asked Gloria, Gloria Layeni, to join us,' said Steve. 'She works in Bob's office here in Port Harcourt. She spent some time in the area. She has a good understanding of the local situation, the local culture. It is possible she may be able to assist us.'

'I spent some time in my teens with a Christian group,' replied Gloria 'We were trying to provide assistance to the poor and disadvantaged and to give some spiritual counselling. Kate and Helen's Mission is only about five kilometres from where we were; it was not so violent then. Port Harcourt is my home now, although I have maintained contact with a few people up there. I could attempt to communicate with them.'

'How?' Yanny asked.

'I need to go there.'

'We cannot let you go, it is much too dangerous,' Steve said.

'It is for you. The risk is acceptable for me. I can blend in.'

'Yanny, you will need to go with Gloria,' said Steve. 'Is that okay with you?'

'It will be too dangerous for her,' replied Gloria anxiously. 'They will spot her easily.'

'Believe me, they will not,' said Phil. 'Yanny is the best there is at blending into a local society. She can keep her head and most of her face covered. A little darkening of the face and she would pass for a local.'

'Then I would appreciate her company and her support. Yanny will need to keep quiet, pretend she has a speech impediment.'

'I can do that,' said Yanny, 'though my Arabic is fluent. It may be useful in certain areas.'

'Possibly, but it is best not to speak,' Gloria said.

'Aluko can pick you up and take you into the area,' Steve said.

'That will not help. Fly us to Abuja, and then we will take local buses. Two women travelling this way should not raise any concern. We are safe as long as we act conservatively, don't ask too many questions.'

'Yanny will be equipped with a satellite phone and a GPS. Is that fine with you both?'

'Fine by me,' Yanny responded. 'Any problems and I will dump them.'

'That's fine by me,' Gloria said.

Three days later, Gloria and Yanny arrived in Maiduguri. Gloria's friends, delighted to see her, offered her and Yanny accommodation without reservation.

'What brings you here?' they asked.

Gloria hesitated, not wishing to be too open. 'I had been planning a trip for some time, and I just took the opportunity to come up with Yanny.'

'We know that is not the truth. Our friendship must allow you to be truthful with us.' replied one of the local women.

'The two white women,' Gloria said hesitantly.

'It is sad as to what happened, but why are you interested?'

'I know one of them. We are aiming to get them back.'

'How? You are only two women.'

'There are others who will rescue them. We are trying to find out where they are.'

'Your friend, Yanny does not speak our language,' said the woman. 'Would she prefer we speak English?'

'That would be appreciated.' Yanny said.

'Yanny, please tell us about yourself.'

'Thank you for your hospitality and assistance.'

'Where are you from?'

'I was born in Senegal.'

'How can we help you, I don't believe we know very much? It does not pay to ask too many questions. We can make enquiries, but do not expect too much. It is best if you both stay here and please, do not venture into the street until you are ready to leave.'

'Thank you. We will abide by your instructions.'

In a concealed part of the compound where they were staying, Yanny used her satellite phone to contact Steve.

'We are safe, staying with friends of Gloria. They will conduct discreet enquiries on our behalf.'

'Good to hear you are both safe,' came Steve's voice. 'Any information will help. Don't stay there too long.'

'We won't.'

'We've received a ransom demand of one million American dollars for each,' Steve added.

'What has been our response?'

'No response. Bob McDonald is desperate to pay. He is organising the money for immediate payment.'

'You must stop him,' said Yanny. 'If we pay too early, they will want more money. He will not get them back any sooner by paying too quickly. He must be made to understand.'

'I've tried, but he is not rational. Anyway, it's up to us to arrange the payment drop-off and a location to pick up the women.'

'You must try harder to deter him. He cannot be allowed to make contact.'

'I need you back here to take control of the negotiations. Two days max where you are.'

'Bob McDonald, does he have their contact details?' Yanny asked.

'Yes, he does.'

'We're in trouble if he agrees to their demand.'

Counter Insurgencies best negotiator, Yanny had seen it before. Invariably, anxious relatives, or inexperienced company bosses assuming a quick agreement, the ideal solution. She knew that a quickly agreed to agreement always resulted in a higher price. Failure to agree to that, and the threats of injury to the hostage would start. She knew exactly what they would threaten: multiple raping by the foot soldiers of Boko Haram. Agreement to the second demand in an attempt to prevent them carrying out their threat would only result in a higher demand. She knew that she needed to be back in Port Harcourt at the earliest.

The first piece of tangible information as to the two kidnapped women came two days later as Gloria and Yanny prepared to leave.

'It is not wise to ask too many direct questions,' Amina, their hostess for the last few days, said.

'Yes, we know,' replied Yanny.

'What we have heard is that the women were seen passing through Baga, about one hundred and eighty kilometres to the north, close to the border with Chad. That is as accurate as I can give.'

'That helps a lot,' Yanny said.

Five minutes later, she was on the satellite phone to Steve.

'The women have been seen. It is not far, although the roads are so bad it may two days to get there. They were spotted by a truck driver.'

'Get back to Port Harcourt as soon as you can,' replied Steve. 'Bob has already contacted the kidnappers. Your worst fears have been realised. Now they want two million dollars for each of them, or else. I needn't spell out what the else is.'

'The fool! Doesn't he realise what he has done?' Yanny angrily replied.

'He does now. I've told him to keep out of it.'

'How did he respond?'

'He didn't like it, but there is no way we can help if he interferes.'

'We are leaving in the next hour,' said Yanny. 'Expect us in two days maximum.'

***

The return of the two white females taken in Maiduguri will cost one million American dollars for each. Payment within one week and no harm will come to them. Any delay will result in their deaths.

'That's the first email we received,' Steve said.

'Can we trace it?' Yanny asked. She had come straight to the temporary office at the Novotel on her arrival back from the north.

'It's a local server, difficult to trace.'

'It's the standard ransom note. Has there been any further contact?' she asked.

'There's this. A video posted on YouTube.'

'That's clearly Kate and Helen. They look unharmed.' She studied the video for a few minutes. 'We could have negotiated from that position. Let me see the damage that Bob McDonald has caused.'

Terms agreed. Money will be available in four days. Please send details.

'He sent the reply the same day,' Steve said.
'Show me their response,' Yanny asked.

The ransom is now set at two million dollars each. Failure to agree and the women will enjoy the undivided attention of our soldiers.

'He saw it?' Yanny asked.
'Almost collapsed on the floor when he read it.'
'It serves him right. Amateurs are the last thing we need. I hope he's keeping out of it from now on.'
'I told him that if he interferes one more time, I'll pull the team out, and he will have to find another organisation to attempt a rescue.'
'You'll not do that.'
'No, of course not,' said Steve. 'But I had to shake some sense into him. So, what do you suggest our response should be?'
'We debate their terms and stall for time. In the meantime, Phil and Harry need to relocate to the north.'
'They'll leave tomorrow. They can take a forward position up close to Aluko,' Steve replied.
'The women were seen up near Baga, close to the Chadian border. Are we going to check it out?' Yanny asked.
'We'll ask Aluko if he has anyone suitable,' replied Steve.

Two million dollars is not acceptable. Any abuse of the two women will render their value as negligible. Please respond in the affirmative, that the women are safe, they are healthy and well-treated, and that no harm will befall them.

'Are you sure you want to send that,' Steve asked.
'If we agree to two, the price goes to three.'
'The money's not the issue.'

'I realise that, but it best to make them think we are not an easy touch, agreeing to every escalating demand.'

The receipt of Yanny's email had the expected reaction. 'This is errant nonsense,' Murtada, the leader of the Islamists, said as he read the email from Port Harcourt. 'Western infidels do not place the value of a deflowered woman beneath that of a donkey. Their worth will not change even if they are abused and beaten.'

'The women – are they safe and untouched?' asked Murtada.

'They are safe,' replied Abacha.

Making sure that Bob was not in hearing range Steve asked Yanny a delicate question. 'What are the chances they have not been raped?'

'They have probably been pawed and groped, but those holding them for ransom realise they have a valuable asset. I wouldn't guarantee that they've not been raped.'

We are aware that the blonde woman comes from a wealthy family. Her ransom is set at three million dollars. The other woman's price remains at two million dollars. Any attempt to negotiate and our soldiers will enjoy the benefits of their company.

'This is a setback,' said Steve.

'No, this is what we want,' replied Yanny. 'They are open to discussion. As long as the price firms, their safety is improved.'

'I'll tell Bob to get the money ready.'

'I don't think we will need more. He has to realise that the money will almost certainly be paid, even if we rescue the women beforehand.'

Bob McDonald had endeavoured to go back to work. At least, he had been sitting in his office in Port Harcourt. Steve met him there.

'We need five million dollars in cash.'

'I thought it was four million?'

'It was, but the ransom goes up when you agree to the first demand.'

'Five million is a small price to pay. Does this mean that the rescue will not go ahead?'

'No, we continue as before. The actions of these people are unpredictable. They could return them unharmed or not, even sell them off to another party.'

'I will leave it in your hands,' sighed Bob. 'I will only complicate the situation.'

Terms agreed. Five million dollars; please respond in the affirmative, that the women are safe, they are healthy and well-treated, and that no harm will befall them.

Agreed. We will send instructions on the money delivery and the transfer point for the women.

'The deal is struck,' said Yanny. 'We have a maximum of four weeks to find the women.'

'That long?' Steve asked.

'Too quick to deliver the money and they will realise that they should have asked for more. Let's lull them into a sense of complacency.'

'We need some luck,' he said.

'Luck maybe, good fortune certainly. Ask Aluko to keep his nose to the ground.'

Chapter 13

Sheikh Idriss Deubet, a proud and noble man with a heritage stretching back one thousand years, was a trader in a trade that in past generations had made his family prosperous and respected. It was his forefather, Mohammad Idriss Habre, three centuries earlier, who had taken the family name to pre-eminence. The tales of his exploits, his daring raids, his treks across the continent and the marches north to the slave market in Tripoli were epic and oft recounted. On one of those trips of seventy days, up through Waday, Bornu, and Bagirmi, he transported close to three thousand slaves. He even pioneered the route down to the slave port of Luanda to service the demand from the Americas.

Mohammad Idriss Habre (the eldest sons of his descendants since that time had been given the name of Idriss in his honour) was a slave trader when slave trading was an honourable profession. Idriss Deubet also traded in slaves, but it was no longer honourable in a world that was overly sensitised and sanitised, and his exploits were not epic. To him, they were dismal, barely worthy of comment.

Mohammad Idriss Habre enslaved thousands, raided hundreds of primitive villages, moved large numbers of savages to the north and into the Middle East. He had not considered the fate of those he sent north into Arabia, the men, invariably castrated, the women, sex slaves, domestics if they were lucky. Those sent to the Americas fared marginally better, but he was no more concerned. They were a commercial commodity, a profit.

Deubet, a nobleman, reduced to selling little boys as goat herders across the border to Cameroon. He also sold young girls, no more than children, but capable to bleed and breed to some degenerate old man looking to regain his youth, his virility at the expense of a frightened child.

How can it be barbaric? he thought. *How can they criticise? They have no issue with their clothes and shoes from India and Bangladesh as long as they are cheap. Do they care about those who slave in countless sweatshops around the world? The fat and lazy Western men who frequent the brothels in Bangkok, Manila, and Mumbai – do they consider the underage girls? Are they not slaves?*

He dressed in traditional Chadian Arab attire, a long robe known as a Jalabiya, with a white turban on his head, a dagger tucked into his sleeve. He was tall and distinguished, a little overweight for a man in his late forties.

His revered ancestor, Habre, traded in thousands while he was fortunate if it was more than two or three.

Business had taken a turn for the better with the Islamic fundamentalists in Northern Nigeria. At least there were more young boys to sell as cattle herders, and the young women, sold across the border in to Cameroon or the Niger Republic as brides. If they had a unique beauty as well as a confirmed virginity, there was always a market in the countries of the Arabian Peninsula. The harems still existed, hidden from view.

The others he sold to whoever would pay the price. He did not ask where, or their fate; he always suspected a brothel in some dreary port, where people tended to disappear and nobody asked questions.

Was it not an ancient Westerner, Aristotle, who put forward the idea of final causes, that a slave is a slave by nature? he asked himself. *Did not their Christian bible embrace slavery in the Old Testament? Was it not true that the Westerners were the worst slave traders in history? Whom did my noble ancestor, Mohammad Idriss Habre, deliver the slaves to in Luanda? It was to Westerners, who embraced slavery as much as he had. What right have they to criticise?*

To Idriss Deubet, the trading of slaves was an honourable pursuit. He saw it as an aberration of a decadent Western society with their liberated views of equality, sexual promiscuity and undue wealth that had taken on one more cause to protest.

He could not see the value of Boko Haram's cause. He was a moderate man, but then, he reasoned, most were poorly educated, easily influenced, and ripe for control by an articulate and educated person. He had to admit that Mohammad Murtada, their leader, possessed both of those attributes.

Still, he reflected, life had not been unkind. His house, situated in a compound on the outskirts of N'Djamena, the capital city of the Republic of Chad, conveyed an air of resplendent tranquillity. The recent upturn in the supply of girls had offered him the opportunity to deflower some of them as they passed through his compound.

He dreamt of the days of his illustrious ancestor. How he wished, he could have been alongside him on the raids. How he would have enjoyed the triumphant arrival at the end of an overland trip with thousands of slaves in bondage. How he wished, he could emulate his success.

It was to the Sheikh that Kate would come. He would come to believe that it was the crowning moment of his career and his life. He was to be sadly wrong.

Chapter 14

It was not often that Sheikh Deubet came to the camp. It was unpleasant, dirty, and isolated, and the five-hour trip across the border from Chad, rough and dusty. He prided himself on his immaculate appearance; out here, it was not possible. He had made an exception on receiving advice of the two white women captives. Blonde, white, and possibly virginal, he knew of someone, someone of great wealth, who would pay handsomely if the virginity were confirmed and the beauty exceptional.

'The dark-haired female is of no value to me,' he said on his arrival. 'She is too old and you have given her to one of your men. She is clearly not a virgin. I am insulted that you lied to me. The other one is unique. It is hard to believe a Western woman of her age is still a virgin. I will need proof.'

'We have a doctor in the camp, he can perform the check,' Murtada said.

'Do you think I would allow a camp doctor to potentially damage her?' exclaimed the Sheikh. 'I must take her on the assumption she is not a virgin. Has she been abused by the degenerates that captured her?'

'She has not been touched. My commander at her capture recognised her value; he ensured she received the most reverential treatment. He had to kill one of his best fighters to protect her. Another, he severely beat. I give you my word, she is chaste and pure.'

'I cannot believe that she has not been abused. I have seen your fighters. You know as well as I do that they are an illiterate disorganised rabble.'

'I would not let anyone else say that to me,' replied Murtada, 'but you are an intelligent man, a valued colleague. They serve the purpose of the cause.'

Deubet was not taken in for one minute with vain flattery. He knew Murtada as a devious and impassioned man, who used the name of Islam to justify the violence and chaos he caused. To present himself as a colleague insulted him, but he would acquiesce and smile in appreciation.

'Have you sent ransoms for the women?' Sheikh Deubet asked.

'Yes, we have contacted the father of the blonde woman. We have negotiated five million in American dollars for the two of them.'

'And what was the response?'

'We have received acceptance from the father.'

'What is your plan now?'

'We will sell them to you if your price is better.'

'They will never pay that much, even if they agreed.' The Sheikh knew that the Westerners would pay the price, but he was not going to let Murtada know. Besides, he was not going to pay anything like that for the blonde-haired woman.

'They will, and you know that.' Murtada knew that the Sheikh was lying in what he had said.

'You will have their militaries down on you.'

'Then the women will die before they can be rescued. I have no compunction about ordering their slaughter if the military of any country is seen anywhere close to here.'

'I will take the blonde woman today, but I will not pay five million, or even one million. Harm their females and the Western military will be here with the Nigerian army and wipe you out.'

'Allah will protect us.'

'You are clearly naïve,' said the Sheikh. 'I have spent time in Europe. I have seen the competency and might of their military, the weaponry they command. Allah may protect you, but he will need to do a lot of protecting to save all of your people.'

'He will save me. The fighters are expendable.'

'You may keep the dark-haired women; she is of no value to me. I will take the other one. I have a buyer, but he will consider your price unacceptable. I can give you cash now, or weapons in exchange for the blonde, but I need to take her today.'

Sheikh Deubet knew her worth if she was indeed a virgin; he would get Dupre, the French doctor, to check her out. She would be worth a fortune if he had confirmation of her virginity. His buyer may well pay more than three million American dollars, possibly five. He could see an achievement to rival that of his esteemed ancestor.

No longer would he waste his time with a black girl, although some had commanded good money in the Arabian Peninsula. No longer a little black boy to a goat herder for thirty dollars. One of the girls had been sold for two thousand dollars, but her beauty had been exceptional; the majority, a couple of hundred dollars across the border into Cameroon. Here was at least five million.

She was unique, ideal for an auction. If her family paid the ransom, she would go back to them untouched and untainted. Either way, he would win.

'I need her now,' the Sheikh repeated his previous demand.

'Then you must give me three million American dollars, and in cash.'

'Your demand is an insult. You know you will never receive that money. I will give you one hundred thousand dollars.'

'It is you who insult me now,' shouted Murtada. 'I have already told you, we have a firm offer of five million for the two. What would possess me to sell her to you for a fraction of her real worth? She is yours for three million dollars.'

'That is ludicrous, and you know it.'

'What I know is that you wish to take her from me, and then collect the ransom for yourself.'

'If I take her, she is no longer your problem. You can send the other one back after they pay, then make it clear that the blonde is no longer in your possession.'

'They will not believe that I no longer possess her.'

'It is easy to convince them. I will send a YouTube video from a location that is clearly not Nigeria.'

'I will accept two million dollars.' The fundamentalist leader realised that the slave trader made sense. It would be easier if he sold the blonde-haired woman to the Chadian and sent the dark-haired woman back as soon as possible.

'Why do you maintain this pretence?' the Sheikh asked. 'You must admit that your success in ransoming of hostages is not an enviable record. You may be able to conduct the negotiations successfully, but those you place your trust in are incapable of carrying out your orders with the finesse required. I have not seen one here in this camp that I would trust with this matter.'

'Allah will assist me.'

'Allah will not assist in an endeavour that he does not condone. Where in the Koran does it mention that what you are doing is allowed?' The Sheikh realised that his anger had allowed him to speak in an irreverent manner. He regretted it.

'My belief in taking Islam to the heathens will require acts of violence. Allah will support me.'

'I was wrong to question your belief. I apologise.' The Sheikh wanted the blonde; he had not come to discuss the semantics of religion with a deluded fundamentalist.

'Let us not argue,' said Murtada. 'As a sign of our lasting friendship, I will let you have the virgin for one million American dollars.'

'I appreciate your offer, and I equally value our friendship,' replied the Sheikh. 'But I cannot give you one million American, certainly not with her virginity unproved. It would be safer to let me take the fair haired woman now at a discounted price.'

'You remember what happened the last time your people attempted a hostage exchange,' Sheikh Deubet said. It was a sore point that hit a raw nerve with Murtada.

'He was the son of a wealthy trader.' Murtada attempted to defend his action in the failed hostage exchange. 'The place, the money and the time agreed, but my people, your description in this instance is apt – an illiterate disorganised rabble. They failed to carry out the necessary security sweep in advance; too busy rejoicing in the conclusion of a successful kidnapping.'

'And they failed to notice the Nigerian soldiers hiding under the cover of darkness.' The Sheikh completed Murtada's sentence.

'Yes, they failed. The hostage was killed in the crossfire, the soldiers took the money, and I lost ten of my men.'

'What about the fighters that survived?'

'I had them killed as a warning to the others.' Murtada paused for a moment. 'It would be preferable if you took the virgin.'

It was fortuitous for the Sheikh that there had been a sighting of a military helicopter twenty kilometres to the south. The alarm went up through the camp, the foot soldiers mobilised and prepared to head south to intercept and take it out.

'What is happening?' the Sheikh asked.

'A military helicopter has been sighted not far from here. They are rushing to take it down. We must vacate the camp.'

'I will give you one hundred thousand dollars in cash for the blonde. If she is proven a virgin and my buyer approves, then I will give you an additional five hundred thousand dollars.'

'Then I must place my trust in you to honour our agreement,' Murtada said, eager to be on his way. 'What about the other woman?'

'Give her to your soldiers after your commander has tired of her. She has no value to me. One hundred thousand dollars, cash in the next five minutes for the blonde.'

'Take the virgin.'

Sheikh Idriss Deubet, delighted at hearing Murtada's words, quickly handed the money over and secured his prize. He knew Kate's worth and he certainly did not intend to come back to honour the agreement, virgin or otherwise.

Chapter 15

'What's the latest on the ransom demand?' Steve asked.

'No change,' replied Yanny. 'It's still three million for Kate, two million for Helen. I cannot stall much longer. Have we managed to narrow the location?'

'No more than what you and Gloria ascertained. We know the nearest community; it's not sufficient for a rescue mission.'

'Bob has the money. When will we need to pay it over?'

'Three weeks' maximum, although it would be better if you keep it to fourteen days. They are starting to get touchy, threatening again.'

'We cannot go blundering into the region,' replied Steve. 'By the time we find them, the kidnappers could have exacted their threats. We need more precise information.'

In the meanwhile, he had to break a promise. A promise he invariably broke most years. The school holidays had started back home in the USA and he had committed to taking Megan and the children on a holiday across the country to Disneyland. It was remarkable that, after all these years, kids still wanted to go there. He had gone at their age though Megan had never been.

'I can't leave,' he said on the phone to her.

'Every year you promise, and every year you let me and the children down,' she said, a little angry.

'I know, but this is too important.'

'What's so important that you cannot make an effort for the children?'

She never asked too many questions. After the trauma of his capture and torture in Afghanistan, she did not want to dwell on where he was or what he might be doing. To know he was potentially placing himself in danger again would have only given her sleepless nights. She was disappointed and asking too much.

'Islamic fundamentalists have kidnapped two white women. One's English, the other is American.'

'Then you must stay. I've no idea how I'm going to tell the children.'

'Thanks. I'll make it up some other time.'

'I haven't seen any reports on the TV.'

'That's the way we want it. The moment it becomes general knowledge, the American and English military will be here marching through the countryside. The women will be dead before they find them. This has to be low-key, discreet.'

'You're not involved in the rescue, are you?'

'No, I have others who will do that.'

'Who else is there with you?'

'Phil, Harry, and Yanny are here. Phil and Harry will organise the rescue. Yanny is dealing with the negotiations and the handing over of the ransom.'

He immediately regretted mentioning Yanny's name.

'How is Yanny?' Megan asked.

'They're all fine, but exhausted. They've been on rescue operations for months.'

'Give my love to Yanny.' Megan suspected there was something in the past between the two of them, but never asked directly. She preferred not to know.

***

Sheikh Idriss Deubet's interest in Kate's compound caused some concern.

'He takes the black girls – the attractive ones, anyway,' one of the local girls told Kate. 'He's interested in you and your friend.'

'What happens to them?'

'We are scared. He may take us as well.'

'What does he want them for?' Kate looked for a consolatory answer.

'He sells them into a forced marriage.' They were more naïve than Kate. The thought of sexual slavery did not enter their minds.

118

'Does this frighten you?'

'Yes, of course,' replied the girl. 'But have you seen what has happened to some of the other girls? Given to the men in the camp, passed around as if they were cattle. You have heard the crying, the screaming at night.'

'Yes, I've heard it.'

'We cannot alter our fate. We can only believe that a just God will protect us and deliver us from this place.'

'I hope your God will look after Helen and me as well.'

'Your friend went willingly. Why does she need our God's protection?'

'She did not go willingly. She did it to protect me.' Kate leapt to Helen's defence.

'How could she do that? How could she bring shame on her family?'

'She is of a different culture. I do not expect you to understand, but what she has done is the most generous and kind act that any of us will ever see.'

'We will accept your word that your friend Helen is an honourable person. We will show her respect.'

Two hours later the Arab entered Kate's compound.

'Please come with me. You will suffer no harm,' he said in perfect English. Kate, no longer associating perfect English as a sign of honesty and decency, protested.

'Why? What do you want? My father will be coming for me. Is Helen coming?'

'You are going home,' he replied. 'But first, you must visit my house. Either you will come peacefully or I will be obliged to use force. Your reluctance will not be tolerated.'

'I want to see my friend.'

'That is not possible. Either you come voluntarily or I will allow my men to use force.'

'I want to go home to my family. I don't want to leave Helen.' She was now crying profusely. There had been some safety, some security with Helen and the black girls in their little compound. Now there was to be none.

'You are going home, but first you must come with me,' he reiterated.

'I don't believe you. I know what you want me for.'

'What you believe does not concern me. You are a valuable asset. I will take responsibility for your auction.'

'Auction?' She was horrified. 'You are going to sell me?'

'Your father can bid or not bid. It is up to him.'

'Who else would pay money for me?'

'I have had enough of your foolish questions. You will do what I say. We leave now.'

'No.'

'Take her, and put her in the back of the vehicle,' he said to two of his henchmen. 'Be careful not to damage her or you will both suffer my wrath.'

Two of his henchmen were immediately at either side of her, pulling her towards the entrance.

'Let me assure you,' said the Sheikh. 'You will be an honoured guest in my house. You will be with my wives. The finest clothes, the most delicate foods will be available. No harm will come to you as long as you follow my instructions.'

Quickly bundled into the back seat of a late model Toyota Land Cruiser, her hands and feet loosely tied; she barely had a chance to say goodbye to the girls that had become her friends.

On the way out of the camp, she saw Helen aiming to rush to her rescue. Abacha caught and restrained her.

The Sheikh sat in the front passenger seat smugly satisfied in the knowledge he had secured a bargain, triumphant in a great asset that would reap him a great financial reward.

How much can I get in an auction? Five million? I may get ten. he thought. The possibilities excited him. An auction between a rich Arab, filled with lust, and a wealthy American, filled with fatherly love. Who will want her the most? Who can pay the most?

He daydreamed as the vehicle slowly bumped along the dusty road back to the civility and the serenity of his house back in Chad.

***

Helen resigned to the fact that she could have done no more for Kate, adjusted to the drudgery of her life. Covering herself with the clothing that was required of the women, she no longer returned to the compound she had shared with Kate.

Abacha's hut, primitive walls covered in mud and an old corrugated iron roof, was both unpleasant and uncomfortable and smelt of sweat and smoke. She now cooked for the two of them on an open fire just outside the only door into the hut. The food he received was markedly better than what he had eaten before – chicken and rice, and millet dumplings. He had shown her how to make the dumplings, the staple diet of his people in Niger.

In the hut at night, he was tender and loving; she had even managed to ensure he had washed before he took her. During the day, he was careful to conceal his newfound softness and showed her the disdain expected by his fellow fundamentalists. His appetite for food only exceeded by his appetite for her.

Each night, she ensured him all the pleasures, all the delights she could muster. It was clear he was not an evil man; poorly educated, limited literacy, a creature of his environment and upbringing. He did not see that what he did was wrong. She could not feign affection for him; he had been responsible for too much destruction in her life to afford him that emotion. However, as much as she wanted, she could not feel hate.

He was disturbed, pleasantly disturbed, that an emotion, a feeling, stirred in him that he had not experienced before. His wife back in his home village, bought by the sweat of his labours, was cold and dull, and would clam up; tighten her muscles when he tried to enter her. Here, with Helen, lovemaking was fluid, relaxed and infinitely pleasurable. She cooked his meals with care, ensured the table was set, and invariably she would find a flower to put in a vase. He enjoyed their time together in that little hut. Abacha had fallen in love.

She would admit that his behaviour had been acceptable, but a man on top of her belonged to the past. She had had more than her share of men, and all she wanted was to return to the happy days at the Mission. Those days, however, were not to return. The Mission was gone, the people as well.

***

'We may have a lead as to where the women are,' Aluko said on the phone to Steve.

'Do you have details?'

'Not yet. It may take a few days.'

'Why so long?'

'We've got to beat the truth out of them.'

'It's best if you give me the full story,' Steve said.

'You heard about the car bomb explosion in the marketplace outside of Abuja?'

'Yes, it's been on the news. Thirty killed, or at least that's what they're reporting.'

'That's for public consumption. It is closer to seventy. They're still peeling body parts off the road.' Aluko said.

'How does this apply to us?'

'Two of the perpetrators were captured.'

'Do they know something about Helen and Kate?'

'They say they do. I have an old friend; he's now the Police Commissioner in Abuja. He phoned to let me know.'

'Who will be conducting the interrogation?'

'The Police will, at their headquarters. It won't be pretty.'

'Pretty or otherwise, we need to know about Helen and Kate.'

'Apparently, they wanted to make a deal. Easy prison term or similar if they told all they knew about the white women.'

'The Police agreed?'

'They'll not entertain it for one moment. Seventy people killed, including the wife of a police constable. There's no chance of a deal.'

'I suppose I can't blame them,' Steve said. 'What can we do?'

'The interrogation begins tomorrow. My friend, the Commissioner, has held it off. He has asked if I wish to be present.'

'How soon can you get there?'

'There is a helicopter not far away from here that can be chartered. If a flight can be arranged, I could be there in four hours.'

'Take it. Refer them on to me, and I will sort out the details and the money. I would like to be present at the interrogation. Can you fix it?'

'That's impossible,' replied Aluko. 'The Nigerian police have a clear mandate of no forced extraction of information. You are a Westerner. Whatever they intend to do, they want it to remain a secret. My friend made it clear that whatever I see is to be kept confidential. I'm sure you understand.'

'Yes, of course,' Steve said, relieved that he was not to be present. He had not seen torture applied; he had only experienced it in Afghanistan. He could imagine the agony that the two bombers were to experience. 'How do we keep the information about the women out of the newspapers?'

'I will ensure the police squash any information leaks. Besides, they don't want anyone knowing that they use torture.'

'I wish I had your confidence. Leaks always seem to get out.'

***

The interrogation commenced at seven in the morning the next day in the basement of a police barrack on the outskirts of the city. The venue, Aluko had to admit, for something that officially did not exist was remarkably well set up.

The two captured bombers were led in. Both severely bruised from a savage beating, one of them requiring support and nursing a broken leg.

'The broken leg, how did he receive that?' Aluko asked.

'His fault,' said one of the interrogators. 'He was too close to the blast. It blew him hard up against a wall.'

He did not believe the explanation, but then he was there for information, not a debate on police brutality.

'You realise why you are both here,' said the lead interrogator to the two men. 'We need information. Is that clear?'

'We need our freedom,' said one of the bombers. 'If you give us that, we will tell you all you want.'

'Your crimes are too severe. We cannot grant you that.'

'Then we will not talk.'

'Suit yourself, but believe me, you will talk. You will even curse your mother and the day you were born before we are finished.'

'Allah will protect us. He will help us endure.'

'Sadly, he will not. You may live for one day down here, but you will not live for two. Let me assure you that before you die, if that is what you choose, you will tell us everything.'

'Allah will protect us,' they both replied in unison.

'If you tell us a lie, we will keep you here until it is verified. If it is proven incorrect, we will bring you back and intensify the pain.'

'Do you want to talk?' asked the second interrogator.

'No,' they both said.

'Hang them up on the iron bar.' The lead interrogator, a burly, hard man who would not give his name to Aluko, issued an order to his three colleagues. It was clear that the procedure seemed automated; this was not the first time they had had some hapless individual in the torture cell.

Hog-tied with their hands behind their backs, it looked as if their shoulders would rip off.

'They'll be permanently disabled.' Aluko expressed concern.

'Do you want to know where these women are or not?'

'Yes, that is what I want.'

'Then let us conduct our business in peace. If you are squeamish, go into the other room. We will tell you when they are more inclined to conversation.'

'I will stay.'

'Good, but from now on be quiet. If they are permanently disabled, so much the better.'

The second interrogator spoke to Aluko. 'Your friend, the Commissioner, asked us to conduct this entertainment on your behalf. Personally, I would have just beaten them to death.'

'The information they hold is too valuable. I will not speak again.'

During the first few hours, Aluko had to leave the room twice to vomit. The beatings to the bodies of both individuals were savage and, whenever they succumbed to unconsciousness, water was thrown in their faces.

Every beating that ended, the same question asked. 'Where are the women?'

'I do not know.'

'Why did you say you did?'

'We hoped you would let us go if we told you.'

'Now you know that we are not going to let you go. Where are they?'

Eventually, at two in the afternoon one of them decided to speak. 'They are to the east of Kano.'

'That is not true,' Aluko said. He had been sitting in one corner, his senses dulled to what he was seeing. 'That is a long way from their location.'

'Why do you say that?' the burly man asked.

'We know they are close to the border with Chad, an area close to Baga. Where he stated is nearly five hundred kilometres from there.'

'Your information, is it reliable?'

'It's our best lead.'

The burly man – it turned out that his name was Solomon – looked to the man who had just mentioned Kano. 'What did I say about lies?'

'It is the truth. I swear that it is.'

'My colleague here says you're not telling the truth. What should I do, believe him or you? Should I string him up alongside you on the bar?'

'I am telling the truth. I swear it.'

'I think we should check with you further.'

'It's time for the generator,' Solomon instructed one of his assistants.

He then turned to Kano man. 'I believe you, but my friend says you are lying. I only know one way to ascertain the truth. You don't mind if I check further, do you?'

'No, I am telling the truth,' cried the prisoner.

'I have a lie detector. It's not very complicated. Mine is simpler than those fancy ones you see on the television police shows, much more efficient. Do you want to know how it works?' He was playing word games with Kano man.

'Yes, tell me.'

'You'll enjoy this. It is great fun. My assistant is going to attach one cable with a clip to your right testicle, and the other with a clip to the tip of your penis.' Solomon grinned at the bomber. 'Are you with me so far?'

'Yes.' Kano man was beyond understanding the details. He was just aiming to be agreeable.

'Then, when we are all comfortable, he is going to wind the handle of the generator.' He turned to his assistant. 'Show him the handle, will you. I want him to fully understand how my simple lie detector works.' His assistant duly obliged.

'Did you see it?'

'Yes.'

'Did you feel the clips on your right testicle and your penis?'

'Yes.'

'Now, what do you think happens next?'

'I don't know.'

'Let me tell you. He will wind the handle and an electric shock will pass through your genitals. You will wish you were dead. You will cry, you will plead, and you will offer to tell anything and everything that we want to know. Are you looking forward to this?'

'I will tell you the truth. I know where the women are. Please, don't do this.'

'I still need to test my lie detector. I need to know if it is working. I will probably have to use it on your friend as well in the next hour or so.'

At that, the other bomber wailed. 'I know where they are. They are not far from Baga. Your friend was correct.'

'I am pleased to hear,' said Solomon. 'I could see that there was not enough room on the bar for the three of you, but first we need to check my lie detector. You will let me know if it is working correctly.'

'Please don't, I will tell you the truth,' Kano man mumbled.

'Is it necessary to continue?' Aluko asked.

'Once on the ground with some food in their bellies, they will start lying again. Do not trust them until they are broken. I may have to give the other one a trial on my lie detector as well.'

'I am overly sensitive,' replied Aluko.

'You are not. I do what I must here because nobody else will. I do not have to agree or approve of my actions. It is, unfortunately, the only way to get the truth.'

'It's time for handle turning,' said the second interrogator.

The handle turned, Kano man convulsed, he stiffened, he cried, one of his shoulder blades disjointed. It was only for ten seconds, but Aluko was in tears at the sight of the agony.

'How was it? Did my lie detector work?' said Solomon.

Kano man, unable to speak, nodded weakly.

'Cut him down. Give him some food and water. He needs a full belly for the debriefing.'

Solomon turned to Aluko. 'You can ask any question. He will not lie.'

'What about the other one? Are you going to cut him down?'

'Not yet. I need a second opinion on my lie detector.'
Solomon made sure the second prisoner heard the conversation.

'I will not lie, believe me,' said the man.

'Okay, cut him down. Give him a feed as well.'

It was best to give them four hours before the
questioning began Solomon told Aluko. Their brains would be
still muddled after the savage treatment they had received. Aluko
took the opportunity to contact Steve.

'We will speak to them in a few hours' time,' he said. 'It is
clear they know where the women are.

'Will they tell the truth?'

'After what I have seen inflicted on them? I am surprised
they are still alive. It was barbaric.'

'I'm sure it was.' Steve knew the treatment they had
received; he did not want details.

'I can meet Phil and Harry at the hotel when I'm free,
probably tomorrow morning.'

'Where do we go from here?' Steve asked.

'I'll send someone undercover to check the location.'

'Is he suitable?'

'Speaks the local language; he will blend in with no
difficulties. He will need at least a week to reach the camp, and
then try to join the group. It may cost him his life.'

'His family will be well provided if anything unfortunate
happens,' said Steve.

'He knows. He is a devout Muslim, abhorred by what is
being committed in the name of his religion. He sees this as his
solemn duty.'

Chapter 16

The two tortured Boko Haram soldiers were more forthcoming after their release from the iron beam and with a good feed in their bellies. 'The camp is to the north of Baga, about thirty minutes' drive,' Kano man said.

'How do you know?' Aluko asked.

'We are both from there.'

'The two white women. What about them?'

'The fair-haired woman has gone.'

'What do you mean, gone? Gone where?'

'The trader took her.'

'Who is the trader?'

'I do not know. We only know him as the trader. He is from across the border. He is an Arab.'

'Why did he take her?'

'I don't know. He sometimes comes and takes the black girls.'

'Why does he take them?'

'We are never told. We think he takes them to Cameroon and sells them as wives.'

'The dark-haired woman, have you seen her?'

'She is still there. She is living with Abacha.'

'Abacha?'

'Abacha led the raid to capture the white women.'

'That makes no sense. Why would she be with the man? You must be lying.'

'No, he is not lying. It is the truth,' the second prisoner said.

'I will accept your statement,' said Aluko. 'You know the punishment for lying, don't you?'

'It is the truth. Do not hurt us anymore.'

'I need the precise location of the camp. I want you to draw a map. Is that understood?'

It took another two hours while they drew a map with the necessary details. It looked correct. Aluko, abhorred as he was of the treatment the men received, had to admit that the openness and the detail they had given him were welcome.

'Keep them securely under lock and key while we check out their information,' Aluko said to Solomon.

'They will not be going anywhere. Any more information you require, just contact me and I will get the lie detector out again. It could do with some further tuning.'

'We have not lied. It is the truth,' repeated one of the men.

***

The last time Kate had seen Helen had been through the back window of the Sheikh's vehicle as it left the compound. The fear that swept over her had been palpable. Her spirit broken, she was almost catatonic. There had been times in the last few weeks when she had felt a degree of calm. Helen had been her support, , her sanity.

Now, as she headed towards an unknown fate, all the doubts, all the fears returned.

They're going to rape me, given to whoever pays for me, she thought. *Why did Helen leave with that murdering savage? Where is my father? Why is he not here to rescue me?*

During the journey, she fluctuated between rationality and self-pity. She did not have the strong personality of Helen or her strength of character. Helen's background had been traumatic and tragic; hers, soft and privileged. She could not change her nature, but she could attempt to emulate her friend.

I will be tough. I will not let them break me. I will survive. Kate made a pact with herself that, whatever was to happen in the future, she would remain resolute; she would rise above the adversity.

With no more tears to shed, there would be no more screaming at her captors. It was clear they cared little for her theatrics or tantrums; she would play the game as required.

With her mind in check, she would drift into a dreamlike state as the vehicle bumped along the road. Mute from her current predicament, she would imagine the good life with her boyfriend if he had lived.

True to his word, the Sheikh had ensured she was well treated; there had been no abuse, no pawing, and no rubbing close to her body. The daydreaming came to a dramatic end as the vehicle pulled up in front of a large, metal gate. To Kate, it looked like the entrance to a prison; to the Sheikh, it was home.

'This is my home,' he told her. 'You will be comfortable here.'

'I will try,' Kate replied resolutely. *If Helen can survive, so can I.*

***

'You're aware of the risk?' Phil said.

'I am aware,' replied Bayo. 'It is my duty to assist. I am the only person who can get close enough to the women.'

'We need to infiltrate the camp. We need to get word to Helen.'

'I will complete my assignment. She will receive a message.'

'Find out what you can about the other woman. Where has she gone? See if you can get a name for the trader.'

'I would have gone myself,' Aluko said.

'Sending you would be tantamount to a death sentence,' Harry said.

There is no way that Aluko could get near,' Bayo said. 'I am from the region. They will accept me as long as I show piety and devotion to their cause.'

Bayo was a deeply religious man. Well-versed in the Koran, he was able to hold his own in any religious discussion.

He had grown up in Kano, in the north, a humble, if relatively impoverished childhood. Islam had been central to the family's life. His father was honest, hardworking and decent, albeit financially strained. A small stall in the bazaar selling fruit and vegetables, which grew on a small block of land at the back of their house, provided a meagre existence.

His schooling had been a Madrassa, and Bayo, of average intelligence, was both literate and numerate. The Mullah, a good man, ensured that he received at least the basic components of a rounded education. A tolerant man, he had instilled in Bayo respect for other peoples, other beliefs, the infallibility of Islam, and the beauty of Sharia in its purest form.

At the age of twenty-nine, Bayo was in the prime of his life. He had a wife, although he had not seen her for six months. They had three children and his last visit had resulted in another pregnancy; he was hoping for a boy this time. A man was incomplete without a male heir; however, although the first three had been girls, he still loved them dearly.

'There is something that I have not told you,' Bayo said.

'Yes?' Harry replied.

'I have not spoken of this before. It may give you reason to doubt me.'

'I see that as unlikely, but tell us anyway.'

'The leader of the group I am infiltrating. I know him.'

'Murtada?' Aluko said. He sounded surprised. 'How?'

'He was a leader in our community,' replied Bayo. 'He comes from Kano. He came to my wedding.'

'Why would he have come?' Aluko was concerned.

'He knew my father from childhood.'

'Does this place any complications on our plan?' Phil asked.

'I met him briefly. It was before he became radicalised. I may be able to assimilate easier into the camp if I remind him.'

'Aluko, what are your thoughts? You've known Bayo for some years,' Harry asked.

'I trust him.'

Bayo, a wiry individual, small in stature, and quietly spoken, hid underneath that modest exterior a determined and resolute personality. He was the ideal person for the job ahead.

Harry instructed Bayo on a plausible story. 'You're a dissolute Muslim living in Lagos, trying to provide for your family. The disparity of wealth and the corruption abhors you, and they dismissed you from your job for wanting to pray five times a day. They even cheated you out of your last three months' pay.'

'Dismissal, non-payment of salary happens all too often,' Bayo replied.

'We can give you a satellite phone.'

'It's best if I do not carry anything that may break my story.'

'Will you take a personal GPS tracker?' It is not too large. If you are challenged or the situation looks dangerous, just dump it.' Harry asked.

'It places an additional risk on me.'

'We need a reliable fix on Helen's location. GPS coordinates would be best.'

'How can I do that? It will be dangerous to take any electronics into the camp. They are bound to search me.'

'Can you hide a small location GPS beacon outside the camp?' asked Harry. 'Go back for it later?'

'I will try.'

After a few days of intensive training in covert operations, Bayo was ready. A willing and capable student, his lack of skills made up with courage and determination.

***

It was after Friday prayers that Bayo left for the northeast and Helen. The bus, old and full of rattles made reasonable progress for the first one hundred and fifty kilometres. The road continued to deteriorate, rendering the vehicle progressively more unreliable. He had purposely taken the cheapest bus, and with unrelenting predictability, it would break down. Anxious hours spent in the hot sun, while a bunch of amateur mechanics attempted to patch it up, only for it to lumber on to the next breakdown.

It was clear to him, as the vehicle inched its way to Baga and Helen, that the effects of the Islamic fundamentalists were all too apparent. The villages they passed through were becoming more conservative, more run-down, more devoid of people, especially females.

It disturbed him. As devout as he was, he did not aim to suppress his wife. She dressed conservatively but she had a voice, an independent spirit, a right to go on the street, to go to the shops, and at home, a right to express her views.

The few churches he saw, neglected and, in some cases, burnt to the ground, while the few women he did see, covered with their eyes focussed on the ground.

The Nigerian military he rarely saw and, for the last hundred kilometres before arriving in Baga, conspicuous by their absence. It was as if he had left his country. It felt to him alien and intimidating. Fifty kilometres out from Baga, they encountered their first roadblock. Boko Haram was very much in control. It was a case of everyone off the bus, baggage searched; they were quick to confiscate anything desirable and demanded payments for the upkeep of the roadblock. At least, that is what they said. Bayo was under no illusions; he saw it go in their back pockets.

'Why are you here? You are not a local,' an unpleasant, short man with crooked teeth and overpowering bad breath asked.

'I have come from the south,' replied Bayo. 'I am a devout Muslim. I wish to embrace your cause.'

'You look like a spy. Your dress, your manner is not of the north. You may not even be a Muslim.'

'I come from Kano.'

'The military try to infiltrate us. We kill them quickly. It would be best if I shot you now.'

134

'Then, you better tell your leader that you shot Bayo, the son of his childhood friend because you couldn't be bothered to check.'

'Do not attempt to threaten?'

'I tell the truth.'

'Lies, it's just lies. Only a fool of a spy would use our leader's name in an attempt to save himself.' He instructed two of his fellow road-blockers, busily sitting on the side of the road playing with an iPad they had just confiscated from a hapless teenage boy to bind Bayo.

No doubt, they will destroy it later, Bayo cynically thought.

'Let the bus go,' the man instructed. 'This one stays with us.'

Luckily, Bayo had dumped the personal GPS tracker out of the window fifty metres down the road; the locator beacon, however, remained in his bag. As much as they had rifled through his belongings, they failed to notice the concealed pouch in the inner lining. They found five thousand Naira, the local currency; after that they lost interest.

'Get the truth out of him,' the crooked toothed man shouted.

'You will regret this when I meet with Murtada.'

'You will tell us the truth, and then we will kill you. He will congratulate us for intercepting a spy. Maybe, he will give us one of the schoolgirls as a reward.'

'You insult the name of Allah with your disgusting mouth and your impure thoughts.' Bayo realised he was in for a savage beating.

'Only a soft, lily-livered Christian would care about a female. They are there for our benefit.' shouted the man.'

'A female is to be respected. What you do is contrary to Islam.'

'It is clear that a captured female is for those who take her. You are a Christian, pretending to be Muslim.' The man looked around at the two who had been playing with the iPad. 'Beat the truth out of him.'

By the side of the road, Bayo received a savage beating. It was good that he was stronger than he appeared. Rifle butts, pieces of wood, fists in the guts and face would have sealed the fate of a weaker man. Bloodied, and barely conscious, the questioning recommenced.

'Who are you?'

'Adebayo.'

'Why are you here?'

'I have come to join Boko Haram.'

'Lies! You are lying.'

'It is the truth. Ask your leader, ask Mohammad Murtada. He will tell you who I am. He came to my wedding.'

'He came from Kano. How could he have gone to your wedding?'

'I told you before. I come from Kano.'

The mention of Kano caused his interrogator to pause, Bayo had mentioned it earlier, but the man had been both too stupid for it to register, too intent on inflicting a savage beating. Within his limited intellect, there dwelled the possibility that the man he had just ordered to be savagely beaten was telling the truth.

'Ease his bindings,' he commanded. 'Give him some water.' He looked at Bayo for a moment. 'If I assume you are telling the truth and I am not convinced yet, what will you tell our leader when you meet him?'

'I will tell him that I have come to join Boko Haram.'

'No, I am not referring to that. I am referring to the treatment you have received here.'

'I will tell him that you were diligent in your responsibility of not allowing potential troublemakers into the region. That you were attempting to flush out spies.'

'Will you do that?'

'Yes, I give you my word.' Bayo saw no reason to mention the savage beating to Mohammad Murtada. He was there to locate Helen and to find out where Kate had gone.

'If you are lying, then those at the camp will deal with you. If you attempt to escape my people, they will shoot you without hesitation.'

'I will not give them a reason.'

***

Held securely in the back of an old Toyota truck, the vehicle moved slowly along the bumpy track. They passed Kukawa as they headed to the camp, close to the western shore of Lake Chad.

'I need to pray.' He had seen the camp, not more than five hundred metres from where they were. The vehicle had run out of fuel at the optimum moment, and his captors were busily attempting to fill the tank from an old metal can that had been on the back of the vehicle.

'You can pray at the camp, it's only a ten-minute walk from here.'

'I must pray now. It is time.' They had noticed that their captive was dedicated in his prayers, more determined than they were.

'Five minutes only.'

'That is fine.' It was his time to prayer; it was also the ideal opportunity to place the locator beacon under a rock. He hoped that he would be able to get back in the next few days and activate it close to Helen.

After he had completed his devotions and loosely bound, they took him from the truck and led him to a small area near the centre of the camp.

'Why are you here?' Abacha asked.

'I have come to join.'

'Why should I believe you? Maybe you have come to cause trouble You look too well fed, too smart for me. I don't trust you.'

'Ask Mohammad Murtada. He will vouch for me.'

'I was told that you know him. I hope your statement is correct. Otherwise, you will die quickly.'

'It is true; I give you my word.'

Murtada was not in the camp, and would not be back for another day. In the meantime, Bayo remained under guard in a hut on one side of the camp. It was dirty and smelled almost as bad as his interrogator at the roadblock, but they showed him a degree of civility and provided him with food and water.

The next day, Murtada returned to the camp.

'There is a new arrival,' Abacha said to him. 'He claims he knows you from Kano. His father was a childhood friend of yours.'

'What is his name?'

'Bayo.'

'I know plenty of men who call themselves Bayo. Have you interrogated him?'

'It appears someone else had before he arrived here.'

'You should have roughed him up, checked his story.'

'I would not want to be responsible for beating the son of one of your friends.'

'It would have made no difference to me,' said Murtada. 'Let me see him.'

Bayo observed that Murtada's hut was larger and certainly cleaner than where he had spent the last day. It even had an agreeable smell.

'I don't know you. Who are you?' Murtada said.

'I am Adebayo, son of Audo Bayero. You came to my wedding.'

'I go to many weddings, but the name of Audo Bayero is familiar to me. How do I know you are his son?'

'My father told me that you both attended a Madrassa in Fagge district. You were friends.

'So did a lot of other people. I will need more convincing.'

'At weekends a group of you would go fishing on the banks of the Kano River. You always caught the most fish.'

'That is true. I was always the best; simpler days long past. Your father, assuming that I accept your story is correct, would not approve of you being here. He would certainly not approve of my actions and those of my group.'

'My father would not recognise the need for violence as a solution.'

'Then why do you not share the views of your father? You are showing him disrespect.'

'I have come from the south. The Christians dismissed me for wanting to pray five times a day, and they failed to pay me for my last three months' employment. They are aiming to suppress our beliefs. I cannot allow that. Hopefully, my father will understand my views in time.'

'Many here are disrespecting the views of their fathers,' replied Murtada. 'It is unfortunate, but in time they will come to believe in the worth of our cause.'

He turned to Abacha. 'I believe he is the son of my friend. He may have his liberty within the camp. Let him train with our men. If he is suitable, take him on a raid at your earliest opportunity. The worth of a man is only proven once he has been bloodied.'

Bayo had first seen what appeared to be a white woman on the third day. He had only seen the back of a heavily covered female, but there was something about the way she stood erect and the way she walked. She was on the other side of the camp. To move closer would have raised suspicion.

The small group he had been assigned to, were taking a break from training and sitting under a tree drinking tea, laughing and joking. Lamido, a good-looking individual who could not have been more than fifteen, was showing off to his adult friends.

'The fair-haired woman the trader took. How I would have worn her out,' he bragged.

'You're just a boy. You would not have lasted five minutes. It's a man she needs,' another joked.

'Who is the trader?' Bayo casually asked.

'We only know him as the trader,' Ado, a scar-faced individual replied. 'He comes here sometimes, buys some of the girls.'

'They call him Sheikh Idriss,' Lamido said quickly, bragging again. 'He comes from Chad.'

'How do you know that?' Ado asked.

'I overheard Mohammad Murtada talking to Abacha.'

'You'll not make manhood if you listen in on their conversations.'

'Is he right?' Bayo attempted to show disinterest.

'That's all he knows; all we want to know,' replied Ado. 'We don't stick our noses in, or ask questions.'

'He comes from Ndjamena,' the young braggart said.

It was clear to Bayo that he had completed his activity in the camp. All he had to do now was to place the locator beacon close to Helen, to let her know help was coming.

How am I going to get the information down south as to where the other woman has gone? he thought.

He could not just walk out of the camp to pick up the locator beacon. He would have to wait for the right opportunity. The chance came after Friday prayers.

It was only five hundred metres away, but in the confines of the camp, it may well have been a thousand kilometres. In the informality of the afternoon, the camp was less restricted, movement not so carefully monitored. He and a group of newfound friends took the opportunity of a walk in the area close by the camp. Bayo steered them in the right direction.

'I need to go to the toilet,' he said. Facilities were limited in the camp; a latrine was behind the nearest tree or in a hole in the ground. His desire to head off the track would not raise concern. Quickly, he retrieved the locator beacon and hid it in the back pocket of his trousers.

Returning to the camp, he ensured they took a circuitous route close to Helen. She was startled when she heard English spoken. 'Help is on the way. Act normal and stay prepared.' The last person who had spoken fluent English had been Murtada.

Standing to one side of her was a small, scruffy man with a rifle over his shoulder.

'You...' she started to speak.

'Don't talk to me. Act angry. Tell me to go away.'

She was quick to understand. 'Keep away, you filthy little man.'

'She told you quick enough,' said one of his friends. 'Abacha is screwing her; you're playing with fire there.' They laughed and joked at his expense.

'If he catches you, he'll have your balls,' said another.

The last laugh, however, was to be on them. He had planted the activated locator on the roof of the hut. Now all he had to do was to get out of there.

***

His way out came sooner than expected. Abacha addressed the group the next morning.

'There's a small military detachment about ninety kilometres to the south. We are going to hit it. There have an armoured vehicle and some heavy duty trucks we could use.'

'Are we taking Bayo?' Ado asked.

'He's going to lead us in.'

'It's his first time. Is he ready?'

'If he's not, he's dead.'

It was clear to Bayo that this was to be his baptism of fire. He had to survive; he had to get a message to the team.

'Okay with you, Bayo?' Abacha asked teasingly. He was still not convinced. It may be one thing to be the son of a family friend of Murtada's; it was another to be a dedicated Islamist.

'I am fine. When do we go?'

'In one hour.'

The journey took the best part of the day. The convoy of three trucks diverted at the sign of any habitation. It was imperative that as few people saw them as necessary. At four in the afternoon, and five kilometres from the military post, they halted.

'It should be easy,' Abacha addressed the group. 'We'll go in at dusk when they're settling in to their evening meal. There are two entrances, and neither is well guarded. I will head in through the rear; Bayo will lead in through the front. All clear with you?' He directed his eyes at Bayo.

'It is fine with me,' replied Bayo.

'You're too confident for my liking. I don't trust you.'

'Murtada does.'

'I know, but you need to prove yourself to me. If you are successful today, then you will also have my trust.'

'We will be successful,' Bayo replied confidently.

Abacha knew a frontal attack would draw the maximum response from the soldiers. It was a suicide mission for the first two or three going in, and Bayo was to be in the first two or three. If he died, so much the better; if he lived, and proved to be a dedicated Islamist, he would be a threat to Abacha's position as a Senior Commander. Better, he was dead.

Bayo realised that Abacha had deemed him expendable. He had not yet relayed the knowledge he had regarding Kate; he had to live. Clearly, there must be a better way to secure a military base than blindly rushing at the gate.

Abacha had moved to the rear, intending to wait a few minutes after Bayo had stormed the front.

'We will be mowed down if we rush the gate,' Bayo said to the eight fighters with him.

'Abacha ordered us to attack,' said one.

'Then he is wrong. Do you want to die?'

'If we do not follow his orders, he will kill us for disobedience,' replied another. A disparate group of individuals, they saw Abacha as their superior in both intellect and authority.

They would rather commit suicide than disobey him, Bayo thought. *What use are they to me? If they want to rush the front gate, so be it. I will not.*

At the nominated time, one of the trucks ramming it broached the gate. The frontal attack group moved in, all except Bayo, who had climbed the wall on the left side of the entrance. The soldiers guarding the military base quickly responded. Of the eight fighters, five fell in the first two minutes. Two of the army personnel gunned down in the confusion.

'Commence the attack.' Abacha had heard the shooting and he felt sure that with the soldiers' attention diverted, he would have the upper hand

Bayo found an office to one side of the yard. There was a satellite phone and it was charged. He needed to be on a roof for it to work. Quickly, he saw some stairs leading up.

He dialled the team. Harry answered. 'I found one of the women. She knows we're coming.'

'We picked up the locator beacon. A rescue team is on the way. What did you find out about Kate?'

'She is with a Sheikh Idriss, an Arab from Chad. Apparently, he lives in the capital and buys local girls to sell as wives in Cameroon.'

'You need to get out of there as soon as possible.'

It was then that Abacha glanced up at the roof. He saw Bayo with a phone. Always a good shot, he levelled his rifle and shot him straight through the heart.

'I intend to leave…' Bayo would never see his newborn son.

Chapter 17

It was up to Harry to pass on the information from Bayo. The noise of the gunshot and Bayo's scream of agony had told him that the brave volunteer had died at the hands of Boko Haram. He chose not to mention it when he contacted Steve with an update. 'Kate is in Chad. We have a precise location on Helen.'

'When can we rescue Helen?' Phil asked. He was with Harry waiting in Abuja. He was ready to move forward to a rescue.

'Let's aim for seven days,' said Steve. 'We need to find Kate first.'

'You're right,' replied Harry. 'Rescue one and the word gets through to the other's captor, it could be precarious.'

'How do we deal with Chad? I don't know anyone there,' Steve said.

'I do,' Harry said.

'You never cease to amaze.'

'Ahmed Sahoulba. His father was the Chadian Ambassador in Paris.'

'How do you know the son of the Chadian Ambassador in France?' Phil asked.

'It's a long story. We spent time at a ski school in the French Alps. We still keep in touch, meet up occasionally.'

'Your family must have been loaded,' Phil said.

Harry had just turned fifteen at the time, and breaks from boarding school always presented difficulties for his father, the honourable Earl. A jealous, possessive man with a rampant, horny teenage son did not gel, especially now he had a new wife. Harry's mother had died when he had reached the age of nine, tragically in a car accident the night the Earl had passed her over for his mistress, who was soon to become his second wife. The latest, his third, an attractive brunette he had met in a seedy strip joint, was no more than five years older than Harry, and sexually precocious.

The Earl, no matter how much he exercised, no matter how many performance-enhancing drugs could not keep up with his young wife's incessant demands. He could not satisfy her, but Harry may have and he would have been easy prey. The Earl was not taking any chances. He knew she was there for the money and title, but he still expected fidelity on her part – or, at least until he had tired of her.

'I'm sending you to a ski school in the Alps,' his father, the Earl Hampden had said.

'Can't I stay here for once?' Harry, the sexually ready virgin, asked. He had seen the brunette and she was making passes at him.

Ahmed and Harry had met the first day at the ski school and formed an extraordinary and deep friendship: one the son of a member of the English aristocracy, the other a Chadian Ambassador. Harry was there because he was a threat to his father's sexual activities; Ahmed because his father was too busy with affairs of state. Regardless of the honourable reason of one and the lasciviousness of the other, both were resentful of their treatment. Weeks spent discussing the validity of the English aristocracy in a modern capitalist system, prolonged discussions on Islam in a secular society, and both aiming to seduce some of the beautiful teenage women during their four-week sojourn.

'There are those in my country who profess a deep devotion to Islam,' Ahmed said. 'Yet they conduct activities contrary to what you would regard as acceptable.'

'What do you mean?' asked Harry.

'The Koran states that a woman is to be treated with respect, yet there are some who subjugate, suppress their women. Keep them in locked houses; treat them as no more than chattels.'

'My father shows them little more respect,' said Harry bitterly. 'They are purely for his entertainment.'

'But they have freedom of movement, and he ensures they are looked after well financially. Is that not true?'

'Yes, you are correct. I am just angry that each holiday he shuffles me off to somewhere or the other.'

'If he had not, we would not have met,' Ahmed said.

'That is true.'

'I have heard that, within my country, slavery still exists,' continued Ahmed.

'Slavery?' said Harry surprised. 'I thought that disappeared last century?'

'That is an official stance, but feudalism, the selling of children as domestic servants to tend animals, is still there. They portray it as indentured labour, but I do not believe that to be the case. My father, a wise man, confided in me that it still occurs.'

***

It had been a few years since Ahmed and Harry had last met. It came as a surprise, a pleasant surprise when Harry contacted him.

'Ahmed.'

'Harry! Where are you? I would recognise your voice anytime. When are you coming to visit?'

'I'll be there in the next few days. Is that alright?'

'Of course it is all right but why the rush? It's not like you to be so impulsive.'

'I need your help,' said Harry. 'It's a matter of great importance.'

'You can rely on me,' replied Ahmed.

'You may be offended by the reason I am coming.'

'I cannot see why.'

'Ahmed, there is a white woman we believe has been bought by an Arab from Chad.'

'That is distressing news.'

'I know I can rely on your confidentiality,' continued Harry. 'It is important that this does not become widespread knowledge until she is rescued. It may be dangerous for her if it is plastered across the Internet and on the TV screens.'

'My discretion is assured.'

'She was taken by Boko Haram, sold to the Arab.'

'Are there any more details?' asked Ahmed.

'What we have is that the trader lives in N'Djamena and his name is Sheikh Idriss.'

'Idriss is not an uncommon name. I will make discreet enquiries on your behalf.'

'Sorry that my visit is to be business, not social.'

'Any opportunity to get together and talk is welcome. I have a sad feeling that, if what you are saying is true, it will reflect badly on my country.'

Two days later, Ahmed phoned Harry. 'I have a potential name.'

'I'll be there tomorrow.'

'I will give you the name now, Sheikh Idriss Deubet. To my shame, I have met him on several occasions.'

'How much have you found out?'

'Not a lot. I knew he was a trader, livestock mainly. I have someone here that you will meet. I trust him to search around, stick his nose in where it is not wanted. He informed me of rumours of the trading of black girls and some boys from Northern Nigeria. The name that kept coming up was Deubet.'

'It sounds possible,' said Harry. 'Do you have any more details?'

'No, we decided not to ask or act suspiciously until you arrived. You are more proficient in these matters than we are.'

'Thanks, I'll see you tomorrow. I'll probably be bringing some colleagues.'

'They're welcome.'

'One's female.'

'We are an enlightened family. She will be most welcome.'

Chapter 18

Kate's introduction to the place that was to become a home for the foreseeable future was more pleasant than she had expected. 'Comment allez-vous? Je m'appelle Fatima.' It was the first friendly face, the first smile that she had seen in two days.

'Je vais bien, merci, et vous?' It was an adequate response, and close to the limit of Kate's French skills. Her least favourite subject in school, and now the one she needed the most.

'Je vais très bien.' Fatima delighted as she was to see the new arrival, was full of trepidation.

'Je m'appelle Kate.'

It was unclear to Fatima as to why the beautiful white-haired woman was there.

Has he acquired a new wife? Maybe, she is a concubine. To her, she looked like a porcelain doll.

It was in her late teens that Fatima had become the second wife. The marriage, arranged and, being the second wife of an affluent man, a member of an honourable and respected family was all she desired. He had paid an unusually high price to her father, a moderately successful businessman in the north of the country. A modest person; she did not see her beauty, her charm, and her education as necessarily desirable traits.

Those first seven to eight years with the Sheikh were ideal, and she had the opportunity to travel to Europe on many occasions. The first wife, a good person, suffered the rigours of five children and was prone to illness and fatigue. To Fatima, the Sheikh was her husband and she learnt to love him, the feeling reciprocated, she was sure.

It was the conclusion of the eighth year that a transformation in his manner occurred. Of his five children, four had been daughters and they enjoyed remarkably good health. The fifth child, a sickly boy of ten, died suddenly, a result of a severe bout of malaria, compounded with intestinal problems. The Sheikh grieved for three months.

His nightly visits to her declined to once every two or three weeks. Her body, she realised, was not the firm and tender delicacy of well rounded and firm breasts and curvaceous hips that she had as a teenage bride; instead, it was sagging and bulging. She assumed that was the reason.

'You are worthless to me,' he said angrily on a visit to her bedchamber.

'I do all that I can to please.'

'My only son has died and you are unable to give me another son.' She had tried to fall pregnant over the years but it was not to be.

'Then you should take another wife.'

He heeded Fatima's advice and another marriage was conveniently arranged to a young, teenage girl of good breeding stock It was remarkable how close in appearance to her she was. A sullen-faced female, she rarely smiled and it became apparent over the next few years that the Sheikh did not favour her with the regular visits Fatima had once experienced.

'She is charmless and frigid,' he complained to Fatima on one of his visits to her.

'She has given you two healthy sons.'

'I must accord her the respect that the mother of my sons is due, but I find her company dull.'

'Then visit me as you see fit. I understand that you must spend most nights with her. You have two sons; there is no reason as to why you should not have more.'

'A man is judged by his sons,' the Sheikh, a proud man, said.

To Kate, Fatima was a beautiful woman with her mixed African and Arab heritage – olive skin, her hair dark, and a face full of allure.

With Fatima, Kate soon came to feel the ease that she had experienced with Helen. The two women quickly bonded. It came as a revelation when Fatima spoke a few words of English.

'I can speak little English,' she said.

'That is good,' replied Kate. 'My French is very bad.'

'No, your French is better than my English.'

In a very short period, and with use, Fatima's linguistic skills became apparent. An enthusiastic student at school, she had regarded English as one of her favourites, although formal schooling finished soon enough at fourteen.

'A woman's place is in the home, rearing children,' her father had said.

'Father, I want to study,' she pleaded.

'You are to be married. What use will an educated woman be?' A moderate and agreeable man, his was a culture that failed to understand the validity of what she was requesting.

After her marriage, the Sheikh provided her with learning materials and access to an English-speaking radio station. She used her time well, and her English, heavily accented with traces of Arabic and French, understandable.

Kate had to admit her surroundings were more suitable than the dirty little camp, and substantially more luxurious than the Pastor's Mission had been. Opulent in design and construction, and furnished to the highest standard, it was a haven.

'What is this building?' she asked Fatima that first day.

'It is the women's quarters.'

'Women's quarters? Do you mean a harem?' Kate replied. 'I didn't think they existed.'

'It is reserved for women only. The only man permitted to enter is the Sheikh.'

'He has concubines?'

'No, he has only the three wives and their children. Sometimes, there are some black girls around the back, but we do not see them.'

'What are they for?'

'They are part of my husband's business.'

'What business is that?'

'He sells them for marriage. That is all I know. Sometimes he visits them at night.'

'That sounds awful.'

'All marriages are arranged in my country.'

'They have been stolen, kidnapped from their parents in Nigeria,' replied Kate. 'I am sure of it.'

'If what you say is true, then I could not approve.'

Some days later, attired in elegant and traditional clothes, Kate resolved to visit the black girls locked in the rear of the building.

'I want to talk the women in the back.'

'It is not possible,' said Fatima. 'Sheikh Idriss will be angry.'

'I need to know what is going to happen to me.'

With Kate determined, Fatima could only make one decision. She would go with her. Besides, if what she had said was true, then how could she regard her husband with any more than contempt and derision?

Had not Kate been kidnapped? Surely, he knew that. Surely, he did not care, she thought.

***

It was late at night, when all the others were asleep in the women's quarters that Kate and Fatima snuck quietly along the narrow passage to talk to the black women.

'Kate, I am Aisha, we have spoken in the marketplace. My father was a merchant there.' The voice was familiar; the English clear and precise, the face concealed in part by the heavy grille on the opening at the top of the door.

'You came there once or twice with the other woman,' she continued. 'She was also white, but her hair was dark.'

'Helen.'

'Yes, Helen, I remember now. Is she here?'

'No, she is still with the attackers of the Mission.'

'That is what I heard.'

'How many of you are here?' asked Kate.

'We are ten.'

'Why are you here?' Fatima asked.

'We were kidnapped, brought here by force.'

'Tell us your story,' said Kate. 'I need to know my, our, fate. Fatima wishes to know the truth.'

Some light filtered into the room where Aisha and her companions were confined. Slowly adjusting to the available light, it was clear to Kate and Fatima that Aisha was an attractive young woman, of about fifteen years of age. Her friends, concealed at the back of the room, seemed equally young, equally attractive.

'We were at school,' explained Aisha, speaking through tears. 'It was an excellent school about fifty kilometres from your Mission. It was late at night when they came in force and with many weapons. There were over one hundred pupils, all female; they took them all.'

'What about the teachers? Where are they?' Fatima asked.

'Two of our teachers attempted to stop them with broom handles. The men killed them with machetes.'

'And the others?' Kate asked.

'Our beloved teachers… they dragged the six that were still alive out of the classrooms.'

'Then what happened?'

'It is too horrible,' said Aisha, crying. 'I cannot speak of it.'

'I will,' said one of the other girls confined in the room. 'My name is Victoria. I will tell you.'

'Thank you,' said Kate. 'We need to know.'

'The youngest of our teachers was about thirty, the oldest at least sixty, but to us they were our friends. We loved them dearly.'

'Go on.'

'They stripped them naked, and then the savages raped them without inhibition or remorse.' Victoria spoke quietly and without emotion. 'We were forced to watch. If we did not, they said we would be raped as well.'

'Did you all watch?'

'One of us, a sweet and dear friend by the name of Blessing, refused. She screamed for them to stop.'

'What happened?'

'They took her, stripped her and raped her repeatedly.'

'Then they killed her,' Aisha added.

'They told us what they had just done was an example to us,' said Victoria. 'It was for us to obey, to comply with anything they asked of us.'

'You must have all been very frightened,' said Kate.

'We were,' replied Victoria. 'We still are. We were forced into a number of old trucks and driven north to their camp.'

'Where are your friends, the other pupils?'

'They are still in the camp,' said Aisha. 'They took them, gave them to the men. We never saw them again, although we could hear them screaming, and the men laughing. We did not sleep that night, or for many nights after.'

'How did you get here?' Fatima asked.

'The trader, he purchased us.'

'Who is the trader?'

'That is what they call your husband in the camp,' Kate said.

'*He is your husband?*' Victoria exclaimed angrily.

'I did not know,' replied Fatima. 'I am sorry. I always assumed that your presence here was at the instigation of your parents and that he was acting honourably as an agent.'

'He is neither honourable nor an agent. He is a slave-trader,' Aisha said.

'I know that now. It is to my shame that I have been deceived.'

'Why were you not given to the men at the camp?' Kate asked.

'It is because we were the prettiest at the school. We are to be sold to whoever is willing to pay.'

'For marriage?' Fatima asked.

'That is what we were told, but we are not so sure,' said Victoria. 'We are aware there are places where men visit and pay money for sex. Could we be sold there?'

'A brothel, it is possible,' Kate said.

'I will kill myself before that indignity.'

'It is best that you do not think such unpleasant thoughts. You are all alive and well. Where there is life, there is hope. Maintain your spirits.'

'We will try,' said Victoria. 'But why are you here? A beautiful white woman must command a high price.'

'My story is similar to yours. I am being held for ransom.'

'Ransom to whom?'

'My father.'

'There are wealthy Arabs from the north who sometimes visit,' said Fatima. 'I had always seen them as business acquaintances. Now I suspect they were here buying women.'

'You mean he may sell me to a rich Arab?' Kate replied with alarm.

'It is a possibility. I hope I am wrong.'

'If your father comes, please take us with you,' Aisha pleaded.

'I will try, but my situation is no better than yours.'

***

Several days later, the only man permitted to enter the women's quarter visited. He had come to speak with Kate. 'I hope you have been shown the greatest respect, and that you have received the treatment of an honoured guest.'

'I have,' she replied.

'I am currently negotiating the terms for you return.'

'You are discussing with my father?'

'Yes, that is correct.'

'You have no right to hold me. I am an American citizen. My father has powerful connections; they will come and rescue me.'

'Your father is a wise man,' replied the Sheikh. 'At least, I hope he is. If he contacts his influential connections, or if I see any sign of deception on his part, then your position of safety and respect will be compromised.'

He stared at her for a few moments before continuing as if to emphasise his point.

'He, or the people that I am in contact with, have been told to maintain secrecy. They have been told not to commit any actions that would be deemed contrary to a peaceful resolution.'

'Am I to be sold to whoever pays for me?'

'I give you my word. As long as your father acts honourably and abides by our agreement, then nobody else will buy you, or act in a manner unbecoming. As a devout and pious Muslim, I give my word. I am a businessman and you are a commodity – indeed, a very valuable commodity.'

They had been offered as comforting words, but neither Kate nor Fatima, when Kate recounted the conversation to her, were fooled. They had met Aisha and Victoria; they knew the truth of the situation. Kate was for sale, and her father was not the only buyer.

'He stated that I would be returned upon payment of a ransom and I will not be harmed.'

'We know he has not told the truth,' said Fatima. 'What are you going to do?' She was now dramatically disillusioned with the Sheikh, dreading a night visit from him. *How would she react? Would he sense her coldness? Would he be suspicious?*

'There is very little I can do. I must place my trust in my father. He will not let them take me. He will come.'

'When he comes, please take me with you.'

Another week passed, and Kate remained confined. A gilt cage it may have been but, as luxurious as it was, it remained a prison. Fatima had been allowed out once to travel into town, but she was not permitted to leave.

It was during Fatima's absence that the Sheikh visited Kate. 'Your father does not agree to my terms. He wishes to negotiate your ransom. This is not the action of a father who professes love for his daughter.'

'I do not believe you.'

'What you choose to believe or not believe is not of concern. I have no option but to offer you to others who will see your value.'

'You gave me your word. You said you were a devout Muslim, and that I would go back to my father.'

'I gave you my word in the belief that your father was an honourable man.'

'Who do you intend to sell me to?' Kate asked, trembling and in great fear.

'I will sell you to the highest bidder.'

'And what will he do with me?'

'That is not of my concern.'

'I am an American citizen! You cannot do this to me.'

'Here, you are a commodity. This is not America. Your fate is in my hands, not your father, and certainly not your country. I will inform your father that his unwillingness to agree to my price has caused me to conduct an auction. It is his decision as to whether you are returned safely to him.'

'He will not let anyone take me,' she replied, her voice trembling with emotion. She was trying to hold back the tears.

'He is not here. He will not find this location.'

With those few parting words, he left. He was elated; she was devastated. The auction, unbeknown to Kate, had commenced sometime previous.

The Sheikh on leaving made a phone call to the one man that had the money and the need of a woman such as Kate. 'I await your representatives in the next few days. The commodity is unique, of the finest quality. You will be well-pleased.'

'I will be disappointed and angry if she is proven not to be a virgin,' the mysterious buyer said.

'Her virginity is guaranteed.' The Sheikh hoped his statement was correct.

Chapter 19

Abdul bin al-Ibrahim had a family history stretching back generations. He was a Prince in his society. His education had been the finest his country and the West could offer. Graduating from Oxford University with a bachelor's degree in economics, he represented the ideal blend of Saudi society and Western values.

He was urbane, polite, and always immaculately dressed, whether it was the traditional dress of his country or the elegant look of an affluent Englishman. His suits were of the finest cloth from Savile Row in London; his shoes handmade by John Lobb.

It was oil that had given his family wealth beyond that of Midas. The substantial investments in real estate in the business districts of New York, London, Geneva and numerous other cities would ensure their wealth and lifestyle would not be hampered by a downturn in oil revenue.

He was portrayed in the media as the agreeable face of Saudi Islam. However, he had a flaw, a weakness. Never reported, it was carefully concealed behind a veil, protected by highly paid and highly professional consultants.

The playboy Prince, they called him. The man who had everything, the man to whom money and the beautiful people gravitated.

His weakness was women. His desire for them, in all shapes and forms, although preferably blonde and young, was insatiable.

'It is time to take a wife,' his father had said. In his mid-twenties and living the life of an up and coming financial consultant in New York at one of the family's banks, he was not prepared, or concerned, for the rigours of Saudi society.

'I am not ready for marriage,' he had protested.

'It is your duty to your family, to your country, to your society.'

The young Prince was obliged to respect the family and, in due course, a marriage was held, a forging of two business dynasties, the marriage of two cousins.

His father had made the arrangement while his mother had ensured the bride was of suitable breeding stock. The young Prince had first seen her face on the day before the wedding and he had to admit that, while not beautiful, she did look pleasant and agreeable. It was on the wedding night that he first saw her body and it was as he had imagined. Her breasts were too small, her hips too large and her skin too blotchy.

'She is good breeding stock,' his father said whenever the Prince complained.

'She may be, but she doesn't excite me.'

'Your marriage to her has secured significant financial benefits and status for us.'

'I accept the marriage. I will fulfil my duty.'

'Give her plenty of healthy boys to occupy her time,' his father said. 'As far as your future wives are concerned, you may choose to your liking, only ensure they come from respectable Saudi families.'

In time, Prince Abdul bin al-Ibrahim learnt to become fond of his first cousin wife, although she never excited him sexually. She had been pleasurable in the marital bed, and three children had ensued. One had died young, but the other two were fine and sturdy. They were boys and he would always be eternally thankful to his wife, Sanaa, for bestowing them on him.

As the years passed, she ballooned in weight and he found no desire, no pleasure in her. Three children and a lifetime of leisure, overindulging in exotic and richly flavoured food had extinguished any passionate interest that he may have once had.

'She is of no interest to me,' he confided in his father.

'She is the mother of two healthy sons.'

'She will give me no more. I will not sleep with her again.'

'Then take another wife. A man is judged by the number of sons.'

To Sanaa, it was a great loss. Not that she enjoyed the act of lovemaking with any enthusiasm, but because she felt procreation was the reason for her being.

The Prince followed his father's directive and acquired another wife four years after marrying the first.

The second wife was to his immediate liking. No longer bound by duty in the choice of bride, he had chosen the daughter of a business acquaintance. She was slender, young (being only sixteen), and of a pleasing disposition. Her body was unknown as she was always covered in the finest robes while her face was hidden by the veil; her eyes, however, were alive and bright. To him, she was all the more mysterious, for his imagination could see what the robes did not allow.

'I admire your choice. She is a cherry ripe for the picking,' his father said.

'She has the body of an angel,' said his mother. 'She will bear you many sons. I have checked her thoroughly.'

On the bridal bed, he had found she was not of the conservative, almost frigid manner of his first wife. This one was fiery, inflamed with passion; she had worn him out the first night. In time, however, as in all romances, the passion subsided, the initial lust diminished and the nights apart grew longer. She was not to give him any sons, only daughters, and her unchallenged beauty held no further attraction for him.

He had, though, discovered one important fact about himself as a result of her. He found a never-ending longing for numerous women, whenever and however he could procure them.

The third and fourth wives proved to be satisfactory as lovers and bearers of children. There had been four more children, two boys and two girls.

Within a few years of his fourth, and last marriage, and at the age of thirty-seven, he realised none of his four wives held any interest for him. Occasional visits to the fiery second wife continued on an infrequent basis, but there burnt within him a need for more. He was seriously dependent on sexual encounters, the more varied, the better.

'I am bored of them all,' he confided to his father.

'What is the problem?'

'I cannot take any more wives, yet none of them excites me.'

'Why is this a problem?' asked his father. 'You have honoured your family responsibilities. They have provided you with good and healthy sons. You are free to pursue other women with discretion.'

His university days in England had been mostly chaste; it would have dishonoured his father if he had indulged too energetically in the promiscuous behaviour of a university campus. At times, he had relented to temptation and partook of the delights. There had been a wild girl from London, who showed no inhibitions, a timid but very attractive red-head from Manchester, and a Jewish girl from California when he worked in New York. His father would have been dismayed at the thought of a Jewish girl but, apart from her religion, he liked her best of all. Had he not been of Saudi royalty, he could have imagined a life with her.

It was on a trip to Dubai that he discovered the delights of the Ukrainian and Russian women who frequented the hotel bars. They were all blonde, fair-skinned and, for a price, devoid of any morals. Their skills, exceptional, their ability to prolong his performance, remarkable, and he lusted after them with a vengeance.

Their beauty was unique, but he would remember his second wife and what she had brought to the marital bed that first night. Not only passion, but also her virginity. It was clear there was one woman that would represent the pinnacle of his romantic and sexual endeavours: a blonde, fair-skinned woman of tender years and exceptional beauty, her virginity intact, her hymen unbroken.

He had set up a house on the outskirts of Riyadh, the capital of the oil-rich kingdom, for his personal pleasure. The walls were high, the privacy ensured. It was here he would bring girls from around the world – Russians, Americans, Chinese, and any shade in between. They were paid handsomely for as long as they stayed, or for as long as they were wanted.

'I want to go home. To complete my studies, to marry, to have children,' Natasha, a blonde beauty from Ukraine told him. 'You have given me the opportunity to achieve that aim,' she added.

'I am pleased to hear you say that,' the Prince said.

He found that the women he brought in from Dubai were normally from good, if desperately poor homes, who had adjusted to the economic realities of their home country. They had one asset to sell, and that was what they were doing. After having spent some time with him, they all appeared to want to go home and to remove their life in Dubai and the Prince from their minds.

'You are free to go at any time,' he would say. 'You will be returned to Dubai, with sufficient money to live the life you choose. I am pleased to have been of service.'

The women would be brought into the country in a private jet and then transported to the compound in one of his many Rolls Royces. Most stayed for two or three weeks though Natasha had stayed for five. He had developed a fondness for her. It was not only sex, at which she was exceptional. She also had a lively mind, an appreciation of art, and he spent many hours in her company just talking. He would miss her, but he would not delay her departure.

***

The Prince, following the call from the Chadian trader was interested, but he needed more information. He did not trust Sheikh Idriss Deubet and an independent assessment of the goods was required. He called in the two men he could trust for such a task. 'Please, gentleman, update me with reference to the blonde woman in Chad.'

He was not a man to move around, cash in hand; he was not expected to sully himself with such issues. If he wanted something, he would get someone to do it for him. He would be hand-on with any women that he intended to pleasure, but in no other matter.

His two agents, Abdullah Al Balushi, an Omani national, and Saleh Al Hasani, a citizen of Muscat, were fully occupied carrying out his business. If the Prince wanted to buy a house in London, an antique car in the USA, a woman in Dubai, or a yacht in the South of France, they would procure. He trusted them without reservation; they knew the consequences of not acting in his best interests, death or maiming was almost certain. Besides, there was no reason to act contrary to his wants, for no one else would pay them as much money as he did.

'Sheikh Idriss, our supplier of black girls we bring here occasionally for your pleasure, has obtained a blonde virgin of exceptional beauty,' Abdullah said. 'She is believed to be American and educated. She is also very expensive. She can be brought here, no questions asked, in secret and compliant.'

Compliant meant drugged. The euphemism was not lost on the Prince, a moral man in all respects except where women were concerned.

'I am interested to find out more,' he replied. 'But I need some assurance the woman is young, a virgin, and she will not be traced back to here.'

Saleh entered the conversation. 'We have a doctor in Chad who will vouch for her virginity. He checks out the black girls that we bring here.'

'Very well, travel to meet with the Sheikh, view the girl, check her out and negotiate a price. When all is ready, then you can arrange for one of my jets to pick her up. Bribe whoever you need to achieve our aims in this matter.'

The Saudi Prince was pleased. His one remaining desire was to be answered.

When he was pleased, his generosity was boundless. 'Please stay tonight and avail yourself of two of my girls. They are leaving tomorrow. I have tired of them, but I can let you know that they are exceptional in their beauty and their talents.'

Saleh chose Yelena, a tall Ukrainian beauty, and Abdullah, a Chinese from Hong Kong, by the name of Yasmin. Early the next morning, exhausted and satisfied, they took one of the Prince's jets and flew to Chad.

Chapter 20

'It is to my great shame that Sheikh Idriss Deubet may be the person you seek.' Ahmed Sahoulba was apologetic. A proud Chadian and a friend of Harry Warburton, he was embarrassed that a fellow countryman was involved in such a shameful business.

'What have you found out?' Harry asked. The three, Harry, Phil, and Yanny, were sitting in the garden of Ahmed's house in N'Djamena, the capital of Chad, sipping tea.

'I have never been naïve about the failings of my country, but to be faced with facts, rather than assumptions, is always difficult. I have asked my cousin to make enquiries. His report is disturbing.

'We must deal with the facts. If Kate McDonald is with him, she must be rescued within the next few days,' said Harry.

'That is understood,' Ahmed said.

'We don't have any option,' Yanny explained. 'The Sheikh, if it is indeed the person you mention, has become difficult, threatening in his ransom demands.'

'My full assistance is without question,' Ahmed said.

'He's threatened to conduct an auction. Highest bidder will take her.' said Yanny.

'Who else would want her, other than her father?' Ahmed asked.

'His indications are that he would sell her to the Middle East as a concubine.'

'Sold as a concubine? You cannot be serious!'

'Unfortunately, we are,' Harry said.

'Do they exist, such places? It amounts to sexual slavery.' Ahmed shocked at the possibility.

'The depravity of man knows no limit. They exist,' replied Yanny.

'What help do you need from me?' asked Ahmed.

'We need to check out his compound.'

'There will be guards.'

'Phil will find a way in.'

'What about the guards?'

'Phil will deal with them if necessary, but ideally we don't want them to know he has been there.' Yanny said.

'They will have dogs,' Ahmed added.

'Then they will be given a tasty treat with some added ingredients,' replied Harry. 'They will sleep for thirty, maybe sixty minutes at least. All the time Phil needs.'

'It is clear, Harry, that you and your friends are well experienced in such operations.'

'We're the best.' Ahmed knew his friend well enough to realise it was not false boasting.

'His compound is located in a densely populated part of town,' said Ahmed. 'If they suspect you are Westerners, they may become hostile.'

'Dress Phil in local clothes, darken his face a little and they will not pick him,' said Harry.

'They will notice his accent – or, should I say, lack of it.'

'Not with Phil. His French is passable, complete with accent, and his Arabic is good.'

'Harry's right, I may not be able to hold an exhaustive conversation in Arabic, but it's good enough to move around,' said Phil.

'Yanny will coordinate our activities and remain here if that is acceptable,' Harry asked.

'An unaccompanied female may give rise to comment.' Ahmed looked at Yanny directly. 'I assume you could adjust your dress and manner as well and your Arabic would be flawless?'

'Flawless, but I am best served coordinating activities here and back in Nigeria.'

***

The next day, an unpleasant little man, his clothes stinking of stale cigarette smoke, and eating peanuts out of a paper bag, came to the house. Yanny took an instant dislike to him. He, to the contrary, found her delightful and desirable.

'Let me introduce Mustapha Tombalbaye,' Ahmed said. 'I have known him for many years. He is the person you need.'

Introductions aside, the situation was discussed. Mustapha wanted to sit close to Yanny. As a result, she had to constantly excuse herself and move around the room.

'Mustapha, please stay where you are,' Ahmed discretely advised. A first cousin, he knew him well, trusted him implicitly, but he knew him for what he was, and he did not want Yanny feeling uncomfortable in his house.

Mustapha Tombalbaye, private investigator, delver into the cesspit of society, was a man of few scruples and even fewer morals. Ahmed used him as necessary: where there was a land deal to be gazumped, a government contract to be secured, political pressure to be applied. He could always find the truth, the lever. Ahmed prided himself in the fact that, in a corrupt society, he had managed to maintain a good degree of honesty. He was not squeaky clean – how could anyone be, when the highest politician to the lowest worker on the street was looking for an angle, a way to make some more money?

He found that Mustapha's enquiries invariably gave him information and knowledge that, once intimated to the relevant person, would cause a change in their stance, their demands, and the money they wanted.

'I've had someone staking out the Sheikh's compound for a few days,' Mustapha said.

'What were the results?' Yanny asked.

'My person has seen nothing unusual – just a few vehicles going in and out. However, he did see some black women in the back of one of the cars, but it was very dusty. He thought they didn't appear local.'

'Why would black women raise suspicion? How would he know they weren't local?'

'They may be domestic servants, but they would walk in and out. Black women in the Sheikh's vehicles – it doesn't sound right.'

'Any sign of a white woman?'

'No, he was keeping his eyes open, but only the black women were seen.'

'What do you make of this, Yanny?' Harry asked.

'They may be recent purchases and the dust would suggest a long trip.'

'Can we arrange for me to go in tonight?' Phil asked.

'Not dressed like that,' Ahmed replied. Phil, dressed in standard Khaki with an Australian Akubra hat, would not have passed for a local.

'I could get you some local clothes,' Mustapha said. 'I just hope you're as good as blending in as you say you are.'

'I am.'

'Good, I wouldn't want to be with you if you are caught. Justice is tough out there.'

'Just get me to the compound wall without being seen. Pick me up afterwards at my signal.'

***

The area around the compound was busy that afternoon as Phil and Mustapha walked casually around its perimeter. It was large, and the walls high.

'How will you get over?' Mustapha asked. He was amazed at the transformation in Phil. His ability to blend was impressive and the way he walked was that of a local. He had even indulged in conversation with a local shopkeeper.

'There's a place around the corner we just passed where the wall is crumbling at the top. That is the best place. I'll go over there.'

'I didn't see it,' replied Mustapha.

'You don't know what to look for. It's hidden from view of the surrounding buildings, but there is still some light in the street.'

'Don't worry, let me know the time, and I'll ensure the light goes off.'

'How will you do that?' asked Phil.

'You tell me the time, and the power to the area will be cut. It's unreliable at the best of time and with some money in the right pockets, anything can be arranged.'

'The Sheikh will have a backup generator.'

'I have taken it into account,' said Mustapha. 'The generator fuel tank was filled this morning. The tanker delivery company will be in serious trouble later; the diesel was full of water. Besides, there is a problem with the starter motor.

'You paid the people delivering? They've disabled the engine?'

'Yes.'

Phil had a newfound respect for his colleague.

At that moment, a Toyota Land Cruiser pulled up at the main gate of the compound.

'That's the Sheikh's personal vehicle,' Mustapha said.

'Yes, but who are they in the back?'

'They look like Arabs, but their dress is not of here.'

'They look as if they are from the Middle East,' said Phil. 'Can you make some enquiries? Find out what you can.'

'I have a cousin at the airport,' replied Mustapha. 'He owes me a favour.'

'We need to know quickly. If they are who I suspect, then we do not have a lot of time.'

'Who do you believe they are?'

'I think they may be the other bidders for Kate McDonald.'

'You can't go in tonight if they are still there. I will ensure the compound is watched. As soon as they leave we can then plan your entry.'

***

It was two days later before it was clear to enter the compound. In the meantime, Mustapha had learnt from his cousin – everyone seemed to be a cousin –the two Arabs had come in on a private jet from Saudi Arabia.

'What else do we know about these two?' Harry asked back at Ahmed's house.

'We know their names,' Yanny replied. 'The names on the passenger manifest show them to be Abdullah Al Balushi, an Omani national, and Saleh Al Hasani, a citizen of Muscat.'

'And what do they do?' Phil asked.

'Our office in Baghdad made some enquiries,' she replied. 'They are procuring agents for some of the wealthiest individuals within the Kingdom of Saudi Arabia, and one person in particular – Prince Abdul bin al-Ibrahim.'

'What do they procure?' Harry asked.

'According to what I have been told, these two individuals travel the world acquiring rare works of art, vintage cars, real estate on behalf of immensely wealthy Arabs.'

'So, on the face of it, they are decent men. But why are they here in Chad?'

'There is more,' Yanny said.

'Please continue.'

'Prince Abdul bin al-Ibrahim has a fondness for women, especially blonde and fair-skinned. His private jet has been known to take some of the Ukrainian and Russian women found hawking their wares in Dubai into Saudi Arabia.'

'Is there anything wrong in that?' Phil said.

'Legally, no, but it's a little perverse,' Yanny replied, shocked at the ambivalence of his statement.

'Why would he be interested in Kate?' asked Harry. 'She appears to be beautiful. But then, so are the majority of the women in Dubai, and they are readily available.'

'You don't get it,' Yanny, a little agitated, replied.

'What don't I get?'

'Flying blonde women into Saudi, just because you have unlimited money and an over-active libido, is not the issue. There is one thing the women in Dubai cannot offer.'

'And what's that?'

'They can't offer their virginity. What if the Prince has a perversion, an unsated desire for a blonde, fair-skinned virgin?'

'Is she a virgin?' Phil was incredulous that a modern, Western young woman would have still held on to the vestige of a more conservative era.

'How would I know?' Yanny replied. 'It's what they believe that is important. Maybe she mentioned it in an effort to make her kidnappers leave her alone.'

'That would explain the interest of the two Arabs,' said Harry. 'We need to get her out as soon as we can.'

'They are the agents. They will not touch her.'

'Can we be sure of that?' Phil asked.

'The Prince wants a virgin, not some woman his agents have pawed,' said Yanny. 'She is perfectly safe, as long as she remains in the compound.'

***

'We wish to see the virgin.' Abdullah Al Balushi was direct and to the point at the meeting inside Sheik Idriss Deubet's compound.

'I have acquired her for the highest bidder,' replied the Sheikh.

'It has been made clear there is to be no auction for the woman,' said Abdullah. 'The Prince, has the first and only claim.'

'His claim is subject to a satisfactory offer. I am aware of her value; I will not let her go for less.'

'You are playing a dangerous game with your arrogant manner.' Saleh Al Hasani knew the anger the Prince would express if they failed. He did not want to contemplate their fate.

'Gentlemen, let us calm down,' said the Sheikh. 'This heated exchange belies our amicable business dealings in the past, the friendship I feel for you both, the respect I feel for the Prince.' He attempted to placate the situation with soothing words. He wanted neither their friendship nor their presence; he just wanted the Prince's money.

'Of course, I will not auction her,' he added. 'She is for the Prince. I was just aiming to ensure the best possible price. You do understand?'

'We understand your desire to maximise your return,' replied Abdullah. 'But be assured, the Prince will pay substantially well for the asset – if, she is, as you say, a unique beauty and a virgin.' He did not like the Sheikh, and he was certain the Sheikh did not like him.

Kate and Fatima had seen the Arabs enter the compound.

'They're not from here,' Fatima said.

'They're from the Middle East,' replied Kate. 'Look how they are dressed. You see the long-sleeved, ankle-length robe? It's called a thobe.'

'How do you know all this?' asked Fatima, surprised at Kate's knowledge.

'I've been to Dubai a few times with my father.'

Abdullah, the taller of the two showed the effects of over-indulgence in the consumption of food and whisky. He could not be considered an attractive man. Saleh, smaller, more youthful, and definitely thinner, with a pronounced nose, the more impressive; however, at forty-eight years of age, he was at least ten years older than his colleague.

'They don't look to be very nice men,' Kate said.

'Why do you think they are here?' Fatima asked.

'I am afraid they are coming for me.'

'Your father will get you back before then,' Fatima said reassuringly, although she was not sure; she had seen these men before. At the time, she had not thought much of it, but now it was clear; they had come for the black girls. This time, they were probably here for Kate.

Meanwhile, the two Arabs from the Prince were becoming agitated. 'When can we see the woman?' Abdullah asked.

'She is being made ready for you. A special showing has been arranged. You will be able to see her, but she will not be aware of your presence.'

'It is important that we are able to see her naked,' Saleh said.

'Do you know what will happen to us if the Prince hears of your suggestion?' Abdullah was visibly angry that his colleague could even suggest such an idea.

'She will be clothed exquisitely,' replied the Sheikh, 'dressed in a sheer and tight Western dress of the highest quality. The delights of her body are for your master, not for anyone else. If he realised you had partaken of any untoward liberties or disrespect, then his vengeance towards you would be without mercy.'

'We would never enjoy the benefits of his women in Riyadh if he were to hear of any liberties being taken,' Abdullah said. 'We would not be capable.'

'What do you mean?' the Sheikh asked.

'He'd have our balls cut off and fed to the dogs.'

'I hope Saleh understands,' added the Sheikh.

'I understand. I allowed myself to be overridden by lust.'

'Let us discuss the price. One million American dollars in either cash or into any bank account you nominate in the world,' said Abdullah.

The Sheikh was offended – to talk about money and business with no respect for local traditions. It was necessary to eat, drink, discuss trivialities before the offensive topic of money was discussed, and besides an offer of one million dollars for an asset worth ten times that amount offended him more.

'It offends me that you discuss financial matters at this early stage,' he replied.

'It is not our intention, but the Prince has made it clear that he wants our negotiations to be concluded in the shortest possible time. He is aware of the sensitivity and the risk of taking an American woman secretly into Saudi Arabia. Even he, with all his wealth and influence, would not be immune to arrest and imprisonment for such an action.' replied Abdullah.

'I accept your apology. I am also under the same pressures. I wish to see her leave these premises as soon as possible.'

'Then the offer of one million dollars remains.'

'I have already been offered ten million by her father.'

'You were told not to enter into any other negotiations.'

'I have not. The group I purchased her from had instigated ransom negotiations, the money agreed by them. I have purely inherited that agreement.' It was not true. The Sheikh had been pursuing an agreement and the amount was three million, not ten, but he did not intend to tell the truth to the agents of a man who counted his millions in their thousands.

***

In the weeks since arriving at the Sheikh's compound, Kate had started to relax, to be more rational in her actions. She retained the belief her father would be coming for her, comfortable in the friendship and trust of Fatima. The latest development had caused her to tense. It was to become a lot worse when the Sheikh entered the women's quarters and spoke to her.

'I will not dress as you require. I am an American citizen. I demand to be sent to the American embassy.' She was indignant.

'I will make myself very clear. The American embassy will never know of your presence in my house and unless you agree to comply, the penalties will be severe. I will not touch or harm you, you are much too valuable, but I can harm others.' He raised his hand as if to slap her across the face but did not.

'You have formed a friendship with Fatima. Failure on your part in any requirement will force me to take her out to the compound and have her flogged. You will watch and you will

hear her scream, and you will realise that it is happening because
of you. Each time you fail a command, I will ensure that the
flogging is doubled and she will die.'

'I will do as you say,' Kate said feebly.

'Good, then we understand each other. Fatima will help
prepare you for the showing, and I will expect to see radiant
beauty and desirability in your look. Failure on both count and
the flogging will commence.'

The dress was Dior, and it was as the Sheikh had
described. It clung to her body, revealed all her curves and the
plunging neckline left little to the imagination. Adorned with
diamonds and jewels and with make-up of the highest standard,
she was of a beauty that no man could resist. Frightened,
confused and ashamed as she was, she could not let Fatima suffer
for her.

'Please, do not do this for me,' Fatima said. 'My life is of
no consequence. I am purely a woman of the harem; you are an
innocent child from the West. I will take the suffering; you must
not take the humiliation.'

'Fatima, you are my friend. I cannot allow you to be
beaten and to die purely for my not wearing a dress. Besides, my
father will not leave me here for long. Once he knows where I
am, he will send people and you will come as well.'

'I hope you are right, but I feel you are misguided.'

'My father will not fail us. We will survive, my dear
friend.'

'Inshallah, God willing.' Fatima was not so sure.

***

'She is ready for the viewing,' the Sheikh said as he led Abdullah
and Saleh to the room he had set up. Both had been there before,
both knew the routine.

The room where they sat furnished with cushions and
expensive carpets on the floor. It was the typical furnishings of a
wealthy businessman, except for the one-way mirror on one wall.

Many black girls had paraded on the other side over the last year. Abdullah and Saleh had purchased a few for the Prince. Other buyers had come and taken a few of the girls to the East. The Sheikh suspected their fate but did not care as long as the price was right.

'Please come in and walk around the room,' he commanded to Kate via an intercom.

She did as she was told. She was beautiful and desirable, but she hunched her back, with her face looking at the ground, and she was crying.

'Hold you head up high. Straighten your back and smile.'

She complied, although the smile was forced and her make-up was streaking down her cheeks from the wet tears.

'If you do not stop crying, and face towards us, I will take Fatima out now and horsewhip her until she is unconscious. Do you understand?' The Sheikh was angry. He had ten million on the line, and the asset was not assisting.

'She is truly beautiful,' Abdullah ventured. 'It may have been best if you had drugged her before we came.'

'I would have done that with the black girls. You would have been able to see them naked, but this is a unique find. I did not want her shown in that manner. They were just donkeys in comparison to the thoroughbred you see before you.'

Kate, fearful of what would have happened to Fatima, complied. She acted as the Sheikh wanted. He was delighted; he knew they would pay him the money.

The two visitors equally knew their master would pay. Their commissions would be high, and he would let them choose whichever girl they asked for back at the compound in Riyadh.

'Is she not as I told you?' said the Sheikh. 'Is she not a flower in the desert, ripe for the picking?'

'The Prince will be pleased,' replied Abdullah. 'He will accept our recommendation.'

'Then let us discuss price. I have only seen one blonde virgin in my time; she must be regarded as truly unique. I could not let her go for less than ten million dollars.'

'The Prince will never agree,' Saleh said with alarm. 'He is not a forgiving person; if he feels he is being taken advantage of, then his anger and cruelty know no bounds.'

Abdullah knew they had to make a deal; the Prince would pay the full price, but they could not agree at this time. Besides, they could tell him the price was ten million and whatever discount they could achieve, divide it between himself and Saleh.

'There must be no other bidders. Is that clear?' Abdullah said.

'That is fully understood. I will not countenance or enter into any agreements with another party until our discussions are concluded.' He had lied. He knew Kate's father would not be able to raise the ten million he was now asking. The three million dollars agreed already would do him nicely, but if he could get a few million more from the Prince, so much the better. He saw a life as a legitimate businessman, in Africa or Europe; he could buy a place in the South of France, live a beautiful life. That was what he yearned for now.

He was tired of dirtying his hands with either deluded fundamentalists or the greedy agents of a Prince, who were no doubt aiming to tell him ten million, then get him to accept less and pocket the difference.

'We will go back to the Prince with your price,' said Abdullah. 'But be warned, his displeasure could be violent. We will contact you tomorrow midday to conclude our negotiations.'

Chapter 21

With the Arabs departed back to Saudi Arabia, Phil and Mustapha returned to the original plan. 'The electricity will go off at one in the morning,' Mustapha said as they both stood to one side of the compound.

'Give me one hour?'

'I will ensure you are given the time you require.'

'Can you see the weak point in the wall?' Phil asked. 'It's lower than the rest. Those drums stacked by the side will act as steps.'

'I see it now,' replied Mustapha. 'I did not see it the other day.'

'The guards, what are they up to?'

'They are dozing, barely conscious. I ensured the food they ordered from the street seller had the minutest quantity of sedative.'

'You are devious.'

'I pride myself that I see solutions to problems.'

'The Sheikh, where is he?' asked Phil.

'He has crossed the border into Nigeria. You only need to worry about the guards, and within thirty minutes, they will be fast asleep. Remember, they are not totally knocked out.'

'Good man,' said Phil. 'If they suspected they had been sedated, they would inform the Sheikh.'

'That is what I thought.'

'How many dogs are inside?'

'I only heard two, but they sound large.'

On schedule, the power went off, and it was clear the generator was not going to start. The guards would have been expected to investigate, but they were sleeping peacefully. Phil quickly scaled the wall and disappeared over the top.

The dogs were curiously sniffing the area nearby, attracted by the smell of raw meat. They were voracious in their appetites and deliberately kept hungry to keep them awake. They soon succumbed to a profound and peaceful sleep.

He had one hour before they would rouse; he intended to be long gone by then. Wearing night vision goggles and with a map provided by satellite surveillance, he made his way across to the far side of the compound.

The general layout was typical. His focus was a large, rectangular building on the far side of the complex. The main house located in the centre was carefully avoided, and within a few minutes, he was outside of what he assumed would be the probable location of Kate. The building was heavily secured, and no light emanated from inside. Skilfully, he moved forward along the side of the walls, looking for a crack, anything that would allow him to peer inside. The few windows, heavily shuttered, offered no help. Despairing that his efforts had been wasted, and ready to leave, he encountered some luck. He had been seen.

It was not luck that gripped him initially; it had been fear, the fear of discovery. The woman – and, judging from what little he could ascertain through his goggles, an Arab woman – was gesturing to him. He had to get out of there quickly before she screamed for help. To his surprise, she did not. In fact, she moved towards him.

'Kate?' she said in a hushed voice.

'Is she here?'

'Yes. You must help her.'

'We will.'

'You must take me as well. Kate is my friend.' The woman looked quickly over her shoulder. 'The men from the north will come back for her.'

'When will they come?' asked Phil.

'Soon.'

'Where is she located?'

'She is at the back of the building. Do you want to see her?'

'No. I need to know she is safe and well.'

'She is safe and well. I look after her. Can we go now?'

'It is not possible. We need to rescue her other friend at the same time.'

'Helen? I know of her. When will you come for us?'

'I am not sure. Within seven days.'

'We will be ready.'

'It will be at night. Ensure that a door is open.'

'The door I came out from. It will be left unlocked. I am Fatima.'

As quickly as she came, she disappeared. He realised he had spent longer in the compound than intended. There was a growling from one of the dogs as it started to wake up. He moved faster than he thought possible, scaled the wall and casually strolled down the street with Mustapha.

'Did you find her?'

'Yes.'

'When are we going to rescue her?'

'Let's talk to Harry and Yanny, but very soon.'

It was close to dawn when they arrived back at Ahmed's house. He should have been exhausted, but the adrenaline kept him focussed.

'Is she there?' Yanny, equally alert, asked.

'Yes, she is there.'

'Did you see her?'

'No, but I was approached by a woman there. She told me that Kate was safe and well.'

'You were seen?' Harry questioned.

'The woman's name is Fatima. She told me she is a friend of Kate's and was looking after her.'

'Can we trust her?'

'I believe we can,' replied Phil. 'She could have screamed and woken the guards, but she didn't. I need to stay here. If there is any attempt to move her, then I will go in and take her by force.'

'Understood,' replied Yanny, 'but it could make Helen's captors nervous if they found out.'

They agreed that Harry would return to Northern Nigeria, Yanny to Port Harcourt while Phil would stay in Chad. Now that both women were located, it was time to execute the rescue.

***

Upon their return to the Middle East, the two agents met with the Prince. 'Master, we have seen the property,' Abdullah said. 'It is all that has been promised. We offer our highest recommendation.'

'Has he agreed to the one million dollars?' asked the Prince.

'He has significantly increased the price. He believes this is a unique commodity and he cannot afford to let it go for any other than the maximum price. He wants ten million dollars.'

'Then he is a fool to think that I will agree to such a price! I am prepared to concede that one million is insufficient, but I cannot agree to ten. He is taking advantage of the situation; he realises that it is a seller's market.'

'The commodity is definitely worth the money,' Saleh urged.

'You have my authority to go as high as five million dollars. I will require proof of virginity, and I want her suitably drugged and compliant on her arrival here.'

The money wasn't important to the Prince; it was only spare change. But there was a principle involved. If he ever suspected the duplicity of his two agents, they would have found out the strength of his vengeance.

Saleh and Abdullah were delighted. The Prince had agreed to five million dollars and he would be pleased with them for some very capable negotiation. All they needed to do was talk Sheikh Idriss down to three million.

As with all negotiations in the Arab world, negotiations are never quick and easy. They would take time, endless cups of tea, and endless bid and counter-bid. Eventually, however, all parties would leave the bargaining table comfortable in their negotiation skills and happy in the knowledge that they had got the better of the other party.

Sheikh Idriss, in the meantime, had sent an updated ransom down south of five million dollars. He knew that both party would pay at least three million, and the first one with the money in his nominated account would take the asset. He may still get the money from the father and sell Kate to the Prince. He was playing with fire, but avarice had taken hold.

***

The discussion over the price for the property was not to be conducted in Chad. It was to be via a phone line. Armed with the Prince's agreement both Abdullah and Saleh were optimistic of a satisfactory resolve. 'Our master will not pay the full amount. He is angry and feels that you are taking advantage of his wealth.'

'Then I will not sell her. I will return her back to her family.'

The Sheikh realised it could end badly for him, personally and financially if he did not bring the negotiations to a conclusion. There was only so far he could go, but he realised that the Prince could act quicker in the transfer of the funds. He preferred to agree with the agents of the Prince, rather than to let they go away empty-handed.

They also realised he had been playing the Prince against the virgin's family. They would seal the deal, get the girl, and then inform the Prince. The Sheikh may have his millions, but he would not have time to spend it.

'That would not be wise,' said Abdullah. 'The Prince will believe that you have been negotiating with other parties. His displeasure will only lead to violent and savage retribution.'

'I have not been entering into other negotiations. The previous owners of the property had attempted a ransom demand, but I have not.

'Let us stop this threatening behaviour and continue our discussions in an open and frank manner,' he continued. 'I cannot let her go for one million dollars, and you do not have the authority to pay ten million. Then let us agree at eight million.'

'Two.'

'Three,' the Sheikh could see taking the money from both parties, giving the woman to the Prince and then disappearing out of sight. He'd still have six million dollars in cash.

'Agreed,' said Abdullah, 'but we need clear proof of virginity. We will arrange payment on proof being supplied. In forty-eight hours we will return and take possession of the commodity.'

Chapter 22

'This is Sally Wilson, BBC in Abuja, Nigeria. There has been a report of an attack on a Baptist Mission in the North of Nigeria some weeks ago. Details are sketchy, but we will keep you updated as soon as we receive more news.'

It had been over four weeks since the Mission had been hit and, up till now, Steve and his people had managed to keep the news quiet. The brief announcement that had been made on the British Broadcasting Corporation's twenty-four hours news channel could not have come at a worse time.

'This is not what we want,' Steve said.

'I'm waiting for the reaction from the kidnappers,' Yanny said.

'What do you think will happen?'

'It depends on what the media finds out.'

'Assume the worst.'

'If the media learn that Kate and Helen are being held for ransom, the kidnappers will become aggressive.' replied Yanny.

'Assume they'll find out,' Steve said.

'I'm still receiving the two hostage demands for Kate. One is clearly from Boko Haram, the other from the Sheikh. He's hinting at more money.'

Conducting a Mission of such danger and sensitivity required stealth, calm evaluation, an analysis of the facts, and the forging of relationships. It did not require the Western media barging in, cameras at the ready.

'We'll need to bring the dates of the rescues forward,' Harry said.

'It's the only option,' Yanny agreed.

It was only to be days before the full flurry of the world's press descended on Abuja, the capital of Nigeria. Further details had leaked. They knew there were Westerners and they knew some were dead.

'This is Sally Wilson, BBC in Abuja, Nigeria. What we know is that insurgents attacked a Baptist Mission in Borno State to the northeast of Abuja five weeks ago. We also know that the leader of the Mission was Pastor Zebediah Johnson, an American citizen, originally from Mississippi. It is believed that his wife, Mary, was with him as well as three other Western citizens. There are reported deaths.'

'It has to be the Nigerian military; our people would not have said anything,' Harry said.

'I had attempted to blanket news of the situation through an old friend of mine; it appears we have not been successful. Let me contact him. See what we can do to prevent any further news getting out,' Steve said.

To Steve, he was Abdul, to those under his command he was Lt General Abdul Ibrahim, Chief of Defence Staff, Nigeria and the senior military officer of the Nigerian Armed Forces. 'Abdul, I need your assistance. You've seen the news reports.'

They had met in the USA at military training school some years previous. Captain Ibrahim and Steve formed a solid friendship during some very strenuous night-time activities. They always attempted to meet up when Steve was in the country. Their last meeting had been two weeks previous at the Radisson Blu in Lagos.

Important as he was, he was still a regular guy who liked to reminisce over a good meal about that particular 'ornery Sergeant Major' who had them crawling through the mud night after night in training.

'We had a detachment taken by Boko Haram ten days ago. Sometimes they join the rebels, some are tortured.'

'Could it be Boko Haram feeding the media?' asked Steve.

'It is possible. Their leader, Mohammad Murtada, is an educated and astute man.'

'That is a remarkably benevolent statement.'

'It is neither remarkable nor benevolent,' said Abdul. 'Did we not study the "Art of War"?'

'If you know your enemies and know yourself, you will not be imperilled in a hundred battles...' Steve quoted. 'If you do not know your enemies or yourself, you will be imperilled in every single battle.'

'You remember. That was drummed into us at training school.'

'How could we ever forget?'

'There is an added complication now. The Nigerian military will need to become involved.'

'You agreed they would keep a low profile, and allow us to rescue the women.'

'I still honour that agreement. But the matter is out of my control.'

'Explain.'

'The Western media asked the President of my country a direct question. What is his country's military doing about the situation? He's also had the American President and the British Prime Minister on the phone urging action.'

'This is Sally Wilson, BBC in Abuja, Nigeria. We have just received information that the attack on the Baptist Mission in Northern Nigeria has resulted in the deaths of three Westerners. The whereabouts of two more Westerners remain unknown, but it is believed they are captives of Boko Haram. Further details will be reported as soon as they become available. We are attempting to get a team into the region.'

'Once they reveal they are females we will have their governments bringing in military detachments,' Harry said.

'Yanny, any change on the ransom demands?' Steve asked.

'They are becoming more aggressive in their tone. Threatening death if any military force attempts a rescue.'

'They'll tighten their security. It's going to be more difficult,' Harry said.

'We need to move quickly. The Nigerian military is forced to act and the last thing we want is them going in with guns blazing.' Steve detailed the situation. 'My friend has done the best he can, but even he can't hold off the military.'

'What's the word from Phil?' Yanny asked.

'It's all quiet there at the present moment,' said Harry. 'The Sheikh returned; it appears he may have brought back some more Nigerian girls. We'll need to take them as well when we rescue Kate.'

'Our concern is Kate,' said Steve. 'Their rescue is secondary.'

'That is callous.' Yanny offended by his remark.

'It sounds callous, but it complicates the rescue. If we can get them out, we will.'

'You sounded racist.'

'You know I am not a racist, just realistic. We must not lose sight of the primary target. Once secured, we will attempt to take them as well.'

'Phil mentioned a local woman, Fatima.'

'We take her,' said Steve. 'She appears to have helped Kate. Leaving her behind, I agree, would be callous.'

This is Sally Wilson, BBC in Abuja, Nigeria updating. There have been dramatic developments regarding the attack on the Baptist Mission to the North of Abuja. We now know that Boko Haram has taken two hostages, Kate McDonald, an American citizen, and Helen Campbell, a British citizen. Their current location is unknown. Pastor Zebediah Johnson, his wife, Mary Johnson, and Duncan Nicholson, American citizens, are confirmed dead.'

As soon as the BBC made the announcement, Abdul was on the phone to Steve. 'I cannot keep the military out; you must realise the situation. The President is in emergency council; I have been summoned.'

'Abdul, I understand. The best approach is perhaps a joint operation – my people leading, your people taking the credit. See if the President will be appeased; tell him there is a rescue plan.

Don't mention Chad at the present moment, but we will need flyover permission to cross into their airspace.'

'I will talk to the President. A swift, decisive recovery; he may go for that. He is looking to regain credibility; he does not want the blood of the two women placed against him due to his inaction.'

***

The President of the Federal Republic of Nigeria was visibly annoyed that the Western media had found out about something in his own country before he did. 'We are being made to look like incompetent fools.'

Timipre Karibo, a Christian from the southern state of Bayelsa in the Niger Delta, had little in common with those committing the insurgency in the north. Elected the leader of his country two years previously, he had based his campaign on a platform of significantly reducing the insurgents' influence in the north. The only problem was that his attempts at reducing their power had achieved little; in fact, they had become more brazen and violent.

Any attempt at discussion or compromise came to nought. They did not trust him, and he did not trust them. He was not of their religion, and there was a history of his making disparaging remarks regarding the influence of Islam in a Christian country.

The President's discussion with his senior military person was blunt and to the point. 'I based my election campaign on significantly dealing with these people, yet here they are, taking white women. What am I able to say in our defence? I will tell you, nothing!'

Lt General Abdul Ibrahim, Chief of Defence and Steve's friend, was at the end of an especially severe ear bashing from the President of his country. He thought that the President was justified in his annoyance.

Karibo, an honest, hardworking and seemingly incorruptible politician, was what the Nigerian people needed. It upset Abdul that he had deceived him for so long.

He had kept quiet about the two women as a favour to Steve. He knew of the work that Steve's people were involved in and he understood the need for secrecy.

'It is clear we need to mobilise our troops in the north and to go after the terrorists,' the President said. 'Failure on our part to act will bring universal condemnation.'

'It is a dangerous move,' replied Abdul. 'If the fundamentalists know we are coming, they will disperse. I recommend no action until it is clear as to how we can mobilise a measured response.' He tried to put forward a rational case, but he could understand his leader's stand on the issue.

'Do we know where they are? Tell me that, Abdul, and please be direct and truthful. Within the confines of this room, we can and must talk freely.'

'We know where the women are. A company specialised in such activities are planning a rescue in the next few days.' He felt he could be honest with his President.

'Then we must be involved,' replied the President. 'We must be seen to be an integral part of the rescue. We must reclaim our honour. There have been too many of these instances and we have not been able to rescue more than a few.'

'Mr President, the company is highly specialised. They are the same group of people who rescued the expatriate oil workers down in the south a few weeks ago. I know the CEO of the company extremely well; we were on military training together some years ago in the USA. He is a good friend of mine. He is currently in Port Harcourt coordinating the rescue of the two women.'

'Then, I want to meet with him. Ensure he is here in my office within the next day.'

***

Lt General Abdul Ibrahim, Chief of Defence Staff, Nigeria and the senior military officer of the Nigerian Armed Forces phoned his friend. 'Steve, the President wants to meet you. Can you be here tomorrow morning? I've provisionally booked Flight 252 at 8.30 am on Arik Air,'

'Okay,' said Steve. 'Book an extra seat for Bob McDonald, Kate's father. He has been funding our activities up till now.'

A meeting with the President of a country normally would have been an auspicious occasion, but to Steve, it was not. The interest of the Western media and the involvement of the Nigerian government were both complications that he would have preferred to avoid.

The next day's arrival at the small and cramped airport in Abuja was not a welcoming site to Steve and Bob McDonald. 'Mr McDonald, would you care to comment?' a reporter asked Bob as his cleared arrivals.

'As the father of one of the kidnapped women, would you be able to tell us how they are?' asked another.

'CNN, as an American and a father, would you be prepared to comment on the response of the Nigerian government? Have they done enough? What do they intend to do? What do you know?'

'How soon will it be before there is a rescue attempt?'

It took the intervention of the police waving batons to regain control of the situation. Steve and Bob were hustled into a secure room at the airport.

'How did they know we were coming?' Bob asked.

'We underestimated them,' said Steve. 'They are like vultures, scavenging over the bones.'

'This is not good for the girls' safety, is it?' Bob asked.

'Unfortunately it only makes the situation worse.'

Twenty minutes later, the door at the rear of the room opened.

'I am Captain Namadi Akintola.' An office, smartly dressed in the uniform of the Nigerian Air Force presented himself at the door with a salute. 'Lt General Ibrahim offers his apologies. I am to convey you to the President's residence.'

'You don't intend us to go through that madness out front?' Bob asked.

'I understand your desire to avoid that madness, as you say. No, I am the chief pilot of the President's personal helicopter. It is waiting outside on the apron. I will fly you there.'

After being hounded by the world's press, they were transposed onto a ten-minute flight in a superbly presented and luxurious Bell helicopter. Landing on the front lawn, they were accompanied in to the building by an exceedingly polite servant.

At the appointed time, the President of the Republic of Nigeria, Timipre Karibo, together with Lt General Abdul Ibrahim, Steve Case and Bob McDonald met at the Aso Rock Presidential Villa in Abuja.

'Welcome, gentlemen,' the President said. 'I am pleased to see you here, although I wish it could be under more agreeable circumstances. Mr McDonald, I can fully understand the pressure and strain that you must be under at the present moment.'

'Thank you, Mr President, it is indeed difficult. I have every confidence in Steve and his people, and we would appreciate any assistance that can be given.'

'Lt General Ibrahim, I believe we should ask Mr Case to give an update on the situation and as to what assistance we can give,' the President said. It was a formal occasion with the President and full titles were the order of the day.

'Thank you, Mr President,' replied Steve. 'The situation has changed dramatically due to the interest of the Western media. We need to bring our rescue dates forward.'

'You must rely on us to assist you in any way,' said the President.

'Let me elaborate on what we do know and where we would appreciate assistance.' Steve had quickly put together a PowerPoint presentation showing the salient facts.

'Firstly,' he continued, 'we know where the two women are. Helen Campbell is in a camp close to the border with Chad.

We have confirmed this visually. Kate McDonald, Bob's daughter, is in N'Djamena, the capital of Chad. She is being held for ransom back to us, or for sale to a buyer in the Middle East. Sorry, Bob, we need to explain the reality to the President.'

'That's okay, Steve. It needs to be stated.'

'What is the significance of the Middle East?' the President asked.

'She will be sold to the harem of a Saudi prince. They still exist, unfortunately, as do the traders who deal with such abhorrence.'

Bob was visibly upset, but the reality was the reality. It served no useful purpose to massage the words to save his feelings.

'This is indeed tragic. We must avoid this at all costs,' the President said. 'You are aware they have taken many of our own women?'

'Yes, some are in Chad, where Kate is located.'

'Are you certain? Are they for sale to a harem as well?'

'Some maybe, but we believe they are also sold into Cameroon as brides. And I must be honest, some are sold into brothels.'

'Your honesty upsets me. I realise the truth must be stated, but it is not easy to hear.' The President appeared shaken by what Steve had said. 'My advisers have intimated this, but I have been inclined to see the best in people. To hear from you confirms what they have told me.'

'The truth is unpalatable,' said Steve, 'but we cannot help if we don't accept the reality.'

'And the other girls, hundreds have been taken. What of them?'

'They would have been given to the Boko Haram soldiers.'

'We must rid our country of such barbaric people. We would appreciate your advice on how to do this.'

'Gladly, but first we must focus on the two women.'

'We must also bring back our own women in Chad as well.' The President made it clear that this was non-negotiable. 'We will bring them.' Steve realised it was to be a bigger operation than he would have preferred. They needed the Nigerian military and the cooperation of their Chadian equivalent.

'Are some of our own women in the camp where Miss Campbell is being held?' the President asked.

'I would say almost certainly. Possibly a large number.'

'We must bring them back as well. Abdul, you are to take responsibility for this.'

'Yes, Mr President.'

'I must tell you; almost all will have been raped. Some may be pregnant or even with babies,' Steve said.

'They are our responsibility,' said the President. 'We will bring them back; give them the assistance to readjust to society.'

'What do you want from us, Steve?' Abdul asked.

'Abdul,' replied the President, 'we will comply with all requirements. The only guarantee I want is that all the Nigerian girls are brought back safely as well.'

'Mr President, I will ensure that we will bring all we can.'

'When is the rescue planned for?' the President asked.

'Six days maximum,' Steve replied.

***

Steve and Harry met Abdul early the next morning at Army headquarters in Abuja. Bob had returned to Port Harcourt. This time, there was not the ignominy of the airport. The presidential helicopter had deposited him close to the steps leading up to the presidential jet. A similar treatment was in place for him on arrival. If it were not for the circumstances, he would have regarded the day's events, the meeting with the president, the VIP treatment, as surreal.

'I'm bringing in a crack team of commandos,' Abdul said. 'They've just completed intensive training in the USA. Is fifty sufficient?'

'Fifty should be plenty,' replied Steve. 'Once we've exited Helen from the camp, you can bring in as many as you like.'

'Helicopters, aircraft – what do you need?'

'We need helicopters, must be unmarked. Use civilian choppers if we have to,' Harry said.

'Two will need to be able to make the trip from Nigeria to N'Djamena,' Steve added.

'Aircraft to take us into the region,' said Harry, 'but we need to stay back at least one hundred and fifty kilometres, preferably two hundred.'

'Anything else?' Abdul asked.

'Do you have any mobilisation close into the area of the camp?' asked Harry.

'It's possible.'

'They need to make a discreet retreat. Not a rush to the south – that may be seen as suspicious. Just make it seem to be a sweeping exercise in a different region.'

'We've pre-empted you on the helicopters. We have two Aerospatiale Pumas for the run into Chad. They can hold up to sixteen people,' said Abdul.

'That should be okay. Do we intend to bring the women back immediately on retrieval?' Harry asked.

'Any Nigerian women we release will come back on the helicopters.' Abdul was firm on that point.

'Gentlemen,' Lt General Abdul Ibrahim said, 'I've asked Major Femi Osuji to join us. He will take full responsibility for our military assistance. Steve, Major Osuji went through the same training school in America where we met.'

'Major, have you been updated as to the situation?' asked Steve.

'I am aware.' Major Osuji, a career military man, was formal and upright.

'I believe that the Major is standing on ceremony due to my presence,' said Abdul. 'This may be a good time for me to excuse myself. Major Osuji has written authority to override any red tape to secure whatever is required. He is, at this moment, equal in authority to me. I am sure he will use it well.'

'Thank you. I will,' the Major replied.

Steve took the opportunity to lighten the mood after Abdul left. 'I'm Steve and this is Harry.'

'Call me Femi. I apologise for my formality before. Standing before the Chief of Defence Staff can be a little intimidating.'

'He was a captain when I first met him. He's a regular guy, one of my oldest friends.'

'Regular, I'm not so sure.'

'Femi, we need to prepare for the entry into the camp. Do we have a forward operating base?'

'We've secured the airfield at Maiduguri. That's about two hundred and fifty kilometres from the camp.'

"How well can we conceal our preparations there?"

'It will not be a problem. Since the attack on the Mission, we have cleaned out the area. No one will come near the base. We can fly the aircraft and personnel through a corridor to the south-west.'

'We need to commence the rescue within four days,' said Harry. 'The media attention is making Boko Haram nervous, and the Sheikh in Chad may attempt to move the other women.

'We can be ready. I need to inform my commandos first.'

'Let's get them to the airfield first,' replied Steve. 'They can be briefed there. We can't risk any more leaks.'

'Fully understood. I will have my people on base within twenty-four hours. What else do we need?'

'We have helicopters arranged for the trip to Chad. We just need to make sure they are at the airbase.'

'I have a logistics manager working on that.'

'I hope he hasn't been told anything?'

'No. He just believes we're reclaiming the area.'

'We need at least four helicopters to take your people into the camp once Helen is secured,' Steve said. 'We can use one of those to drop the initial assault team fifty kilometres distant.'

'Why so far?'

'We can't risk the helicopters being seen.'

'We could have gone in closer than fifty kilometres. Thirty would have been fine.'

'We'll discuss at Maiduguri.' Steve believed that a longer distance was ideal, but it would be difficult carrying heavy weapons. It would take close to two days to cover the ground under cover of darkness. *Femi may be right*, he thought. *If they can get closer, then we could bring the date of the rescue forward.*

'The plan needs to include the retrieval of the Nigerian women as well,' Femi reminded.

'That precludes gunships coming in once we've secured Helen. It will need to be more of a ground battle.'

'Do you know where the women are in the camp?' Femi asked.

'The problem is they could be dispersed.'

'Then, I will take one hundred commandos and additional helicopters for transportation.'

'We take Helen first, and then Harry will leave immediately for Chad with ten of your commandos. Is that agreed?'

'I agree. I am aware of the President's directive in this matter. My concern is for the Nigerian women as well.'

'Helicopters need to look as though they are civilian,' added Steve. 'You'll get closer that way. Not the helicopters for Chad, leave them in military markings.'

'We will ensure the helicopters are suitably camouflaged. I am told that the Nigerian military will receive due credit at the conclusion of this exercise.'

'The Nigerian military will receive full credit. We prefer not to advertise our exploits too openly. We just want the two women.'

'I appreciate your expertise in these matters. We will follow your lead and ensure that both of our outcomes are successful.'

'They will be,' said Steve. 'We have done this before. If we work together, success is guaranteed.'

Chapter 23

Pierre Dupré had been the outstanding student of his year. They even spoke of him eclipsing his father, Francoise, Head of Surgery at the Hopital de l'Hotel-Dieu, and widely regarded as one of the best surgeons in France.

'You're destined to take my place at the hospital in due course,' his father would say.

In the eight years it had taken for him to qualify as a doctor, Pierre had surpassed all others. In an intensely fierce programme, where only the top seven to ten per cent passed through to the subsequent year, he had constantly been in the top one per cent. There was not one subject where he failed to achieve a distinction.

A junior position at his father's hospital on graduation, he soon gravitated to cancer surgery. His operating skills were superb while his calm and authoritative manner with patients and staff alike garnered respect.

It was only a few months after graduation that he had befriended, bedded, and ultimately married his darling Amelia. A fellow doctor, she was equally destined for greatness and, in time, would become head of staff at a hospital close to Lyon, some distance from Paris.

She had given birth to a son, Charles. He was a healthy, bouncing boy until just after his first birthday when he started to show signs of destructive behaviour.

'He's just a baby, he'll grow out of it,' Amelia and Pierre both said. It was three months later when they had him diagnosed. They were both doctors and devoted parents. As parents, they wanted to believe his behaviour was normal; as physicians, they knew it wasn't.

'He's bipolar,' the paediatrician announced. Both were shocked; Amelia was inconsolable.

'Where did we go wrong?' she asked Pierre, half-accusing him.

'It is not my fault,' he replied.

In the next year or so, with Charles' condition worsening and Amelia blaming Pierre, the marriage started to crumble. Intimacy with her had been virtually non-existent since that day at the paediatrician's, and Pierre, a tactile and virile man, was left with no outlet for his needs.

'I want to be with you, I want to share your bed,' he would plead.

'I have no time for such foolishness. There are our careers. There is Charles,' she would say.

It had never been an overly passionate pairing of two people. They had loved each other fiercely in the year before Charles had come along, but she was a passive lover, whereas he was adventurous, always willing and wanting to experiment. She was basically a once a week, on a Saturday morning lover, while he was ready at anytime and anywhere, wherever and whenever the mood took him.

As infrequent and impassive as she was, she had kept him in check; and, whereas their bedtime activities were not always the most satisfying, he had managed to control his urges outside of marriage. He would see female patients, attractive women in the street, or at the cafe he would frequent during his work days and fantasise about making love to them.

With Amelia's growing coldness, he could no longer hold back, he needed an outlet. The local prostitutes came to know him well, and he quickly found his need becoming an irrational obsession.

One day, a female patient came to see him. She was in his room at the hospital; young, dark, with a short skirt and skimpy top and high on recreational drugs. She kept slipping into unconsciousness, unaware of her surroundings. How she had managed to find herself with a doctor was not fully understood.

It was then he committed the unforgivable; he took advantage of the situation. He betrayed a sacred trust that exists between patient and doctor. He touched her. At first, on the arm, then the leg, then the breast and then he put his hand between her legs.

What's the harm? I can claim I was conducting a routine medical inspection, he thought.

The young woman revived and left; he was never sure as to what had been wrong with her, other than the drug she had ingested or inhaled. The indiscretion he had committed thrilled him to a level of ecstasy. It was more exhilarating than any of the romantic moments with Amelia. It far exceeded the laborious labouring on top of a fat, drunken tart down by the Bois de Boulogne.

He knew he had a problem. He had not been the top student at the medical school to not realise that he was debauched, an immoral and wicked person and that he could not stop.

Over the next couple of years, his lust for the prostitutes continued, but his desire to abuse the doctor-patient trust remained paramount. There were a few opportunities; sometimes, a woman would come in delirious, drunk, or full of drugs and he would avail himself. It could only have been eight or ten, and two of them were so far out of it that he had penetrated them. The last one, however, had somehow regained a degree of sanity while he was on top of her and had screamed 'rape'.

'You are a depraved and worthless man!' Amelia screamed as she slammed the door in his face.

'I have resigned my position at the hospital as a result of your actions,' his father stated. 'You are no longer welcome in my house.'

His career was over. Amelia divorced him, and he spent eighteen months behind bars before being released early for good behaviour. The bottle occupied him for a few years, but he was not really a drinker and coupled with the cost of alcohol and Amelia cleaning him out financially after the divorce, he was rendered almost penniless. She had a problem child and the judge had been generous in the extreme towards her. He tried selling insurance but was no salesman; he even tried labouring on a building site, but the other men were uncouth and loud-mouthed.

***

In time, Pierre drifted to the south of the country. He first saw the man lying on the street in Marseille, covered in blood and with his face lying in his own vomit.

'What has happened? Let me help you,' said Pierre. Destitute as he was, as dishevelled and unkempt as he appeared, he still retained the vestige of a doctor, a health giver.

'They threw me out of the bar,' the man replied.

'I will get you some medical treatment,' Pierre said, his licence having been revoked at the time of his conviction for patient violation.

'Thank you, sir.'

The man, he took to Hopital Edouard Toulouse on Boulevard Danielle Casanova, not far from the docks. There, they sobered him and tended to his wounds. They were not severe, nor life-threatening.

'You'll live,' the doctor said. 'Just go easy on the wine for a few days.'

Discharged and looking fitter, Pierre's new friend spoke. 'I am Captain Alexandre Archambault. I owe you a debt of gratitude.'

'It is not necessary.'

'You look as though you could do with a good feed. Let me buy you lunch.'

The two men went to a small eatery not far from the hospital. After a good lunch and a bottle of red wine, they were firm friends. The captain failed to heed the hospital doctor's warning.

'You should have listened to the doctor,' Pierre said.

'They all say that. I can handle my drink.'

'That's not what I saw when I rescued you off the street.'

'That was bad luck. I had a bet with the captain of another ship that I could down a full bottle of an unpleasant wine before him.'

'Who won?'

'I did, of course.'

'Then why were you out on the street, lying in your own vomit?'

'Just a casualty of the love of the fermented grape. Let's not talk about it anymore. Tell me about your life.'

'There's not much to tell.'

'We are good friends here. I can see that you are an educated man down on his luck. What can I do to help?'

'I am not sure there is much that you can do. My life has been on a downward spiral for some years. I cannot see how it can be changed.'

'Do you have any money?'

'Very little.'

'Then, I can help. How would you fancy a trip out to sea?'

'A trip out to sea? Yes, why not?'

'I have a small boat, a tramp steamer. It moves around the Mediterranean taking cargo here and there. Would you be willing to come onboard and work for me?'

'I have no experience of boats,' said Pierre. 'I may be seasick all the time. But yes, I would be pleased to come and work for you.'

'Then it is settled. Let's have another bottle of wine to celebrate.'

He spent two years sailing up and down the Mediterranean with the good captain; it was the first time since those events in Paris that he felt anything close to contentment. At each port, the captain would take off to sample the local wine while Pierre would take a different direction, the route to the nearest brothel. As fate would have it, they had docked in Algiers, the capital of Algeria on the northern coastline of Africa.

A fellow patron made idle conversation while waiting for Maria, a voluptuous and highly in-demand woman from

Morocco, at the bordello favoured by sailors and Frenchmen down close to the water's edge. 'I'm looking for a partner for my medical practice,'

'I am a doctor,' he continued, 'mainly French expatriates that have retired here, or have been left over from the days when France ruled the country. It's a cushy number; they prefer a Frenchman to a local with their grubby hands. It's mainly old people's diseases and ailments, piles with the men, arthritis and incontinence with the woman. A few tablets, a few kind words, and they pay well enough for my regular visits to the best brothels in Algiers.'

'Sounds ideal to me,' said Pierre.

'Ideal? It's paradise. Are you interested?'

'I don't have much money.'

'We can figure something out.'

'Why so generous?'

'Let's talk later,' replied the doctor. 'Maria's free and I'm horny.'

Later that night they met, Pierre Dupré, the disbarred doctor, and Docteur Auguste Lefevre.

'I'll be honest,' said Auguste, 'I've got cancer. Two years at most. I don't want treatment or pity. I just want to go out with a bang. You give me a commission for every patient I send you, and I'll be happy.'

'Cancer can be treated,' Pierre ventured.

'Prostate, and what use am I afterwards? They'll destroy the nerves in my dick. I won't be able to get an erection. What kind of life is that?' He shook his head. 'Anyway, I would need to go to France for the treatment.'

'Any issue with France?'

'There's a little issue back there. She was willing, and I was young and full of hormones. They don't like it when you do it in your surgery, even if it's harmless.'

'Did she make a complaint?'

'Complaint! Hell, no. She loved it. It was only when the receptionist came in. Silly old bat, I was planning to sack her. If I'd got rid of her a week earlier, I wouldn't be here now.'

'What did she do, the silly old bat?' asked Pierre.

'Only reported me to the ethics committee. They advised me to go and practice somewhere else.'

'That was tough.'

'It's fine now. I much prefer my life here, nobody asking too many silly questions. I just wish I had more than a few years. What about you? You must have a tale to tell. You wouldn't be floating around in a rusty tub if you hadn't committed some indiscretion, upset the sensibilities of a group of prudish old men.'

'My story's similar.'

'No matter, I don't need to know. Do you want to work with me?'

'Yes, I would like that very much.'

In the short period that followed, Auguste went off to the brothel every day. Pierre made the money and joined him as often as he could. Both enjoyed their lives immensely. Auguste lived on for two and a half years more before they wheeled him out to the local Christian cemetery. Never had so many prostitutes gathered over one coffin as on that day.

***

Pierre continued with the surgery, his manner oozing charm, attracting more clientele than he could manage. His visits to the brothels were severely hampered by the demands of work, and his obsession was not being satisfied. It was at the end of an unusually long week that he received a new and unexpected patient.

'We found her disorientated on the street,' the Gendarme said. 'She is French. We thought you were the best person to bring her to.'

A fresh-faced woman in her mid-twenties, it was clear she had experienced a bad trip with some cheap hashish. According to the passport she was carrying in her trouser pocket, her name was Yvonne. She was also very attractive and almost comatose. He had given her a sedative to calm her symptoms.

No one will know, a little examination can only be beneficial to my diagnosis, he thought.

She was lying on the examination bed in his surgery; he loosened her blouse.

I need to check her heartbeat, he said to himself.

It was then he saw her breasts, firm, proud and succulent. He could not resist; he fondled them warmly. With his blood hot and his erection firm, he loosened the belt on her jeans and eased them down to her ankles. Now, devoid of any restraint, he climbed on top of her.

At the moment of climax, a commotion at the door and in burst Michel, her boyfriend. Tall, strong and muscular, he pulled Pierre off and flung him to the ground. While Michel was temporarily occupied with caring for Yvonne, Pierre made a dash for the door. His worldly possessions amounted to very little and, grabbing his backpack, he rushed down the road. The distraught boyfriend attempted to follow, but he did not know the back streets, the alleys of the town, and Pierre quickly shook him off.

There was no time to consider the options; he had to get out of town. It was a ten-minute taxi ride to La Gare Routiere, the local bus station, in Hussein Dey. The next bus leaving in ten minutes, would be headed for Tamanrasset in the centre of the Sahara Desert, nearly two thousand kilometres down the Trans-Saharan Highway. He boarded the bus. Dry and dusty, Tamanrasset offered little for him. It was to be another three months before he reached N'Djamena, the capital of Chad.

In time, he set up a small clinic catering to the diplomatic corp, a few French people, and some of the more Westernised locals. It was to be his final destination. In the intervening fifteen years, and now in his sixties, he no longer cared.

There had been the occasional woman in the backstreets who had come up from Cameroon, but he had now reached an age where, although the mind was willing, the libido was not.

It was Sheikh Idris Deubet who contacted him with a special request. 'I have someone special that I wish you to examine.'

'Another black girl?' Pierre asked enthusiastically.

He always relished their examinations. The girls were heavily sedated, vaguely aware of his probing and fondling. As with the women in Paris, and then with the backpacker in Algiers, he could not resist himself. In the security of the small room at the Sheikh's compound, he had availed himself of their vulnerability. He had declared them all virgins, even if, on leaving the room, some were not. Tarts on the street may no longer have excited him, but those little black girls did.

'This one is unique. It requires the utmost discretion on your part. Are you willing to do this for me?'

'Yes, what will the payment be this time?'

'Two thousand American dollars.'

'You usually pay me two hundred. This woman must be special.'

'She is. She is white.'

'I understand. For that amount of money, my discretion is assured.'

'If she is harmed in any way or abused, then your life will be forfeited. Is that clear?'

'She will receive only the best attention from me.'

***

The examination was to be conducted in the same room where he had examined the black girls. They had entered alone. The next day in the morning the examination commenced. The woman that entered the room was mildly sedated; the chaperone was not.

'I am here to check that Kate is treated well,' said Fatima. The Sheikh had shown Fatima the horsewhip when she protested that there was no way she would allow Kate to be examined. Kate had intervened and had told the Sheikh that she would comply.

'That is fine,' said Pierre. His appearance was unshaven and untidy and though not visibly drunk, he smelt of stale wine and stank of cigarettes. Fatima was abhorred and could barely look as he commenced his examination.

'Bonjour, Mademoiselle, I am Docteur Dupré,' he said as he breathed over Kate and tried to look down the top of her dress. Fatima did not like him at all, Kate barely noticed. 'I will conduct the examination, which I can assure you will be quite painless and, possibly, pleasurable.' He spoke in a combination of French and bad English, but Fatima understood perfectly what he was saying and inferring.

To Pierre, the blonde, fair-skinned woman was exquisite in her beauty and innocence. The black girls had excited him, but with Kate he was delirious with pleasure. She had reawakened stirrings below his belt that he had not experienced in years. Fatima could see the ever-expanding bulge in his trousers.

'Please lie down comfortably,' he said to Kate.

She was relaxed and dreamy as the doctor commenced his examination. He probed her vagina to check her hymen was intact; he massaged her breasts to check they were natural, and all the while his breathing became heavier and his nervous trembling more noticeable.

Eventually, Fatima grabbed Kate and made for the door. The doctor closed the door behind them and relieved himself of his tension with a few swift motions of his hand on his erect member.

An official certificate was produced by Docteur Pierre Dupré stating virginity intact. It was what the Sheikh wanted. The two thousand dollars for the examination had been well spent. He would ensure the Prince would have a copy within the hour.

Fatima, deeply upset by the doctor, his visible excitement, his probing hands and his extended finger pushed into Kate's vagina, had spoken to the Sheikh.

Dragged back to the Sheikh's compound from the small rundown one bedroom apartment that was Pierre Dupré's home, he crouched in the presence of Idris Deubet. 'Your actions have condemned you,' the Sheikh in a rage screamed. 'You were told to treat her with the utmost care. You could have broken her hymen, taken her virginity with your finger. She is worth three million dollars to me, possibly more, but you could have rendered her worthless.'

'I apologise. I had been drinking. I made a mistake,' Pierre mumbled. Heavily bound and severely beaten, his trousers stained with wet urine.

'If Fatima had not been there, you would have raped her.'

'I apologise. Please let me go. It will not happen again.'

'It will definitely not happen again. You will not be alive.' The Sheikh turned to the two henchmen standing close by. 'You know what to do.'

'It will not happen again. I am sorry.'

'Remove him from my sight. He disgusts me. I do not want to see him again.'

A brilliant career destroyed for one single flaw in his character; an obsession that could not be restrained. It had led him to this. Docteur Pierre Dupré, top of his class, destined for greatness, trussed and bound in the back of a four-wheel drive, heading out of town to an undisclosed and remote location. Abakar and Mahamat were masters of their trade. If there was an assassination, some torture required, information to be extracted, they were the best. Unpleasant both in appearance and manner, they had an unparalleled record of acts of senseless and indiscriminate violence. It was to them that the doctor had been entrusted.

'I know a good place where we can take you. We'll be all by ourselves,' Abakar said to Pierre.

'Please. I will pay you well. Let me go.'

'You know we can't do that. Our word is our bond. We have accepted the commission from Sheikh Idriss. What kind of businessmen would we be if we accepted your offer? Besides, he pays us well, much more than you could ever offer.'

'It is a good profession. We get paid to enjoy ourselves,' Mahamat said. 'Your death will be most pleasant.'

Pierre, already wet with urine, defecated in despair. 'You can clean that up before we start,' Abakar said with a smile.

'We're taking you out towards the Ennudi Plateau,' said Mahamat. 'It's very scenic. You'll have a lovely view as we remove your balls.'

'Why are you doing this? What did I do to you?'

'You have done nothing to us,' replied Abakar. 'Do you think we care that you couldn't keep your hands to yourself with some women? It is purely business. He paid, you die. It's nothing personal.'

'Don't you feel guilt for what you are doing?' said Pierre.

'Guilt? No. Why should we? We have already told you. To us, this is a pleasure. We are cruel people.'

In due course, the vehicle arrived at its destination. Pierre was removed and tied to a convenient post. He could tell this was not the first time they had been there.

'Take his balls,' Mahamat said. 'You better gag him first. I don't want him vomiting on my shoes.'

With one swift motion of the knife, Pierre was separated from his manhood.

'Stuff them in his mouth and gag him again,' Abakar said.

'I'll cut him across the belly. Make the blood flow.' Mahamat had some work to do before his business was concluded.

'Cut him hard. Make the blood ooze. The vultures will have a good feed.'

They both laughed as they drove away down the rough and dusty track. Pierre Dupré would never be seen again.

Chapter 24

Activity at the airfield in Maiduguri had been intense since the decision to mount the rescue operation with the cooperation of the Nigerian military. A sleepy regional airport had in the space of three days been transformed into a forward base for the military. All the helicopters, aeroplanes, and personnel were on base. The secrecy still held; the media unaware as to what was about to happen. They were still speculating, criticising, attempting to corner any politician or key player, including Bob McDonald, who was attempting to keep a low profile.

Major Osuji had been tasked with making the opening statement at the operational briefing. 'Secrecy has been the primary reason that the full details of the operation have not been revealed to you all before. President Karibo and Lt General Ibrahim are fully aware of our presence here and have given full and unequivocal approval for what is planned. Harry Warburton of Counter Insurgencies will give you details of the operation.'

'Thank you,' Harry said. 'As you are well-aware, there was an attack on a Mission not far from this base some weeks ago. Three people were killed and two kidnapped. You have no doubt seen the reports in the media. The two kidnapped are women – one is American, the other British.

'Counter Insurgencies has been contracted to affect a rescue by the father of one of the women. We have found them both. One is with Boko Haram, about two hundred kilometres from here, the other is in the Republic of Chad.

'What we have also found is that there are a large number of kidnapped Nigerian women with Boko Haram and a smaller number in Chad. It is a clear directive from President Karibo that we are to rescue all of the women. This presents complications with Boko Haram in that, once they are aware of our presence, they will start shooting, and numerous women will be killed in the crossfire.'

'Are the women isolated?' a young Captain asked.

'They are dispersed throughout the camp.'

'I realise Harry does not want to say this directly,' Major Osuji preferred to give the facts. 'Our women have, with the exception of a very few, been given to the foot soldiers. They have been raped; some will be pregnant, some with babies.'

'It is most unpleasant to consider.' the captain said.

'The women we will rescue in Chad have probably fared better,' Harry said.

'Harry, please continue,' the Major said.

'The operation has several components and timing is critical. Firstly, we need to establish at least twenty of our people in a holding location close to the camp. To achieve this, we need to fly to within thirty to fifty kilometres of the camp, offload, and for them to trek in. At a nominated time, they will cause a diversionary tactic, grab Helen Campbell, the English woman and quickly move her to a waiting helicopter three hundred metres away.

'Any Nigerian women with her will be brought out at the same time. Now, here is where it gets complicated. How do we maximise the number of local women to be rescued?'

'Harry, it needs to be said. There will be collateral damage,' the Major clarified the reality.

'It seems inevitable,' replied Harry. 'We may be able to remove a few in the initial stages, but a helicopter landing nearby will raise the insurgents to arms. They will almost certainly start randomly shooting the women in the camp.'

'Let us worry about how we rescue them. You focus on Helen Campbell and the other woman in Chad.'

'Major Osuji, I'll leave it to you. Secondly, once Helen is rescued, hopefully with as many local girls as we can at the same time, three helicopters based at the base here will commence the flight into Chad. Now, we need these to be concurrent operations. We cannot allow activities at either location to be relayed to the others. The women's lives will be in further jeopardy, both here in Nigeria and Chad if that occurs.'

'Are you taking any Nigerian Army soldiers into Chad?' the young captain asked.

'At least ten, which is why we have three helicopters. There may be up to twenty women to bring back.'

'Will the Chadian government allow us fly in their airspace in army helicopters?' The young captain persisted in asking questions.

'They will meet us as we cross into their airspace and then escort our helicopters to the landing area. Once on the ground, there will be sufficient vehicles. We will then proceed to the compound where they are being held. We have someone in the field and, on receiving word that we are on the way, will secretly enter the compound. Any guards found there will be eliminated, peacefully or otherwise. There are some dogs, but he will deal with them. The retrieval of the women in Chad should be trouble-free.'

'Why do you need ten commandos?' Major Osuji asked.

'In case of complications,' Harry replied.

'Complications?'

'There is an interested person from the Middle East aiming to secure Kate McDonald, the American female there. If he or individuals acting on his behalf are there or make any action to claim her, we may need to respond.'

***

At the end of the third day, and ahead of schedule Aluko and five of his men were dropped thirty-five kilometres out from the camp along with twenty commandos. The commandos had attempted to give Aluko and his team a crash course in commando tactics in preparation, but they were neither regular soldiers nor of the physical strength required. Their role was to coordinate the rescue of Helen, and to let Harry know that all was proceeding according to plan.

The commandos, Harry had realised, would be focussed on taking out the Boko Haram fighters and rescuing as many women as they could. It was clear that some would be killed. Their style of retrieval was not subtle, more crash and burn. Helen was the prime objective, and Aluko had to make sure she was secured before the shooting began.

'Yanny, I need you up here for when Helen is brought back,' Harry phoned. 'You've met her. She'll appreciate a friendly face.'

'When will she be there?'

'Tomorrow night, around ten is the plan.'

'Won't you be there?'

'No, as soon as we have word Helen is secured, we will be lifting off for the flight into Chad. We should be close to N'Djamena by the time she lands.'

'Bob's bringing up a private jet with a full medical team,' Yanny replied. 'I'll get a ride with him.'

'It's not necessary. The Nigerian military have set up a field hospital. It's excellent.'

'We cannot stop him. He's brought in the family doctor from the States as well, and Kate's mother. She's been heavily sedated since the kidnapping.'

'He's premature, although I suppose we can't blame him. I only hope Kate is up to all the attention. She's likely to be spaced out after so many weeks. Did anyone contact Helen's parents?'

'Bob's already done that. They're on a plane from Manchester down to Abuja. We're bringing them up as well.'

'I'm not sure the military will be pleased with all the civilians here.'

'Bob contacted President Karibo. He cleared it.'

***

Progress from the landing point to the insurgent's camp had been slow and laborious. Walking at night, heavily laden with weaponry and no lights, was challenging. The Army commandos appeared to revel in the trek. Aluko was close to collapsing from exhaustion as they edged the last two hundred metres towards the camp.

'All quiet,' the eager young captain said to Aluko.

'I need to let Harry know we're here. Did you see any trouble in the last thirty minutes?' Aluko asked.

'There was some. We were seen by some men on their way back to the camp.'

'What did you do with them?'

'Garrotted them.'

'Then I am pleased I didn't see them.'

'You'll never make a commando if you can't kill without hesitation.'

'Harry, we're on target,' said Aluko, making contact with Harry using the satellite phone he carried.

'Helen?'

'She is here but she's not alone.'

'Abacha?' Harry asked.

'It seems likely.'

'You better let one of the commandos deal with him.'

'Yes, I am aware of their particular skill,' Aluko said.

'Grab Helen at the time agreed. Deactivate the beacon if you can. Have they located any local girls?'

'Some are close to Helen. About ten from what we can see. The remainder are scattered throughout the camp.'

'If they can run fast enough, bring them with Helen.'

Ending the phone call to Steve, Aluko turned his attention to the immediate situation. 'Are there any more women?' he asked the captain.

'They're dispersed. We've seen quite a few, but they look to be in a bad way. We'll have to clean up the camp.'

'Clean up the camp?' asked Aluko.

'We have to kill all the insurgents.'

'You realise that you'll end up with a few dead women.'

'I know,' replied the young captain. 'My men are eliminating a few of their soldiers on the periphery, but there'll still be a substantial number left.'

'Let me get the white woman and the Nigeria women in the hut close by,' said Aluko. 'We'll aim to take them out on the helicopter.'

'Then go now before the ruckus starts.'

'It is ten minutes early, but I can see we have no option,' Aluko said. 'The white woman, she is in the hut with a man. Can you deal with him?'

'My best man will go with you.'

Aluko and the captain's best man moved towards the hut. The commando started to throw pebbles on the corrugated iron roof. Less than a minute later, Abacha, interrupted from his nightly entanglement with Helen, angrily came out of the door naked. As he looked up, looking for the disturbance to his romantic interlude, the captain's best man closed his hand over Abacha's mouth and stuck a thin knife into his back. He collapsed silently to the ground. He was then garrotted. Aluko understood why he was the captain's best man.

Aluko entered the hut and found Helen, equally as naked, in the bed. Confused, she jumped from the bed, hit him on the head with a thick piece of wood and kneed him firmly between his legs.

'Helen?' Aluko groaned in agony. Almost bent double, he held on to the arm of an old wooden chair for support.

'Yes.'

'Helen, you know me. I am Aluko. There is a helicopter three hundred metres from here. We need to go now.'

'Abacha?' she said, slightly shocked at the intensity of the moment. 'What if he comes back?'

'He will not trouble us.'

'Why?'

'He's dead.'

'Oh!' It was all she could say. Savage, barbaric as he was, he had treated her well. She could not like him; she could not hate him. She was only sad.

'We need to go,' urged Aluko.

'The girls in the next hut, they are my friends.'

'We will try to bring them, but we do not have much time. We need to exit the camp before the shooting starts.'

'Shooting?'

'Shooting. I am not alone.'

They had barely left the hut when the first shots were fired. One of the Boko Haram fighters had not been dispatched successfully. Regaining partial consciousness, he had raised the alarm. The insurgents were slow to respond, but respond they did. They began randomly rushing around, shooting anyone that seemed suspicious. They even killed a few of their own men by mistake.

'Protect the women at all costs!' the young captain shouted before he was hit by a bullet in the leg and collapsed to the ground. In agony and incapacitated, he continued to issue commands and shoot with his pistol.

The battle would continue for thirty minutes before the commandos gained the upper hand. It was not a one-sided battle; the insurgents gave as good as they received. Five of the commandos were killed, and over fifty Boko Haram fighters died. Mohammad Murtada, the insurgent's leader had craftily slipped out the back of the camp when the first shot was fired. He had been lucky – the most he received was a bullet graze to his right leg.

The commandos, devoid of compassion, and upset over the death of their captain, systematically eliminated all the captured fighters, but only after they had extracted as much information as they could. It had been a bloodbath.

The information extracted excited the Nigerian army soldiers. 'Major, we know where there are another two camps,' Lieutenant Oni said over the satellite phone as the battle at the camp came to a conclusion.

'Why isn't Captain Mukhtar phoning me?' Major Osuji asked from the base in Maiduguri.

'I have assumed command, sir. Captain Mukhtar has died in battle.'

'I am sorry to hear that. He was a good man.'

'We all thought so as well. He will be sadly missed. He fought bravely.'

'Did we achieve our aim?'

'We did, sir. We are aware of two other camps? We want to move on them now.'

'Do you have enough men?'

'No. We need all the men in Maiduguri.'

'Are there women at the other camps?'

'It is believed so.'

'You have my permission,' Major Osuji said. 'We don't want more women than necessary to be killed.'

'That will not be possible. We will need to go in with full force.'

'Understood. I will dispatch eight hundred men by road in the next sixty minutes to support your operations. Please ensure I have the locations as soon as possible.'

'Thank you, sir. I will send the coordinates.'

The raid at the primary camp had resulted in seventy-eight women being rescued, along with three babies. Ten of the women were pregnant, all were heavily traumatised. It was clear that a number of women had been killed in the crossfire but, given the intensity of the battle, the numbers were less than expected.

***

The exit from the camp for Helen, the run through the surrounding bush, was hectic and completed without delay. Barely able to stand up for the last one hundred metres, she was held between two commandos and virtually dragged along. Her legs were scratched and bleeding, but otherwise she was unharmed.

I am free, she thought. *What about Kate?*

It was five minutes later when Aluko contacted Harry. It was only then that he realised he had been shot, adrenaline suppressing the pain.

'Target secured plus nine,' he said as the helicopter carrying him and Helen lifted off from the ground.

'Casualties?'

'Four of our men. I've taken a bullet in the shoulder. The commandos, similar number.'

'Collateral damage?'

'You'll need to ask Major Osuji. We ran out of there as fast as we could. We missed the action.'

'Not all of it. You took a bullet.'

'I'll be fine.'

'Be prepared for the reception committee at the airport. Bob McDonald's jet landed sixty minutes ago. Helen's parents are here as well,' Harry said.

'Have you told them we are coming?'

'No need. We could see them celebrating the moment our three helicopters lifted off the apron. That was the signal that you had been successful.'

Aluko was to miss the welcome. By the time the helicopter landed, he was unconscious due to blood loss. He was to survive.

It was Helen who had acted as his guardian angel on the trip down. She applied bandages as she could, nursed him in her arms, kept talking to him. She did not want her saviour succumbing to death. By the time they landed, she was covered in blood. Her parents virtually collapsed on the ground at the sight of her. They, not her, needed Bob's medical team. All she needed and wanted was a hot shower and a cup of tea.

Chapter 25

As the three Aérospatiale SA 330 Pumas of the Nigerian Air Force crossed into Chadian airspace, they were met by two Mil Mi-24 helicopters of the Chadian Air Force. After identification protocols had been formalised, they proceeded in close formation to the international airport in N'Djamena. Major Osuji had made a call to their military once Harry and the commandos had lifted off from Maiduguri, to inform them of the expected time of the border crossing.

'There has been a development,' Phil said over the radio to Harry in the lead helicopter.

'What is it, Phil?'

'The jet from the Middle East landed about an hour ago. It seems clear they are serious about taking Kate.'

'What do you mean?'

'They have brought some additional support. They look like mercenaries and they look professional.'

'How many are there?'

'I've seen five so far, and they are well-armed.'

'Where are they now?'

'They are just about to head off to the compound. At least, that would be the assumption.'

'Can you get Kate out now?'

'Not without a gun battle. There was a French doctor at the compound a few days ago. I never saw him leave.'

'What do we know about him?' Harry asked.

'A dishevelled character by all accounts. Mustapha thinks he may have been brought in to check Kate.'

'Understood, virginity intact,' said Harry.

'That would be the assumption. The Sheikh knows you're coming.' Phil said

'How did he find out so quickly?'

'It's on the news. Three camps of Boko Haram have been attacked by the Nigerian military. It mentions a large number of women being freed. He must have put two and two together.'

'What has been his reaction?' asked Harry.

'He's brought in additional security for the compound. At least ten locals and they look solid as well.'

'So, we're going to have to fight our way in?'

'It looks that way,' Phil said.

'What about Kate and the other women?'

'Still in the compound, although now we can't just walk in and take them.'

'It may have been easier if you had taken Kate that night you went into the compound,' said Harry.

'That's speculation.'

'True, let's discuss the current situation.'

'Mustapha is following the Arabs from the airport,' said Phil. 'I am outside the compound.'

'The vehicles we need. Where are they?'

'Close to the airport, but now they'll see you coming in. They're bound to inform those on the way to pick up Kate.'

'There's not much we can do. We are committed to the airport. If we divert, it may give them enough time to grab Kate and exit the country,' Harry said.

'How long to touchdown?'

'Thirty minutes.'

'We better move fast once you arrive.'

'Can you take out any of the guards at the compound prior to our arrival?

'Not before you arrive,' said Phil. 'That would be a clear signal that a rescue was imminent. Once you land and are seen, then I will try to take out two or three. I won't be able to get them all.'

'Reduce a few. It may help.'

***

The Prince, safely ensconced in Saudi Arabia reacted with alarm at the developing news. 'I am determined to have that woman.'

'That is why we asked to bring additional support to secure her for you,' Abdullah Al Balushi, his lead agent, said. 'With such a prize, and the deviousness of Sheikh Idriss, we contemplated all possibilities.'

'The news from Nigeria was unexpected. But, with the people you so graciously supplied, we are ensured of success,' Saleh Al Hasani, the second of the Prince's agents, said.

'Don't aim to suck up to me. I do not appreciate sycophants.'

'What about the Sheikh? It is clear that he has deceived us and that he was conducting an auction,' Abdullah asked.

'Why do you ask me? You know what happens to people who abuse my generosity.'

'His death will be swift.'

'If you don't bring me the girl intact, then you both can stay there and join the Sheikh in Jannah, in Hell. Do I make myself clear?'

'We will ensure the virgin is with you tomorrow,' replied Abdullah.

The additional security that they had brought was not for a fight with the army of any country. It had been insurance in case Idris Deubet attempted to double deal, or to move her to another location in a bid to secure additional ransom money.

The three helicopters carrying Harry and the commandos landed on time. They were clearly marked as military, and they were no more than three hundred metres from the Prince's jet. Their landing and the subsequent disembarking of a number of heavily armed soldiers could only mean one thing to those watching from across the apron: they had come to rescue the woman.

'We need to hurry up,' Abdullah said to Adeel, the lead mercenary. 'Those helicopters mean trouble.'

'We came here to deal with a Chadian Sheikh, not fight the Nigerian and Chadian military,' Adeel replied. A tough and aggressive fighter from Libya, he had supported Gadhafi. When the dictatorship was doomed, obviously going to lose, he skipped the country and joined a mercenary organisation. Any conflict in the Middle East, any ideology – he did not care, as long as the money was good and the fighting minimal. Fighting against the armed forces of any country was risky, and he did not intend to get himself killed.

'You took the Prince's money. It is now time for you to justify his generous payment.' Abdullah reminded him.

'We will go to the compound with you and fetch the woman, but we will not fight the military,' replied Adeel.

'We go now, and with luck it should not take more than two hours to be back here at the airfield. Let us hope we can leave then.'

'Why don't we leave now and forget the woman?' Adeel said.

'You do not know the vengeance of the Prince.'

'What do I care about him? It is my life that is important to me, not his need to get his leg over a Western woman.'

'It is the Western woman that is responsible for your payment. If we fail to return with her, he will ensure that you, as well as I, will not survive to see another full moon. Do I make myself clear?' said Abdullah.

'Do not threaten me. Neither you nor your precious Prince can harm me,' Adeel arrogantly responded.

'Do you not know of the reputation of the Prince, the wealth that he commands? Do you really believe he would not find you?'

'We must leave now. Your debating can wait for later,' Saleh interjected.

The four Toyota trucks and the Sheikh's personal Land Cruiser were out of the airport and heading down Rue de la Gendarmerie within three minutes. Their progress had been swift, but the traffic, they still had twelve kilometres to travel, had slowed. It was mid-morning and the traffic was reaching its peak.

***

'They're heading your way,' Harry said.

'Where are you? Are you on the road?' Phil asked.

'Not yet. The vehicles are not here. I am told five minutes.'

'How the hell did that happen?' said Phil angrily. 'I can't hold off all those coming for Kate.'

'I realise that. You'll just have to engage in some delaying tactics.'

'I'll get Mustapha on it.'

'Fine, let's do that. When we're fifteen minutes from you, you can start reducing the numbers at the compound.'

'Agreed. We are still going to have a gun battle.'

The vehicles that Phil had organised had been stuck in traffic; it had been a miscalculation on his part. Meanwhile, Harry ascertained the situation at the airport.

'We need to ensure the private jet cannot leave,' he said to the pilot of the helicopter that had accompanied them from the border to the airport.

'They are requesting their plane to be refuelled,' replied Captain Mornadji Déby. 'They will find that our people are remarkably slow today.'

'You've spoken to the crew of the fuel tanker?'

'It seemed an appropriate course of action.'

'Thanks. Great thinking, but if we are slow in refuelling, they may just leave and fly east to the Sudan. They'll pick up fuel there, no questions asked, as long as they throw enough money around.'

'We could impede their access to the runway.' the Chadian captain said.

'Let's do that, a few trucks in the way, something similar.'

'Consider it done.'

While the plan to halt the departure of the Prince's jet was being discussed, the promised vehicles arrived. They were now thirty minutes behind the Prince's people, and they still had to battle the traffic outside the airport.

'We're just leaving,' Harry said to Phil.

'This is not what we planned.' Phil sounded agitated. 'There's no way you can get here in time, and I just don't see how we can hold them off.'

'Did you get any more men to help?'

'Mustapha organised five locals, but they're just rent-a-gun.'

'They'll not be much use in a serious fight,' Harry said.

'If the Prince's people are professional, they'll be close to useless,' replied Phil.

'There's not much we can do at this moment. Just see what Mustapha can do to slow the Prince's people down.'

'He has already organised a few interesting diversions. Not sure if it will hold them up for very long.'

'Update me when I get there. See if he can hold them up for at least twenty minutes.'

'How are you going to get here in twenty minutes? The Prince's men set out thirty minutes ago and they're not here yet.'

'We're getting a full police escort.'

'How did you arrange that?'

'The pilot from one of the helicopters that escorted us in, his cousin is in charge of the police station at the airport.'

'Everyone is related to everyone else here,' said Phil.

'In this case, it is to our advantage,' Harry replied.

'There's been a car accident up the road from here. It's probably Mustapha. It looks like chaos.'

'That means they've arrived, and we're only just clearing the airport.'

'I will not be able to hold them if they get to the compound before you do.'

'Do what you can,' said Harry.

'In that case, I'll start reducing the numbers.'

'Any reduction will help.'

'It won't help much.'

'Can Mustapha get any more help?'

'He tried, but we had very short notice. We thought it was going to be a relatively straightforward operation.'

'We assumed the Prince would just send his two agents with the money, and the Sheikh would have grabbed Kate and taken her out to the airport. Their bringing in heavies has changed the scenario.'

'We've miscalculated,' Phil realised they had made a serious mistake. It had seemed a simple exercise to grab Kate – just poison a couple of dogs and remove four guards at the most. Now they had fifteen armed men to deal with, and most of them were disciplined and well-trained.

'We did not miscalculate,' replied Harry. 'I have some very professional soldiers with me. It's unfortunate that they're in the wrong place at this time.'

'Just expressing my frustration out loud.'

The police escort, meanwhile, was doing a good job. Sirens blaring, they weaved through the traffic with bravado. Any vehicle that was likely to halt their progress, duly rammed to one side. With one police car in front and another at the back, the pace was impressive. In the frantic dash, vehicles were being damaged, every traffic violation in the book broken.

'We're close to the compound now. What's the situation?' Harry asked.

'Mustapha's delaying tactics have just about been exhausted. They should enter the Sheikh's compound in the next few minutes.'

'How about the guards, did you manage to reduce the numbers?'

'I took out two who had left their post to get some food on the street. They're lying dead in an alley.'

'That leaves us with about thirteen to deal with,' stated Harry.

'We're outnumbered here. Have you prevented their plane leaving?'

'I left Captain Déby and a couple of the Nigerian soldiers to deal with it.'

'Can he be trusted? Is he up to the task?'

'We can trust him. Whether he is up to the task, I don't know.'

'They're entering the compound now,' said Phil. 'I can't take them on at this moment. I'll need to wait for you.'

'Ask Mustapha to delay their leaving.'

***

'We have come for the woman,' Abdullah said.

'I need the money first,' the Sheikh responded, obviously agitated by the situation.

'You have no right to any money. It is obvious the Nigerian military are here because you continued to conduct an auction with her father.'

'That is not true. I only kept her for the Prince.'

'Lies, it's just lies. The Prince knows of your treachery. If you survive this day, it is he who will decide as to whether you spend your money or whether you will die.'

The Sheikh's fate had already been decided, but with the situation so precarious, now was not the time to send him to his grave. The immediate need was to grab Kate and to exit as soon as possible.

'Here is your money,' said Saleh. 'Enjoy it for the little time that you have left.'

'I cannot take it here,' said the Sheikh. 'It will be impossible for me to get it out of the compound, out of Chad. We are soon to be attacked by Nigerian soldiers.'

'That is your problem,' replied Abdullah. 'We have upheld our part of the deal.'

'Take me with you. It is the only hope for me. The Chadian government will not let me be free here,' pleaded the Sheikh.

'Why should we?'

'I can get you out of the country.'

'We can deal with it ourselves.'

'I am told they have blocked your plane's exit.'

'We can bribe our way out.'

'It will be easier with me there to assist.'

Abdullah thought for a moment. 'Your presence may help. We will take you and your money with us. If your assistance at the airport is advantageous, then I give my word that we will transport you to a country of your choosing.' *An open door at one thousand feet would provide an adequate solution to the double-dealing Sheikh,* he thought.

Abdullah had seen an advantage if they survived and the Sheikh did not. The Prince had paid five million dollars. Both he and Saleh could claim the money was lost in the exit from Chad, and then divide it between the two of them. A half share of five million was better than sharing two. He knew Saleh would not have any problem with the solution.

'I accept your word.' The Sheikh did not believe or trust either Abdullah or Saleh, but he had few options. If he stayed, the Chadian government would have him arrested and imprisoned, probably tortured. He was an embarrassment to the country and they would be sure to make an example of him.

The Nigerian soldiers were also on their way, and they were not likely to be partial to his holding women from their country. There was the added complication that two of the girls currently imprisoned had been drugged and raped by him; his knew his chances of survival were slim. No longer would he be seen as the natural successor to Mohammad Idriss Habre, the notable and honoured slave trader and ancestor. His legacy, he could well see, was the descendant who brought dishonour and shame. The three million dollars looked to be of small consequence now. He would gladly give it all back for his life, but his life was no longer his to control.

'Bring the woman now,' Saleh commanded.

'My money, I want my money first,' said the Sheikh.

'Here is your money. Spend it well.' Saleh thrust a suitcase containing three million dollars in cash into the grasping arms of the Sheikh.

'She is in the building at the back of the compound. You are free to take her.'

'Is she suitably prepared?'

'Yes, she has been given a mild sedative. She will be compliant.'

Abdullah and Saleh made their way in haste for Kate. Time was of the essence. There was to be a battle to exit the country and neither was partial to violence, especially when it was directed towards them.

'Put the Sheikh in the lead car. We may need him to get us out of the country,' Abdullah commanded Adeel, the lead mercenary.'

'I do not take orders,' Adeel, a singularly unsavoury character responded. 'I will put him in the car purely because he may be of assistance.'

'Just ensure he is there when we leave.'

'He will be there.'

'Good. We will get the woman.'

Pandemonium erupted when the door to the women's quarters was broken down. The other women, unaccustomed to the presence of a male inside their domain other than the Sheikh, cowered in fear.

'Where is the white woman?' Saleh asked.

'She is not for you.' Fatima instinctively stood before the Prince's agents to protect Kate, concealed in a small room off to one side.

'We have paid the Sheikh. She is now our property.'

'Then you will have to kill me first.'

'If we must, then that is what we will do.'

At that moment, a rustling in the room where Kate was concealed, accompanied by the noise of something falling to the ground indicated her location.

'She's in there,' Abdullah said.

'I'll grab her,' Saleh said.

As he attempted to open the door, Fatima attacked him with a vengeance. A small man, he was thrown off balance and flung to the ground. She was savage, gouging at his eyes, kicking him as best she could. Adeel, hearing the commotion, rushed in and quickly picked up Fatima and threw her hard against the wall; she was barely able to stand.

'Grab the white woman. We have to leave,' Abdullah shouted. 'Don't harm her. The Prince has paid a great deal of money for her in pristine condition.'

Adeel deposited Kate in the lead vehicle, and even he was enamoured by her white hair and her porcelain features. As the vehicles moved to exit the compound, Fatima, now sufficiently recovered, rushed towards them.

'Take me. She is my friend. I will look after her for you.'

'Put her in the car as well,' Saleh said. He had taken a shine to the beautiful if ageing woman who had severely beaten him. He was determined to tame her. *What is the use of a skinny Russian tart when I could have a buxom African woman?* he thought.

***

Frustrated by his lack of action, Phil phoned Harry. 'They're exiting the compound.'

'We're here. What can you do? What can you see?'

'Four vehicles. They may have left one behind. I'm not sure at the present moment.'

'Can you see Kate?'

'She's in the lead vehicle,' said Phil. 'She is with the woman I spoke to that night when I climbed the wall.'

'Fatima?'

'Yes, it's her. The Sheikh appears to be in same vehicle as the two women.'

'Can you take out the third and fourth vehicles?' asked Harry. 'It would even the numbers for us.'

'Mustapha is here. He is listening in on our conversation.'

'I will organise some road works, accidents on the way to the airport,' said Mustapha. 'It should be possible to prevent the last two vehicles reaching there in time.'

'Let the other two through to the airport,' Harry said. 'We still need some of the Nigerian soldiers here. The Sheikh's guards are here looking lost, not knowing what to do.'

'Can you manage with three soldiers?'

'Three will be alright. With the rent-a-guns and the soldiers we should be able to take them with not too much trouble.'

'Consider it done. We need to get back to the airport. We're dispatching one vehicle to you now.'

'Thanks, we'll take out the guards. If we liquidate a couple, the others will probably make a run for it.'

'We need all the black girls. The other women in the compound are not our concern. We'll grab Kate and Fatima at the airport,' Harry said.

'I'll ask Mustapha to get some extra vehicles,' said Phil. 'A bus would be best. We'll get out to the airport as soon as possible.'

'We'll wait for you.'

***

With Helen safely back in Maiduguri and a sufficient amount of time elapsed since the helicopters had left for Chad, Yanny felt the time was appropriate to phone. 'What's the latest?'

'It's not gone as well as we hoped,' Harry said as the convoy weaved its way through the early afternoon traffic. The police escort was moving at speed in the reverse direction to which they had come just thirty minutes earlier.

'What about Kate?'

'She's with the Prince's men.'

'How did that happen?'

'I'll explain later. Is anyone listening in on our conversation?'

'There's only Steve and Major Osuji.'

'That's okay. The Prince brought in some mercenaries, seriously menacing guys, and the Sheikh had apparently heard about the attacks on the Boko Haram camps.'

'That's unfortunate. We asked that the attacks be kept out of the news while your operation was in progress, but the Western media are here now. They chartered a couple of private jets. The place is crawling with cameras and reporters with microphones sticking them in the face of anyone who looks as if they may not what is going on,' said Yanny.

'Didn't the military stop them from landing?' asked Harry.

'From what I can see, they encouraged them to come.'

'Why would they do that?'

'After the criticism they've been receiving lately, they see this as a public relations triumph. They'v rescued a total of two hundred and ninety-four women in the three camps and removed the Islamist threat in the north.'

'I suppose we can't blame them, said Harry. 'But it would have been better for us if they had waited a few more hours. How's Helen?'

'She's okay, and Aluko will pull through.'

'Has she spoken to the media yet?'

'Not yet, but she is remarkably calm. She said she would make a statement once she knew Kate was safe.'

'Do the Western media know what we're up to?' asked Harry.

'Officially, no, but they have figured it out. They are aware that three helicopters left after news of Helen's rescue was confirmed.'

'How did they find out?'

'It was an accident. They caught Kate's mother off guard and she blurted it out.'

'It doesn't matter now,' said Harry. 'Phil is going after the Nigerian girls in the compound and we are heading to the airport to get Kate and Fatima. Talk to you later.'

Chapter 26

The trip back to the airport for the Prince's men was slow. They did not have the benefit of a police escort and were forced to take advice from a person they did not trust, Sheikh Idriss Deubet. Their precious cargo, oblivious to the problems slipped between a hazy daze and semi-consciousness. Fatima, her protector, made her comfortable the best she could as the convoy weaved in and out of the traffic, ran the red lights, ignored the traffic police and the other cursing motorists.

'Why is our return to the airport taking so long?' Abdullah asked.

'It is normal for this time of the day.' The Sheikh preferred it slow. He was not anxious to leave the country in the Prince's jet. He did not trust either Abdullah or Saleh.

'There was an accident on the way to the compound,' said Abdullah. 'It looked too convenient to me. It is as if someone is trying to slow us down.'

'Accidents are all too common,' replied the Sheikh.

'Not this one. I'm sure it was set up to delay us.'

'Let's just focus on getting out of this awful place,' Saleh said.

'What can we do about this traffic?' said Abdullah exasperated. 'It will take forever to get to the airport.'

'Take a left down Boulevard de Sao, it may be quicker,' the Sheikh said.

'How can we trust you?' asked Abdullah.

'You must. Why would I delay my exit from here? My future lies with you and the money in the case.'

'You may have contacts here, people who can smuggle you out of the country. You have enough money to buy your way out of trouble. You could even bribe half the politicians in the country.'

'I don't know anybody, and the President of my country has stated that he is against indentured labour. I have been involved in human trafficking – how do you think the politicians will react? They will happily take my money, but it would be political suicide if it were found out. Believe me; I want to exit the country as much as you do.'

The Sheikh, desperate as he was, as despondent as any man can be who had lost his country, his possessions, his respect in the community, did indeed have an alternate escape plan. The jet at the airport was not his preferred choice. He knew his fate was suspect if he went with them. He had realised that he had to exit the compound, but where to was unclear.

'We will follow your directions,' continued Abdullah, 'but if there is any sign of treachery on your part, then Adeel will dispose of you without hesitation.'

'At the bottom of Boulevard de Sao take the right exit of the roundabout and head up Avenue Mobutu,' said the Sheikh.

Mustapha, meanwhile, had been following close behind. He had seen an opportunity. It was dangerous; he had to cause an accident on the roundabout.

'Where are you taking us?' Kate had momentarily stirred from the sedative she had been given.

'I thought you had drugged her?' Saleh said.

'She is sedated, not drugged,' replied the Sheikh. 'You don't want to be seen carrying a woman onto the plane. She can walk as long as someone holds her arm.'

'You were my husband; how can you do business with these people?' Fatima asked. 'How can you condone your actions?' She diverted her eyes when she spoke to Sheikh Idriss. She could not bear to look at him.

'It is my family's heritage and besides, you did not care where the money came from when you were spending it on your trips to Europe.'

'Stop this nonsense!' Abdullah shouted. 'I am not interested in your petty squabbles. I am only interested in getting to the plane.'

As the convoy approached the roundabout, Mustapha seized the opportunity. He realised that they would take the third exit to the right. He dropped a gear and floored the accelerator pedal. His small Renault reacted violently but lurched forward. He quickly overtook Abdullah's convoy, careened dangerously around the roundabout, and rammed another car close to the exit. The damage to either vehicle was minor, but in a country where insurance was a luxury, there were bound to be the inevitable arguments, fighting possibly and a large crowd to watch the afternoon's entertainment. A minor incident would hold up the traffic for at least thirty to forty minutes.

'Quick! Go straight ahead before the traffic blocks the roundabout,' said the Sheikh.

'Follow his instructions,' Abdullah commanded.

'Where are you leading us to now?' Saleh asked.

'It is a different route. It will take us down close to the river. It is fine.'

'We've lost two of our vehicles. They're stuck in the traffic,' Adeel shouted. 'We have to go back for them.'

'Do you want to stay in this country? Do you know what will happen if we are caught with a drugged American female?' Abdullah shouted back.

'You are right. They will have to look out for themselves,' Adeel had no alternative but to agree. One of those left behind was a cousin.

Mustapha was pleased with his work. Now all he had to do was sort out an agreement with the highly annoyed and potentially violent driver of the Toyota Corolla he had just damaged.

Before the inevitable cursing and arguing he quickly phoned Phil. 'Two vehicles down.'

'Great. That evens the numbers.'

As the two remaining vehicles moved down close to the Chari River, the Sheikh considered his options. He had a friend with a hotel close by who could get him out of the country without too much difficulty. He wasn't sure where he would head, or how he was going to blend into another society; but, he reasoned, with three million dollars in cash, there must be possibilities.

Just then, the vehicle slowed for a donkey and cart crossing the intersection. Seizing the opportunity, he opened the rear door of the Land Cruiser, grabbed his suitcase, and made a run for it. The only problem was that running can only be slow with a suitcase.

'Grab him!' Saleh shouted to Adeel. Quickly, he slammed on the brakes and Adeel caught the Sheikh before he had covered thirty metres.

'Let me go,' screamed the Sheikh. 'You have the woman; I have the money. It is a fair deal.'

'You asked to leave with us and that is what you will do,' Adeel said.

'Put him in the back and restrain him,' Abdullah said.

'I will find my own way out of the country. Let me go.'

'Is this gratitude after we offered you a free plane flight to wherever you wanted to go?' Saleh smirked.

'I do not need your flight. I can make my own arrangements.'

'No, it is our honour to assist you with your newfound wealth.' As difficult as their situation was, Saleh still saw the humour in the Sheikh's predicament.

'Where to now? Have you driven us down a false road?' Abdullah asked.

'No,' replied the Sheikh. 'This is the correct road to the airport. I swear it.' He was, by now, in great fear of his life. He had seen through their plan. If they could have his money and the Prince could have the woman, then what need was his to him?

'I don't trust him,' Saleh said.

'Neither do I,' Abdullah agreed. 'What should we do with him to ensure he tells us the truth?'

'Make sure he cannot run away again. Adeel, incapacitate him.'

Without hesitation, and without deviating from his driving, Adeel swung round and shot the Sheikh in the ankle.

'*You barbarian*,' Fatima screamed. Kate stared vaguely into space.

'Where to, Sheikh? Or else he will shoot you in the other ankle,' Saleh asked.

The Sheikh, in severe pain, responded weakly. 'Stay on this road.'

'For how long?'

'Three or four kilometres, and then the road will veer into Boulevard de Strasbourg.'

'And then?'

'You come to a roundabout. Take the third exit.'

'What's the name of the road?'

'Rue 1011. It will take you directly to the airport.'

'I hope you are not lying, or you will be shot again.'

'It is the truth. Please, leave me here.'

'We will let you go when we are safely at the airport,' Abdullah said. 'The Prince will not appreciate your blood in his aircraft.

Sheikh Idriss had told the truth and, within fifteen minutes, they reached the airport.

'What about him?' Saleh gestured towards the Sheikh.

'It would be best if we do not kill him here,' replied Abdullah. 'At this moment we have not committed any violence in this country. We will take him with us.'

Abdullah turned and looked at Fatima. 'You! Tend to his wounds. Make sure he is not going to mess the Prince's jet with his bleeding. And tell him to shut up moaning or I will have him gagged.'

'I will do as you say,' Fatima responded. He was her husband or had been. Degenerate, worthy only of contempt, she could still feel some affection. She could still reflect on their early years together, still remember the love that they had once felt for each other. She would do what she could to ease his suffering.

***

Phil's reinforcements at the compound presented themselves. 'Captain Ambrose Oyekan of the Nigerian Army at your service. We are here to assist.' A tall, distinguished and exceptionally sturdy soldier stood to attention and saluted him.

'Pleased to meet you,' Phil said.

'Do we have the authority of the Chadian government to conduct a military activity outside of the airport?' asked the captain.

'They gave us permission to enter their airspace, not necessarily to fight in the suburbs.'

'If the local people see us in Nigerian Army uniform, they will become hostile. They may end up assisting those holding the compound and our women.'

'It is a distinct possibility. It may be best if I make a phone call, and see what can be done.' Phil said.

'We want our women. We don't want to be fighting and possibly killing innocent locals. The implications are too severe to imagine.'

Phil had not thought through this scenario before. He had initially planned an entry by stealth. Now it was apparent there was going to be a battle, and that the neighbourhood would be roused. Unimpeded, they would soon gather to look, and the sight of the uniform of a foreign country would rile.

He called Steve. 'What is the situation with the Chadian military? Are they going to help us at the compound?'

'Do you need help?' asked Steve. 'I thought it was going to be straightforward.'

'That was the plan.'

'The plan has changed?'

'Correct. We'll talk later as to why.'

'If you need their military, I'll call Ahmed and see what he can arrange.'

'Thanks.'

'What is the situation on the ground?' Steve asked.

'I have five locals as well as Captain Oyekan of the Nigerian Army with two of his men. They are in military fatigues.'

'I see the problem,' said Steve. 'Nigerian military attacking a compound, the locals won't understand.'

'Precisely, how soon can Ahmed get some of his country's military here?' asked Phil.

'Let me phone him. I'll get back to you in five minutes.'

Steve ended the call and immediately phoned Ahmed. 'Ahmed, Phil is at the compound. He is with some Nigerian commandos. It is likely to be a gunfight. We need Chadian military personnel there. Otherwise, there will be an international incident.'

'I understand. I have a good friend at a local military post. I should be able to get people in uniform there quickly. Will that be okay?'

'That will be fine. They don't need to take part in the attack, just to be present.'

Steve then made contact with Phil again.

'Ten to fifteen minutes, is that okay?'

'Fine, we will wait.'

True to his word, within twelve minutes a Toyota pickup truck with four soldiers in the back arrived.

'Lieutenant Mahamat Oueddei at your service. I am informed that the President of Chad has accorded you his full support and assistance.'

'That is correct, although we did not expect to be engaged in a gunfight.' replied Phil.

'I am told that you come from Australia, but you have the appearance of a Chadian.'

'It's just a skill I've picked up over the years.'

'What do you require from us?'

'Purely to keep the people in the area calm. If they see Captain Oyekan and his soldiers in Nigerian military uniform attacking the Sheikh's compound, they may get violent.'

'May I ask what the purpose is? What is of interest in the compound?' asked Lieutenant Oueddei.

'The Sheikh has been indulging in slavery. Buying women from Boko Haram and selling them to whoever will pay.'

'A distasteful business. It will reflect badly on my country.'

'Your President has given us his full cooperation. The people of Chad will be able to show the world that they regard the activities of the Sheikh as abhorrent.'

'It will still reflect badly.'

'There are probably ten to twelve Nigerian women still in the compound. It is for us to free them.'

'We will secure the neighbourhood. I will ensure that the local police block the roads in the vicinity and that they keep the locals at a safe distance. Is there anything else you need?'

'A bus to transport the women to the airport would be appreciated.'

'I will see what I can organise.'

Time was no longer the issue. It was necessary for Phil to calm the situation, to let the guards at the compound believe that they were safe, to lull them into a state of complacency.

Forty minutes later, Lieutenant Oueddei updated Phil. 'The main roads into the area are effectively closed. The police will be moving through the streets in the immediate vicinity dealing with any people who venture out.'

'Thank you. I am going over the wall in five minutes.'

'Any assistance required from my men?' Lieutenant Oueddei asked.

'Just be visible,' said Phil. 'Captain Oyekan is well briefed and it is his country's women that he is rescuing. I would not wish you or your people to be harmed.'

Five minutes later and Phil was over the wall, the same spot as before, the same dogs who found the juicy steaks to their liking. This time they would not stir from their sleep.

Two guards prowled the grounds while two more were asleep in a quiet corner. With little hesitation, Phil systematically eliminated all four with a knife in the back, a hand over the mouth, and a tight cord around the neck.

'Four down,' he whispered into the two-way radio.

'Inform when the women are found,' Captain Oyekan responded.

'Will do.'

Phil slowly and stealthily moved around the compound until he reached the women's quarters. As he attempted to enter, a woman screamed out in a shrill voice. He had momentarily forgotten that it was not only the Nigerian women in the compound; there were the Sheikh's other wives and their children.

'Attack now!' Phil issued the command.

There were only six guards remaining, and two of them were heading towards him. He quickly dispatched one with the pistol he always carried, the other he missed. The guard was strong and determined. Phil was taking a savage beating and close to exhaustion when Captain Oyekan came up behind the guard and struck him hard across the back of his head with the butt of a rifle.

'Thanks, he was tough.' said Phil.

'Glad to be of service,' the captain answered, pleased that the four guards had been dispatched at the entrance with no injuries to his men.

'I heard the shooting. How did it go?' asked Phil.

'We're okay. One guard did a run for it, the other three we killed.'

'What's it like out of the road?'

'Lieutenant Oueddei is dealing with it. Where are the women?'

'A room at the back, according to what Fatima told me.'

As soon as Phil had recovered slightly, they moved to find the women.

'Stand back,' Captain Oyekan said. 'I am going to break the lock.'

'Please get us out of here.' Victoria cried in tears of fear and joy.

'Come out into the open,' Phil said. 'Do we have transport?' he asked of the Nigerian Captain.

'I'll check with Oueddei.'

'Thank you for rescuing us,' Aisha said. 'Where is Kate?'

'We are attempting to rescue her now.'

'And Helen?'

'She is fine. She is with her parents in Maiduguri.'

It was left to Phil to inform Steve of the situation. 'We have the Nigerian women.'

'How many?' asked Steve.

'Twelve.'

'Are they able to travel?'

'I think so. Badly shaken up, but they look okay.'

'Do you have transport?'

'Soon,' said Phil. 'We had some assistance from the Chadian Army. They will organise transport.'

Phil made contact with Harry.

'Harry, we have twelve Nigerian women.'

'Any trouble?'

'It was okay. We killed nine guards, but we are all fine.'

'The women, how are they?' asked Harry.

'They should be at the airport within the hour. How about Kate and Fatima?'

'They're at the airport, arrived some time ago. The Sheikh is with them. He appears to be in a bad way.'

'Where are you?'

'We should be entering the airport in the next few minutes.'

***

The Prince's jet was a scene of utter panic and fear. 'Has the plane been refuelled?' Abdullah asked as soon as he reached the plane.

240

'Not yet,' the pilot replied.

'Why not?'

'They said they were coming, but they had some mechanical issues with the truck.'

'I don't believe it. How much fuel do we have?'

'Not enough to get to Saudi. We would have to refuel in the Sudan on the way.'

'Is that possible?'

'The fuel supply there is unreliable. We may be stuck on the ground for a day or so while they find fuel for us.'

'That's no use,' said Abdullah. 'Besides, I don't want our cargo waking up, or being seen by prying eyes. Once we leave here, this plane's details will be relayed to all the police and government agencies in the region.'

'I'm sure the reason for the tanker delay is not a mechanical problem,' the pilot said.

'They're being paid to go slow. Why didn't you bribe them?'

'We tried, but we didn't have enough money.'

'Give them what they want! Just make sure to get that tanker over to the plane.'

The fuel tanker crew and their boss had acted on the request of a Chadian Air Force officer previously. The pilot of the Prince's jet conducted his request with twenty crisp fifty dollar notes, a thousand dollars; the Chadian military officer didn't have a chance. Five minutes later and the plane was receiving sufficient fuel to make the four thousand kilometre trip to Riyadh.

'Get everyone on board,' Saleh shouted. 'We're leaving.'

'We need clearance before departing,' the pilot said.

'Forget it; just get us out of here.'

Adeel dragged the Sheikh onto the plane. Fatima helped Kate up the steps, a gun pointing straight at her back. She had seen the furious activity over near the helicopters on the other side of the apron. She was sure they were there to rescue Kate.

'They had some trucks across the apron to block us,' the pilot said. 'They were forced to remove them when an Egypt Air Airbus came in from Cairo.'

'Get us out of here quickly before they block again,' Abdullah shouted.

Over by the helicopters, Captain Déby saw clearly the changing situation. 'How long before you are here?'

'Six minutes,' replied Harry. 'What's the situation?'

'They've got fuel. They're preparing to leave.'

'How did they get fuel?'

'They must have bribed someone.'

'Have you blocked their exit?' asked Harry.

'We had some trucks in front of them, but they were removed by the Airport Authority.'

'Block them again quick,' ordered Harry. 'Move up one of the helicopters, land at their front.'

'We're already planning to do that,' said Captain Déby, 'and I've got some more trucks moving into position. The only problem is that it is a busy time at the airport. There are four planes scheduled to leave within the next thirty minutes, one is an Air France Airbus departing for Paris, the other three into the Middle East.'

'Hem in the Prince's jet. I don't care what you do. Shoot the tyres out if you have to.'

The Prince's jet, engines now running, prepared to move forward. Ignoring any instructions to the contrary, it came close to touching wings with a flight from Abu Dhabi that was taxiing to disembarkation after landing.

'Captain Déby, have you managed to halt the plane?' Harry asked anxiously after a couple of minutes. 'We're here at the entrance, but now the local police have woken up. They realise something is going on; they are stopping all the traffic. We are having difficulties. I've got seven guys in Nigerian military uniforms and the police are waving their guns at us.'

'I thought you had a police escort?' replied Captain Déby.

'We do, and they're now arguing with the police at the roadblock.'

'I'm not sure how this can be resolved,' said Captain Déby 'We'll not stop the jet leaving at this rate; they only need to throw enough money around.'

'The helicopter – where is it?'

'They started shooting at its fuel tank with a semi-automatic. We had to move out of their way.'

'The only way we'll get onto the airfield is if the Chadian Army come and fetch us,' Harry said.

'You had some assistance down at the compound. Isn't that correct?'

'Yes, we did. How we are going to get anymore now is difficult. We're hemmed in by traffic.'

'The airport is also a military base. We could get someone from there.'

'I'll phone Ahmed again.' Harry said. 'We're stuck outside the airport, and the police are very nervous. Seven soldiers, heavily armed in the uniform of a foreign power, and the police are freaking out. I can't blame them really, but we need to get on to the airport apron within the next few minutes otherwise the Prince's plane will take off.'

'I'll phone the base. By the way, the President of Chad is aware of what is happening. He has issued a presidential command to all Chadian military forces to assist. Expect help within ten minutes.'

'It may be too late,'

Harry immediately phoned Phil after ending his conversation with Ahmed. 'We can't get to the airport. Your Chadian officer, can he get some help to us? Ahmed is doing what he can. We have the necessary authority to get what help we require. Only problem is, it's not where it is needed.'

'I'll ask him to do what he can. We are on our way to the airport with a police escort. Give us sixty, maybe ninety minutes. We are not hurrying; some of the Nigerian girls are showing signs of shock. Flashing Sirens may be too much for them right now.'

Harry then phoned Captain Déby for an update 'Captain, what is the situation?'

'The plane is temporarily blocked; I've got some trucks in its way. There is an Air France flight leaving in fifteen minutes, and the airport authority will release the Prince's jet before then.'

'There is a Presidential command if we need to use it,' said Harry.

'That's fine, but I doubt if even that will stop an Air France flight leaving.'

'Can you get some soldiers over from the base at the airport? You can state the Presidential command.'

'If I do, they will want to check, verify and double check. It will take hours. I will use another method. Our helicopters are based over there; I should be able to get a few people quickly.'

'Thanks. Do what you must. Just don't let the Prince's plane leave.'

Due to the efforts of both Captain Déby and Ahmed, it took only fifteen minutes before the Chadian Army arrived at the roadblock.

'Release these men immediately,' the Chadian Army officer ordered.

'They are Nigerian soldiers,' replied the lead police officer at the roadblock. 'We cannot let them go.'

'I am acting on the command of the President. Do you want to personally explain as to why you are delaying these men on a vital mission?'

'I need authority from my superiors before I can let them go,'

Harry pointed to his watch. 'We don't have time for this delay.'

'Release them now, or I will be forced to take restraining action against you and your officers.' The police officer relented when the soldiers levelled their rifles and pointed them at him.

'Take them, but I will be making a full report.'

'Make your report if you wish,' said the Army officer, 'but what I have told you is true. We do not have the time to wait for you to check.' He turned to Harry. 'We have seen the situation at the airport. We will follow and assist in any way we can. We are yours to command.'

'Thank you,' replied Harry. 'We need to stop the aircraft leaving. There are two women on board as captives. Do not shoot at the plane, just stop it.'

***

The Sheikh was receiving the anger of the Prince's men. 'This is your fault!' Abdullah, the Prince's lead agent screamed.

'I did not auction the women,' the Sheikh replied.

'You are lying.'

'It was the Islamists. They are the reason for the trouble.' The Sheikh, still in severe pain attempted to defend his position.

'How are we going to get out of here?' said Abdullah.

'Bribe your way out,' the Sheikh said.

'How can I bribe my way past the Army?'

'Offer to leave the woman.'

'And then the Prince will deal with us all,' replied Abdullah.

'Do you want to give your money back?' Saleh shouted at the Sheikh. He had already spent his initial share on the purchase of an apartment in the South of France. He, like Abdullah and the Sheikh, was in an impossible situation.

'Of course I do not. I have no home. It is only the money that will secure my future,' replied the Sheikh.

On the other side of the apron, Harry now backed up by seven Nigerian commandos and another ten Chadian soldiers, planned his next move.

'We need the two women unharmed,' he said. 'They are our primary focus.' The commandos, who wanted to storm the plane, concerned him. 'We will need to negotiate. We may have to offer them safe passage if they release the women.'

'Our military will not allow them to leave,' Captain Déby said. 'They have committed too many violations in our country. They have brought shame to us all.'

'What you do after we have the women is not my concern,' said Harry.

'Then we will follow your plan until you have the women. After that, it will be up to the Chadian military.'

'I agree,' said Harry. 'Have we managed to successfully halt their exit?'

'It is halted for the moment.'

'What do you mean "for the moment"?' asked Harry suspiciously.

'There is still the issue of the departing international flights.'

'I thought we had a Presidential command?'

'We do, but not all will abide by it.'

'What do you mean?'

'The head of the airport authority is aligned with the opposition party in Chad. For him to accede to the president is akin to working with the devil. He will not listen, and he will command free movement for any flights leaving the country.' Captain Déby explained.

'That is lunacy,' said Harry, clearly exasperated. 'Do you mean to say that he will condone the Prince's actions?'

'He is neither condoning nor disapproving. It is how politics works here.'

'What about the local soldiers? What will they do?'

'They will follow the command of the highest ranking person present.'

'You mean the head of the airport authority?'

'That is correct.'

It was clear to Harry that the situation was tenuous. If the plane stayed where it was, it would soon be free and on its way to Saudi Arabia. He had to come up with a counter-plan.

Chapter 27

Harry knew he had to communicate with the Prince's plane on his arrival back at the airport. Captain Déby immediately offered him the use of the radio on his helicopter.

'TT-1OF to A40-AU4, do you read?' said Harry sitting in the Chadian helicopter.

'A40-AU4 to TT-1OF, we read you.'

'I am Harry Warburton negotiating for the release of the two women on your plane.'

'We do not have any women on board. We are here on a trade-related mission. You have no right to hold us.'

'Let me talk to one of the Prince's agents.'

'We know of no Prince.'

'Who am I communicating with?' Harry asked.

'I am the chief pilot on this civilian flight to Oman.'

'Let me talk to one of the agents who took the American woman.'

'We know of no American woman. We are purely a trade mission.'

It was going nowhere. Unless Harry could talk to one of the agents, there would be no peaceable agreement. Eventually, either the Chadian military would let it go on the command of the head of the Airport Authority or the Nigerian military would storm it. Either way, it was going to be an unsatisfactory result.

'What's he saying?' Abdullah, the Prince's lead agent, asked of his pilot.

'He wants to talk to you. I have told him that we are a trade mission. He does not believe me.'

'Of course he doesn't believe you,' said Abdullah angrily. 'We are not invisible here. They would have seen us bring the woman on board, and then we had the Sheikh sitting on the steps of the plane being bandaged. Let me talk to him.'

'Is that wise?'

'How would I know? We are not going to get out of this by procrastinating.'

Abdullah took hold of the radio. 'You have no right to hold us. We are an internationally registered plane. It is for you to grant us immediate departure.'

'I assume that you are the agent of the Prince?' said Harry.

'I am nobody's agent.'

'I want the two women,' said Harry firmly.

'We want safe passage to exit the country.'

'I can only attempt to secure you safe passage if you hand over the two women unharmed in the next five minutes.'

'Attempt, what does that mean?'

'I am not a citizen of Chad. It is not my decision as to whether you receive safe passage,' Harry said.

'There can be no further discussion until that assurance is given,' replied Abdullah.

The communication ended in an impasse.

'What's the situation?' Saleh asked.

'It's not good,' said Abdullah. 'If we give over the women, they may allow us out of the country.'

'May or may not? Which is it?'

'The person I spoke to said it is not for him to decide. It is up to the Chadian authorities.'

'What did they say about the women?' asked Saleh.

'He said that we are to hand them over.'

'Then we have no bargaining position. The Nigerian and Chadian soldiers would attack. What are our options?'

'The best we can do is to agree to fly to a neutral airport outside of the country where they have no jurisdiction,' replied Abdullah. 'Give them the women and then we fly back home.'

'Then we disappear and divide the five million dollars between us? It sounds a good solution.' Saleh saw wisdom in Abdullah's plan.

'You don't get it,' said Abdullah angrily. 'Use your brain for once. What will happen if we do not return with the American women? What will the Prince do?'

'He will ensure we do not have an opportunity to enjoy our newfound wealth. So, why are you planning to hand over the women?'

'I'm not. We only *agree* to hand them over. Once we are out of the country, then we can renege on the deal. You are using your dick instead of your brain. I see you lusting after the other woman.'

'She is most desirable.' A naturally intelligent man, although unfortunately Saleh's intelligence invariably focussed on activities below his waistline.

Abdullah continued. 'If we go to a neutral country, let's say the Sudan, we can bribe our way out. Even if we gave them several hundred thousand dollars, we would still be ahead. There is no way that either the Chadian or Nigerian military could follow us. The only person who could possibly follow is the Englishman I just spoke to.'

'It sounds a perfect solution.'

'It is if I can convince them to take the bait.'

At Maiduguri, the Western and local media were frenetic; another planeload of women had since arrived. The Nigerian military was shuttling the hundreds of women from the three Boko Haram camps to the base. Helen Campbell was coherent and responsive and Aluko, conscious and talking. Phil had updated that twelve Nigerian girls had been freed from the Sheikh's compound and were on their way to the airport. News of events at N'Djamena International Airport was slowly filtering through. The one piece of news that all those assembled at the airfield in Nigeria were anticipating was the release of Kate McDonald.

The Western media, in their blundering, were badgering her parents as to whether she was at the airport in Chad. Were the rumours of a Nigerian and Chadian military standoff with an

Omani-registered jet correct? If Kate was on the jet, what was the prognosis for a successful outcome?

Harry from his vantage point inside the airport in Chad could see the build-up in activity on the perimeter of the airport. The standoff was starting to hit the local news, and crowds were forming to watch the action.

'This is not ideal,' he said. 'We are too visible here. In situations like this, people get nervous, they panic, and that is when people get killed.'

'What do you want us to do?' Captain Déby asked.

'Ideally, move the plane to a more isolated spot.'

'If we give them any freedom to move, they may well just take off.'

'It may be a risk we have to take.'

Suddenly, the radio in the helicopter buzzed into life.

'This is A40-AU4,' said Abdullah. 'We are willing to discuss a compromise agreement.'

'We are not open to compromise,' replied Harry. 'Give us the women and you are free to depart.'

'I have not seen clarification by the Chadian authorities.'

'What is your compromise?' asked Harry.

'We will fly to a neutral location, preferably an airfield in the Sudan. We will give you the cargo that you require, and then we will depart for the Middle East.'

'I cannot agree to such an agreement. What proof do I have that you will honour it?'

'Then we will render the cargo valueless before you attempt to claim.'

'Any damage to the women will ensure your safety is jeopardised.'

'We are without any safety as long as we remain in this country,' replied Abdullah. 'The soldiers that you have will not let us go, and they are now starting to bring up anti-aircraft guns on the other side of the airport.'

'I have not seen that,' said Harry.

'You better look. They are there, and they will use them on us if we give you the cargo.'

Harry had not looked. The Prince's man had been correct. The Chadian military were bringing in some heavy weaponry; there was no way they were going to let the jet leave. The question was how to prevent them acting before the women were freed. Killing an innocent American woman due to some trigger-happy Chadian soldier would not reflect well in the international press, and what Chad did not require at this time was bad publicity.

Harry made contact with Steve. 'You need to get the Nigerian president to talk with his counterpart again. You also need to get your friend Abdul, the head of the Nigerian military, to speak to their Chadian head of the Armed Forces. The military are bringing up some serious weaponry. I do not want an unfortunate accident before we have figured a way to get the women back.'

'I'll organise it. Abdul is here with me now,' Steve replied. 'He will deal with the situation. Phil has phoned; he is waiting at the international terminal with the women. He will not move until you give the all clear. You are on the TV here, by the way. We're all watching.'

'That's the last thing we want,' said Harry.

'What are you planning to do?'

'It's not clear at the present moment. They've offered to fly to a neutral country, offload the cargo, and then they leave for the Middle East and we return to Nigeria with the two women.'

'You don't trust them?'

'Not for a minute but I may need to offer a tentative agreement. This is Yanny's expertise. I could sure use her now.'

'It would take about ninety minutes by helicopter for her to get there,' said Steve. 'Do you want me to send her?'

'I'm not sure we have that much time. Do you have a jet?'

'Yes, it could make the trip in twenty to thirty minutes.'

'Put her on a plane within five minutes,' replied Harry. 'She can speak Arabic to them. It can only help. Instruct the

251

aircraft to taxi to the end of the runway on arrival, and make sure it has no military markings.'

'Bob McDonald is listening over my shoulder. He's nodding that we are to use his jet.'

'He is *not* to come,' ordered Harry. 'It is to be only Yanny. Anyone else who attempts to board the plane, arrest them. We do not want well-meaning, emotional assistance.'

'It will be only the pilots and Yanny,' confirmed Steve.

'Don't fail me on this,' said Harry. 'These are unpredictable people, pushed up against a corner. They know how desperate the situation is. They must realise that their chances of exiting the country are slim. If they go down, they will take whoever they can with them.'

'What is the situation at the airport? Are there any flights coming in or leaving?'

'It appears the airport has virtually closed down. I haven't seen a flight for the last twenty minutes.'

'You better let them know a private jet is coming in with your lead negotiator who speaks fluent Arabic.'

'I'll let them know, although they will be suspicious. I just want to see Yanny get off the plane at the end of the runway, and for it to turn around and leave. It is important. I do not want them thinking there may be some more Nigerian commandos inside.'

'Don't worry,' replied Steve. 'I'll personally stand guard until it leaves. Yanny is already on board, and the pilots are starting the engines as we speak. She will be there in less than thirty minutes.'

Harry realised the limitations of his negotiating skills. He would rather focus on how to board the plane and release the women while Yanny kept them occupied over the radio.

He picked up the helicopter radio again.

'TT-1OF to A40-AU4, we are considering your request.'

'We will give you ten minutes,' replied Abdullah. 'Otherwise, we will start off-loading some of the cargo. Do you understand?'

'We understand, but we need longer than ten minutes. We are discussing with an airfield in a neutral country to accommodate your request.'

'You are stalling. We have no need of an airport. We fly to the capital of Sudan and, if required, pay whatever money they want. We give you the cargo and leave.' Abdullah knew that, with enough money spread around, they could leave and keep the white woman.

Steve had some trouble with Bob McDonald, but in the end, he managed to reason with him as to what was best. Yanny was on the plane, the only passenger. It was no more than two hundred kilometres, and twenty minutes would see her on the ground in N'Djamena. A car was already heading down the runway to pick her up on arrival.

'What is the delay?' Abdullah demanded of Harry.

'We are bringing someone in who can discuss with you in Arabic.'

'My English is sufficient. You only need to agree and then our problems are resolved.'

'It is not so easy for us to arrange. I am in communication with my superiors for agreement. They are also facilitating a place for the transfer in the Sudan.' Harry realised that he did not have the skills or the diplomacy required.

'You are delaying us. The Prince's lead agent sounded agitated. 'You are preparing to storm the aircraft.'

'That is not true,' Harry kept his voice calm. 'We would not do anything that would place additional risk on your cargo, as you prefer to call the two women.'

'My patience is not infinite. We will move in ten minutes or we will throw the valueless cargo out of the plane.' Abdullah raised his voice in anger.

'You must realise that, with your cargo valueless, there will be no chance of a peaceful resolve.'

'Then that is what fate has decreed. Do not bandy words with me.' Abdullah replied angrily.

As Abdullah responded to Harry's mediocre attempts at a resolution, Bob McDonald's plane landed. The airport was now in full lock-down mode.

'You have brought in extra troops from Nigeria?' Abdullah shouted. 'Your cargo is forfeited.'

'You can see the plane from where you are. Only one person will exit and then the plane will leave.'

'I will wait, and if what you say is not true, I will personally render the cargo worthless and push it out of the front door of the plane.' Harry could only hope that Steve had kept Bob McDonald from boarding the plane.

Both Harry and Abdullah were focussed as the aircraft came to rest. Yanny exited and, as planned, the plane taxied to the other end of the runway and took off.

'It is a woman! Why would I want to talk to a mere female?'

'She will speak in Arabic. She is more skilled than I am in such discussions.'

'There are no discussions. Our position is resolute. We leave now.'

In two minutes, Yanny had met up with Harry.

'What's the situation?' she asked.

'They are demanding to leave for a neutral country, probably the Sudan, where they will let us have the cargo,' replied Harry.

'What is the cargo?'

'That is how they refer to the women. They have not directly referred to either of them by name.'

'I need to talk to the women first,' she said.

'Is that wise?'

'Yes, I think so. It will defuse the situation if both parties are referring to the same commodity.'

***

Quickly Yanny seated herself in the Chadian helicopter ready to make contact with the jet and its cargo. 'My name is Yanny. I will need to talk to the women before I can accede to your demands.' She spoke in fluent Arabic. With Yanny focussing on the discussions, Harry was free to put a rescue plan into action.

'We only have cargo here. I do not want to talk to a woman,' said Abdullah.

'You have no alternative. If you wish to leave, then I would suggest that you let me talk to at least one of the women.'

'I will not agree to a request that I cannot possibly achieve. We only have cargo related to our business interests in Chad.'

'We have seen you with the women. We have binoculars, and we have seen you at the Sheikh's compound. We know what you have. Give them to us, and you are free to leave.'

'Assuming that I agreed with what you say, how can I trust the military that are closing in on our position?'

'Let me talk to the women, and I will ensure they pull back.'

'What authority do you have to issue that command?'

'I have the full authority of the President of Chad. He is anxious to avoid further escalation.'

'I will let you speak to the local woman.'

There was a pause and then a woman's voice could be heard on the radio.

'We are well,' said Fatima. She was speaking in Arabic.

'What is your condition?' asked Yanny.

'I am unharmed. Kate is still sedated.'

'Her condition?'

'She is fine.'

'Who else is there?' asked Yanny. 'I am told the Sheikh is there as well.'

'He is, although he has been shot,'

'He is not of any concern to us.'

'No more!' Abdullah said as he seized the headset and microphone from Fatima.

'I have kept my word,' he said to Yanny. 'Now it is up to you to keep yours.'

The Chadian military, on the other side of the airport, had been slowly mobilising and coming in closer to the besieged jet. Abdullah had made it a condition during the discussions with Yanny that they were to back off. She had to comply. She spoke to Harry. 'We need to pull the military back.'

'Have you agreed on that?' he asked.

'It was a condition of talking to Fatima.'

'What about Kate? Did you talk to her?'

'Fatima says she is sedated.'

'Did she talk about her condition?'

'She said she is fine.'

'If you have made an agreement, then we must comply.'

Major Moussa Abbas of the Chadian Army had joined Harry. A career soldier, he had received a phone communication by the President of his country to assist in any way possible.

'Major, we need you to pull your troops back a suitable distance.'

'I can't see the wisdom,' replied the Major.

'Yanny made it part of an agreement to be able to talk to the women,' explained Harry.

'My men are prepared to attack the aircraft to free the women.'

'You realise that will almost certainly get them killed?'

'I have my orders.'

'Do you also have the personal authority of your President to act as you see fit?' asked Harry.

'I will accede to your request.' Major Abbas issued an order to all military personnel to pull back two hundred metres.

Yanny again made contact with Abdullah. 'The military have complied with your request.'

'You are now to remove the obstructions to our movement and to let us move to the runway,' said Abdullah.

'I can only agree if you are willing to make a token gesture.'

'Enough! You are playing us for fools.'

'I am not. I have received a request from the military to confirm that you are holding the two women.'

'You have spoken to one of them. What more do they want?'

'They want the Chadian woman.'

'She stays here,' Saleh said to Abdullah, nudging him in the back.

'I cannot agree,' Abdullah responded.

'The Chadians are adamant. They will not let you take one of their citizens against her will.'

Abdullah turned to Saleh. 'We have to play their game.'

'I wanted her for myself,' said Saleh.

'You're still thinking with your dick.'

'You are right. As long as we have the fair-haired woman, they will not attack.'

Abdullah spoke into the radio. 'We agree. You can have the local woman.'

'Please send her out,' Yanny replied.

'I will not leave Kate,' Fatima screamed, overhearing the conversation.

'You have no choice,' said Abdullah. 'Adeel, grab her and put her out on the tarmac.'

Fatima fought and clung to Kate, but she was overpowered and they were wrenched apart. Separated from Kate, she could only look at her forlornly.

Yanny, meanwhile, was seeking assurance from Harry and Major Abbas. 'We need to make it clear that, once we have Fatima, the Chadian military will pull back out of sight. Is that clear?'

'It is understood,' Major Abbas said. 'I assume you are not ceding to their demands? You don't intend to let them leave?'

'No, it is just a tactic to weaken their resolve,' replied Yanny. 'They are not leaving this airport and we are going to get Kate back unharmed. If they are willing to agree to concessions, it means they are weakening.'

'I will concede to your wisdom in such matters,' replied the Major. 'Our military will comply, but we will stay prepared.'

Fatima's reluctance was causing concern. 'Throw her out of the aircraft!' Abdullah commanded. Adeel immediately complied.

With binoculars trained on the jet, Harry had seen the door open and Fatima flung out 'She's out on the apron. We need someone to go and pick her up.'

'I have an airport ground support truck outside. I'll go,' Captain Déby said.

'Not dressed like that,' said Harry. 'Take off your uniform. Put on some overalls.'

In a matter of minutes, the Captain had transformed from military officer to airport worker and was driving the three hundred metres to where Fatima lay on the ground. Adeel had not bothered with lowering the steps; she had just been flung the out of the open door to the ground. Landing badly, she struggled to stand.

'Get in quick,' urged Captain Déby. 'I am here to help.'

'What about Kate?' she asked.

'We can do no more here. You must come immediately.'

Once Fatima was safely in the vehicle, Yanny phoned Steve.

'Steve, we've got Fatima.'

'It's being streamed live on the Internet,' he said. 'Well-done.'

'How's that possible?' asked Yanny. 'How can we be on the Internet?'

'It seems that an American TV network was in the country monitoring the drought in the north of the country. They were at the airport preparing to leave when this unfolded. They appear to be up on the roof of the main terminal building zooming in on you.'

'Not exactly what we want, but there's not much we can do about it.'

'What's the plan now?' asked Steve.

'Pull the Chadian military out of sight,' Yanny reiterated.

***

As agreed, the Chadian military made another strategic move back. 'We have complied with our side of the agreement,' said Yanny. 'The Chadian Army have moved back from their previous position.'

'It is not far enough. I can still see them on the other side of the airport,' Abdullah complained.

'It is the best that can be hoped for.'

'I still have the most valuable cargo here with me.'

'The Chadians are conscious that there is an American television crew streaming this around the world,' said Yanny. 'Their armed forces will not allow themselves to be seen as submissive and incompetent.'

'Stop the Americans with their cameras!'

'That is not possible.'

'Instruct the Chadian police to shut them down.'

'That will not happen. What you and the Sheikh have done has brought derision on the people of Chad. They are attempting to reclaim some credibility with a successful outcome.'

'I do not accept your explanation,' said Abdullah, 'but for the moment, we will continue. Has a suitable place been chosen for the exchange of the cargo?'

'We are in discussions with government in the Sudan.'

'We wish to change it to Southern Sudan. It is a different country to the one that you are suggesting.' As far as Abdullah was concerned, a governmental agreement in the Sudan could only mean one thing: a trap was evolving.

'The only airport suitable in Southern Sudan is under the control of the United Nations,' said Yanny. 'You would be arrested if you landed there.' Yanny knew it was a lie, but it sounded plausible.

'Remove the obstructions and allow us to leave.'

'Once we have confirmation from the Sudan we will release the plane. We also need to move people to the nominated airport to receive the cargo.'

Time was moving slowly, and those holding Kate were becoming more flexible in their demands. Yanny was working towards a resolution whereby Kate would be released at the airport and the plane would be allowed to leave.

'Saleh, we cannot return to Saudi Arabia.' Abdullah said.

'Why? If we have the woman, I don't see the issue.'

'You are remarkably stupid. Don't you understand that there is nothing to connect us with the Prince?'

'Everybody knows it's the Prince.' Saleh expressed his consternation at Abdullah's statement.

'Everybody knows, but nothing is proven. Where is the connection to the Prince?'

'What about this plane?' asked Saleh.

'The plane is chartered through Oman and separated from the Prince by a number of offshore companies and bank accounts. It is unlikely that it could ever be traced back to him.'

'They know that we work almost exclusively for the Prince.'

'Where's the proof?' asked Abdullah.

'I suppose there is none,' agreed Saleh.

'If we leave with the woman, the Prince will never risk claiming her. He will be covering his tracks as we speak.'

'His country will protect him. They will not allow him to be implicated.' Saleh stated the obvious.

'Saleh, at last you are using your brain.'

'Then what do we do?'

'We must protect ourselves, and then disappear somewhere the Prince can never find us.' Abdullah paused for a moment. 'A remote desert community in Oman or Muscat may be possible. In time, the Prince may forgive us. It is all we can hope for.'

'We still have two and a half million dollars each,' said Saleh.

'If we can keep it, we will be fine,' Abdullah sensed a solution. 'I will talk to the woman again. She said her name was Yanny.'

Fatima, meanwhile, severely bruised and exceedingly concerned about Kate, was responding to the medical treatment that the Chadian army had arranged. The Chadian military had moved away some distance and were giving the impression of passive observers. The live streaming continued, picked up by all the major news channels around the world.

'We are willing to leave our cargo here, subject to guaranteed safe passage to a country of our choosing,' Abdullah conceded.

'I cannot guarantee safe passage. You have committed a crime.'

'That is for you to guarantee. We may as well die here alongside our cargo.'

Yanny was elated with the latest compromise from the aircraft. It was what she wanted. If they could secure Kate's release in Chad, the plane could leave.

'I will speak to the Chadian authorities and see if they can give you a guarantee,' she replied.

Yanny spoke to Major Abbas and Harry. 'You have heard what they want. Safe passage and they will leave Kate here.'

'If they leave Kate, then they can go where they want, even to Hell,' said Harry.

He realised that Yanny had achieved a possible conclusion to the situation. It was something he would not have been able to achieve; he did not have the language skills, the diplomacy, and the intellect she had brought to the situation.

'I cannot see how the Chadian government will agree,' said Major Abbas. 'These people have committed a serious crime in our country. We can't just let them go free.'

'It is imperative that we agree,' replied Harry. 'Once we have Kate, then you can do what you like.'

'You are saying that we agree only until we have safely retrieved the woman?'

'Yes.'

'Then it may be possible to comply with your requirement.'

'Is that a yes?' Yanny asked.

'It is a yes. You are free to inform the plane. Do what you must to secure the American woman.'

It was time for Harry to coordinate the activities to allow a smooth handover of Kate and to allow the free movement of the aircraft to leave.

'What's the plan?' Yanny asked.

'We let them taxi to the end of the runway,' replied Harry.

'But won't they take off?' Major Abbas saw a problem.

'It will not be possible. Their plane is a Gulfstream G650; it needs at least one thousand six hundred metres to reach speed before it can take off. We just need to place a truck up the runway at a distance of one kilometre. Their pilot will realise that a lift off is impossible.'

'Perfect,' said Yanny. 'It's far enough to calm the kidnappers but close enough to deter the pilot.'

She then made radio contact with the plane.

'A40-AU4,' she said, 'we have an agreement.'

'We will release the cargo once we have a clear exit confirmed?' replied Abdullah.

'That is agreed.'

'We are ready to leave.'

'You are to taxi to the end of the runway for a take-off. Is that agreed?'

'That is agreed.'

'Two vehicles will accompany you at a distance of fifty metres to your rear until you are within two hundred metres of the runway. They will then withdraw.'

'We agree.'

'Once you are at the take-off point, a solitary ground support vehicle will approach the plane. Is that understood?'

There was a slight pause before Abdullah responded. 'It is understood.'

'The Englishman you spoke to earlier will be the driver.'

'That is understood.'

'We will remove the current blockages to your movement in five minutes,' said Yanny, 'and then you will proceed to the agreed point. Prior to leaving that position, you will allow your cargo to leave the plane. You are then free to go.'

Saleh, as usual, was quick to see a possible opportunity to satisfy his avarice. 'Why don't we just take off and keep the woman as well? That way, the Prince will get her and we will get the money.'

'It is possible. I'm sure if we can conceal the woman in a remote part of Oman and Muscat, there will eventually be a way to get her to him.' Abdullah could only agree with Saleh.

Abdullah, relieved that they may get away with their lives, was also susceptible to avarice and acutely aware that avoiding the wrath of the Prince was certainly more conducive to a long and fruitful life.

***

Five minutes had transpired and, as agreed, the vehicles blocking the plane were removed. The pilot quickly seized the moment and throttled up, released the brakes and the plane slowly moved forward. Captain Déby and Major Abbas were each in a couple of Toyota trucks following at the agreed distance.

'They're letting them go with Kate!' Bob McDonald shouted at the television screen they were all watching in Maiduguri.

'Relax; Yanny and Harry know what they're doing,' Steve said.

At the agreed point, the Captain and Major Abbas pulled back and let the plane move forward without any vehicles at its rear.

'They're not behind us,' Saleh jumped up excited. 'Let's make a run for it. Let's keep the woman.'

'I agree; we have nothing to lose. We have tricked them,' Abdullah said.

'No, we have not!' shouted the pilot. 'There are two trucks halfway up the runway, about one kilometre away?'

'What do they matter?' Saleh shouted back.

'They matter. I cannot get the plane airborne in that distance. I need at least five hundred metres more.'

Abdullah picked up the radio. 'You have tricked us. The runway is not clear for us to leave.'

'We have not tricked you,' Yanny replied. 'You are free to go, once we have the woman. We always realised that, if you sensed an opportunity, you would take it.'

'What proof have I that you will keep your word?' Abdullah asked.

'My word is honourable, yours is not.'

Abdullah turned to Saleh.

'We have no option. If we kill the woman, they will blow up the plane. If we give them the woman, they will let us go. They are Westerners, even the Arabic-speaking woman. They may well honour the agreement.'

'Then we must comply.' Saleh saw no other option.

'The cargo is yours. Send your pick up.' Abdullah said disappointedly.

'He is waiting to the left of the plane,' said Yanny. 'He will be there in two minutes.'

Yanny contacted Harry. 'Pick up Kate. You are to stand off at about fifty metres and let them bring her to you.'

'I'll be there.'

'Please send someone with the cargo if she is unable to walk,' said Yanny to Abdullah. 'Once she is seated in the vehicle, the block on the runway will pull back and you will be free to leave.'

'She can walk,' replied Abdullah. 'She is conscious.'

The plane door duly opened and Kate, bleary-eyed, slowly exited the Princes' jet by the front steps.

'Over here, Kate,' Harry shouted.

'I am coming,' she said in a whisper. He could barely hear her.

'Kate, please get into the vehicle.'

Harry opened the vehicle door for Kate to enter

'Fatima?' she whispered. 'How is she? Helen?'

'They are both fine,' 'Fatima is with us. Helen is at a military base in Nigeria. Are you up to a helicopter flight?' Harry asked.

'Yes, that will be fine,' she responded weakly.

'I have Kate,' Harry proclaimed. Yanny and Harry were ecstatic. In Maiduguri, there was immense jubilation.

The Prince's jet commenced its take-off and rose into the air. As the pilot veered left, he saw the two Mikoyan MiG-29 combat aircraft of the Chadian Air Force lined up at the end of the runway that they had just left. It would be fifty-five minutes before the Prince's Gulfstream left Chadian airspace and crossed the border into the Sudan. It was not going to make it.

Chapter 28

'How is Kate?' Steve asked over the radio.

'She's badly traumatised but appears to be unharmed,' Yanny responded.

'Is she lucid? Is she up to speaking with her parents?'

'Probably, but she wants to talk to Helen first.'

'Helen is here. Is Kate ready?'

'Yes.'

There was a pause and then Kate's voice came over the radio.

'Helen, it's Kate. How are you?'

'I am fine,' said Helen. 'We saw you on the television.'

'I don't remember much of it.'

'We are all waiting here for you,' replied Helen, crying with joy. 'Are you coming soon?'

'Soon, we are waiting for Victoria and Aisha and the other girls.'

'Then we'll see you when you get here.'

It was only a short conversation. Kate was still not communicative and it was apparent that she was not ready for the glare of cameras. The television crew that had been relaying the events at the airport in Chad were desperate for interviews with all the parties involved.

'The television crew here want to put me on camera,' Yanny told Steve. 'Are you okay with that?'

'Go ahead if you want to. Remember, we were just advisers. All credit is to go to the governments of Nigeria and Chad and their armed forces.'

'Did the cameras pick up the Air Force jets taking off?' asked Yanny.

'Yes, it was clear as to their mission.'

'I will ask Major Abbas and Captain Déby to speak on behalf of the Chadian government.'

'How long before you leave?'

'One to two hours. We need to ensure Kate is fine, and the Nigerian girls are treated for any trauma. We're also getting their names, so you can get their parents to the airport in Nigeria if possible.'

'Fatima, how is she?'

'She's badly bruised, but no broken bones. Kate is clinging on to her.'

'Fatima is coming as well on the helicopter?' Steve asked.

'She's insistent.'

'Bob wants to send his jet.'

'Please don't, Kate is not ready for her parents here.'

'Okay,' replied Steve. 'I'm sure the Nigerian government will want their return to be on Nigerian military helicopters. They are making a major public relations exercise out of this.'

'I will talk to the TV crew here, but not back in Nigeria.'

'Agreed, but do not say too much. Leave it to their military to grab the credit.'

This is Jessica Samson, American Broadcasting Network in N'Djamena, Chad. I am standing on the apron of Hassan Djamous International Airport at the successful conclusion of the hostage rescue that we were fortunate to be able to relay live to all our viewers.

I have with me three of the main people involved in the rescue – Captain Mornadji Déby of the Chadian Air Force, Major Moussa Abbas of the Chadian Army, and Yanny Schmidt. I am informed that both Captain Déby and Major Abbas have a reasonable degree of fluency in English.

Yanny, what was your role in the rescue of the two women? One is known to be Kate McDonald, an American citizen who was kidnapped in the north of Nigeria.'

It was inevitable that the camera would focus on Yanny first. Her exotic looks, coupled with her part in the major news event around the world that day, were to make her an instant celebrity.

'I was purely the mediator between the Chadian and Nigerian military and the kidnappers on the plane,' she replied.

'I am led to believe that your role was more significant,' Jessica Samson continued to probe. 'It is due to your efforts that there was a satisfactory resolve.'

'I am a member of a team, an experienced team that has been proud to assist.'

'Captain Déby, what was your role in this operation?' asked Jessica.

'I was the pilot of the lead helicopter that accompanied our Nigerian colleagues to the airport. I have primarily acted as a liaison at the airport since our arrival.'

Quickly the focus came back to Yanny. 'What was the significance of the two military jet fighters that left soon after the kidnapper's plane took off?' the determined broadcaster continued to question.

'That is not for me to comment. I assisted in the safe return of the two women. Major Abbas may be able to offer further information.'

'Major Abbas, can you please comment?'

'The two fighters have taken off on a training mission.'

'Surely you do not expect our viewers to believe that?'

'I am unable to comment further. Chadian military operations are subject to confidentiality,' replied the Major firmly.

'Major Abbas, we are aware that a number of Nigerian women have been recovered from a compound in a suburb located fifteen kilometres from the airport. Are you able to confirm?'

'Your information is correct. Twelve Nigerian nationals, all female, were recovered and are present here at the airport. They will be repatriated in the next few hours to their own country.'

'How does this reflect on the people of Chad?' the broadcaster with the scoop of her career continued to ask questions.

'What do you mean?'

'It is clear from reports in Nigeria, and the limited information we are receiving here in Chad, that there is modern-day slavery in your country.'

'It is clear that the President of Chad, the military and the people of Chad are abhorred by such practices,' replied the Major. 'If what you say proves to be correct, it is clear by the actions that have transpired here today that neither Chad nor Nigeria will tolerate such barbarism.'

Focus soon came straight back to Yanny. 'What are your plans from here?'

'I will be accompanying Kate McDonald and the Nigerian women back to their loved ones in Nigeria.'

The camera constantly focussed on her. It was only a matter of days before the international media and the social media were scrutinising this beautiful mystery woman. She would regret the day she consented to give the interview.

'Yanny, how much longer before you can leave?' Steve asked shortly after the TV interview.

'Ninety minutes. Everyone is here, and the Chadian Army medical team is ensuring that all the women are fit for the trip.'

'Are there any concerns?'

'They all appear to be fine. It's important that you keep them away from the media when we arrive.'

'We've already ensured that they will be kept at a distance. They're like scavenging vultures,' Steve said.

'I know,' said Yanny. 'I've just experienced them.'

'They kept their camera on you for virtually the whole interview.'

With flights slowly returning to normal at the airport and the onlookers dissipating, it was time for the flight back to Nigeria. It had taken longer than the ninety minutes at the airport, more like two hours, and then there was an additional ninety-minute flight back to Maiduguri.

'We're ready to leave,' Harry informed Yanny.

'Is everyone in the helicopters?'

'They're all on board,' said Harry. 'You will be travelling with Kate and Fatima. I'll be in the second helicopter and Phil in the third.'

'We better say goodbye to Captain Déby and Major Abbas,' said Yanny.

'Don't bother,' replied Harry. 'They're coming as well. They are bringing the head of their armed forces. The Chadian President is claiming it as an important moment when two countries acted in cooperation to rid the world of an abomination. It's a major public relations coup for the Chadians as well; they are going to milk it for all it's worth.'

***

Late afternoon, the three Aérospatiale SA 330 Pumas of the Nigerian Air Force lifted off, accompanied by the Mil Mi-24 piloted by Captain Déby. He would lead to the border with Nigeria, and then the position would reverse with the helicopter carrying Kate, Fatima and Yanny taking the lead. The flight was uneventful apart from the excitement of all returning home. At eighty-six minutes after lift-off, they had a tail wind, the four helicopters landed at Maiduguri.

The usually tranquil airfield had been transformed. More media crews had chartered in on private jets. The Nigerian TV crews were also on the ground. As Steve had arranged, the helicopters landed some distance from the increasingly boisterous crowd.

It was up to Yanny, Captain Déby, Major Abbas along with Phil and Harry, as well as the Chadian Head of Military, to deal with the accolades and the media scrum.

Kate was reunited with her parents and Helen, the Nigerian women with theirs. There was to be a need for counselling for many of the returnees, especially Kate. Her mental strength over the last few weeks had been due to the support of Helen and Fatima. In the next few days, her condition would worsen as she relaxed and remembered Zebediah and Mary, as well as Duncan.

Helen would also mourn; Zebediah and Mary had been like second parents to her. She would mourn them more deeply than Kate, but within a few weeks, she would recover and devote herself to continuing the good work that they had started.

Sammy the horse, their friend, was grazing in a field at the back of the airfield. Aluko had arranged it. Helen and Kate were delighted to see him.

'Bob, we need to take part in the press conference. The Nigerian government, as well as Chad, are anxious to take the opportunity to show the world that they have acted in a courageous and dynamic manner.' said Steve.

'It is your team that should take the credit.'

'That is not what we want. The companies and individuals who need our expertise know whom we are and where to find us. Let them have the glory.'

'By the way, was Kate?' Bob had nonchalantly broached a sensitive subject.

'According to Helen and Fatima, she was untouched.'

'We are just glad to have her back,' said Bob. 'It is good to know she still remains the same dear person that was taken.'

***

The press conference, convened in a hangar at the airport. The area at the front festooned with microphones from all the major news channels around the world plus the local television stations. The first to speak, Lt General Abdul Ibrahim, Chief of Defence and head of the Nigerian Armed Forces set out the conditions for the conference. 'Prior to our talking to the media, there is one condition I must place on you and which you must honour. If there is any attempt to ask questions of Helen Campbell, then this interview will conclude immediately. She will make a statement and leave.'

'Will Kate McDonald be present?' Sally Wilson from BBC News, Abuja, Nigeria asked.

'Kate's father, Bob McDonald, will make a statement on her behalf,' replied Abdul. 'She is fine, but in need of rest. Let me commence these proceedings by outlining the events leading up to the successful conclusion, as you have all seen today.

'We are all aware of the attack on the Mission close to this airfield that resulted in the death of three American citizens, Pastor Zebediah, his wife Mary, and Duncan Nicholson. During that attack, Boko Haram took both Helen Campbell and Kate McDonald. It is unfortunate that, due to the sensitivity of the situation, we kept that news from you for as long as was possible.

'Steve Case, you will no doubt learn, is an old friend of mine from Army training we conducted together in the United States when I was a humble Captain. His company is involved in similar hostage ransom and rescue situations around the world. Normally, he would prefer to keep a low profile but, due to the enormity of the actions of the last few days, he is willing to abstain from that profile and address you.

'Before we ask Steve to speak, I would ask my counterpart from Chad to make a few words.' Abdul turned to the man sitting to the left of him.

'Lt General Ibrahim, members of the world's press,' General Youssouf Kabadi said, 'It is clear that there has been a travesty, committed by certain individuals in Chad.

'When he became aware the situation, the President of Chad in his wisdom did not attempt to conceal. My fellow officers and soldiers in the Chadian military, of which I have the honour of leading, have played a decisive part in the freeing of Kate McDonald and twelve Nigerian citizens. I applaud the efforts of all on this successful outcome.'

'General Kabadi,' Sally Wilson interjected, 'there are reports of a plane crashing two hundred kilometres north of N'Djamena. Initial accounts indicate that it is the same plane that left immediately after Kate McDonald was freed.'

'I am led to believe it may be the same plane.' the General replied.

'Is there any significance that, less than five minutes after it departed, two fighters of the Chadian Air Force also took off?'

'I am not aware that they are related,' said the General. He knew the truth, but this was neither the place nor time to reveal that a single Vympel R-27 medium air-to-air missile fired from one of the fighters had downed the plane.

'I would ask Steve Case to make a statement now,' said Abdul, attempting to deflect the questions away from his counterpart.

'Thank you,' said Steve. 'Firstly, I would like to acknowledge the assistance of the Nigerian government, specifically President Timipre Karibo, who Bob McDonald and myself had the honour of meeting. It was at that time that we received his unqualified approval of our plan and the full support of his military. The resources, the expertise they provided were critical to the success of this operation. Without them, this successful result would not have been possible. My company brought our expertise to the operation as advisers. All credit must be given to the Nigerian government, as well as the government of Chad, especially the President and their military personnel, who assisted greatly.'

'Yanny, does she work for you?' Fred Wilkinson, CNN, Abuja, Nigeria asked.

'Yes, she is one of our most valid operatives.'

'Will she be making a statement? Will she be present at this press conference?' The media pack in unison clambered for an answer.

'Yanny was not the only member of the team,' replied Steve. 'And no, she will not be present here. She is with the rescued women.'

'I would ask Bob McDonald, Kate's father, to make a statement.' Abdul again attempted to deflect unnecessary and pointless questions.

'I will only make a short statement,' Bob said. 'I, along with Steve, would like to offer my appreciation to both the Nigerian and Chadian governments. My daughter, Kate, would like me to say on her behalf that she appreciates your interest and concern. I can tell you that she is fine and unharmed. Two people have been instrumental in her well-being. Firstly, Helen Campbell, who will address you shortly and secondly, Fatima, who befriended and ensured Kate's safety during troubling times in Chad. My wife and I hold them in the highest esteem.'

'Where did they intend to take Kate?' The assembled media throng were after an answer.

'They were taking her to the Middle East,' replied Bob.

'Why?'

'I am not willing to indulge in conjecture. Just let me say that my wife and I are delighted that Kate and Helen, as well as Fatima and the Nigerian girls, are safe back here today.'

'I would ask Helen Campbell to make a short statement,' said Abdul. 'Please do not ask questions, or subject her to unnecessary strain. She has been through a traumatic time. Although she is holding up well, as you will see, she must naturally still be fragile.'

There was a flurry of camera clicks and flashes as the media attention turned to Helen. 'I would like to thank all those who facilitated our rescue,' she began. 'The last weeks have been traumatic and painful. Both Kate and I are fine, although we now need to mourn the death of our beloved friends at the Mission, Zebediah, Mary and Duncan. They were truly lovely people whose early deaths, for no understandable reason, leave us both severely upset. At another time, I will give a fuller explanation of what has transpired since we left the Mission, but for now, you will need to excuse me. I should add that I have an unparalleled love for Africa, and it is my intention to stay and carry on the good work that Pastor Zebediah and Mary Johnson set out to do.'

Epilogue

Kate McDonald, in time and with the counselling and support of a stable family unit back home in the United States, gradually adjusted back into society. She had recovered better than most would have expected. It was to be another year before she met Edward Albright, an up and coming local politician in New Orleans. In the years that followed, she would move into the Louisiana mansion in the countryside that she had envisaged with Bill Cleavers. There were to be two children, and life was good for her. She would never again visit Africa; the memories were too painful, too suppressed for her to return.

Her friendship with Helen and Fatima remained intense and, whenever the opportunity arose, they would meet up. She was an avid supporter of Helen's work, regularly organising fundraising events amongst the socialites of Louisiana.

Helen Campbell, remarkably unaffected by her ordeal, would spend the rest of her life on the African continent. As she had stated at the press conference in Maiduguri after their rescue, she would dedicate her life to continue the good work of Pastor Zebediah and Mary Johnson. Initially, she had opened a home for disadvantaged children close to where the old Mission had been. In time, there were to be many more missions around the country. Liberia, the Congo, Somalia, Southern Sudan and several other countries were all to feel the benefit of her devotion to the continent.

It was on a lecture tour of England that she again met Sally O'Rourke, her school antagonist and so-called friend when the promiscuous Sally had needed a fat friend to ensure that the best-looking guy available laid her. No longer pretty, the years had aged her. The three husbands and the screaming delinquent children had driven her to despair. There was no malice on Helen's part and she treated her as an old friend.

275

Feted now as a saintly figure on the African continent, there was even mention of a Nobel peace prize, but Helen remained unaffected by the attention. She only wanted to be in Africa with her people. The lecture tours and the awards were a necessary part of attracting funds for the ever-expanding missions. There was always a Duncan Nicholson building or room, and the homes were always called the Pastor Zebediah and Mary Johnson Home for the people of Africa. Sammy, the horse, lived for another three years in resplendent luxury in the north; he always received a carrot every time Helen passed.

Edith Smith, her saviour that day on the side of the Mersey River, would occasionally visit. Helen was always sure to spend a few days with her when she was in England. Benny, the dog, succumbed to old age, but another Benny, who was equally fond of her, had replaced him.

Her parents devoted their time to generating funds for Helen; it was their interest that kept her father active beyond his years, and he died at the age of eighty-five. Her mother died soon after. There was never to be a man in her life again.

Fatima quickly bonded with Helen, and she became an integral part of her activities in Africa. They were to become lifelong friends and colleagues.

She was to be the silent partner, a position she cherished. She would never speak of her past, and that she had been married to Sheikh Idriss Deubet, the slave trader. Whenever there was a lecture tour for Helen in the United States, she would accompany. Both Helen and Fatima always ensured to spend several days at the mansion in Louisiana with Kate.

The End

ALSO BY THE AUTHOR

The Haberman Virus

A remote and isolated village in the Hindu Kush mountain range in North Eastern Afghanistan is wiped out by a virus unlike any seen before. A mysterious visitor checks his handiwork clad in a space suit. He makes a phone call. "The field trial has been successful. Implementation of Phase Two can commence."

The virus Sam Haberman has genetically engineered, on the orders of the American President, has given him the means to redress the imbalance of the occupier and the occupied in Palestine.

His plan is flawed. The results are catastrophic as continent after continent is decimated. The ultimate bioweapon in the hands of terrorists who will stop at nothing to achieve their aims.

The Vane-Martin Conundrum

The Islamic State is creating chaos in England with a concerted bombing campaign. The Prime Minister cannot stop the carnage, but the tough-minded Anne Argento, a senior member of his government can. She needs to oust him.

Frederick Vane and Andrew Martin are sure the Prime Minister is to be assassinated.

Do they allow the assassination to continue? Do they tell DCI Isaac Cook, a tall black man of Jamaican heritage? Do they inform Anne Argento? Can either be trusted with the information?

Malika's Revenge

Malika waits in a smugglers' village for someone to pay her price, a few scraps of heroin. A Russian gangster on the run from the KGB finds himself there against his will, but where else can he go - they want him dead.

A drug lord, an Afghan warlord and the Russian Mafia are entwined in a plan to raise the quantity of heroin shipped out of Afghanistan. The drug lord sees the Russian mafia taking his business. He will not let it happen without a fight. The Afghan smugglers' leadership, double-dealing and treacherous as ever sense an opportunity to play the Tajikistan drug lord off against the Russian mafia.

The Afghans only care for their money, not who they deal with and if that means death to a few or many, concerns them little. Profit is what they want for their disparate causes, and the cost of a life has little value.

ABOUT THE AUTHOR

Phillip Strang was born in the late forties, the post-war baby boom in England; his childhood years, a comfortable middle-class upbringing in a small town, two hours drive west of London.

His childhood and the formative years were a time of innocence. Relatively few rules, and as a teenager, complete mobility, due to a bicycle – a three-speed Raleigh – and a more trusting community. It was the days before mobile phones, the internet, terrorism and wanton violence. An avid reader of Science Fiction in his teenage years: Isaac Asimov, Frank Herbert, the masters of the genre. Still an avid reader, the author now mainly reads thrillers.

In his early twenties, the author, with a degree in electronics engineering, and an unabated wanderlust to see the world left the cold and damp climes of England for Sydney, Australia – the first semi-circulation of the globe, complete. Now, forty years later, he still resides in Australia, although many intervening years spent in a myriad of countries, some calm and safe – others, no more than war zones.

Printed in Great Britain
by Amazon